Yellowstone Brigade

Other novels by Alfred Dennis

Chiricahua
Lone Eagle
Elkhorn Divide
Brant's Fort
Catamount
The Mustangers
Rover
Yuma
Sandigras Canyon
Shawnee Trail
Fort Reno
Ride the Rough String
Trail to Medicine Mound

To see more books by Alfred Dennis visit
www.alfreddennis.com

Yellowstone Brigade

Alfred Dennis

WCP

Walnut Creek Publishing
Tuskahoma, Oklahoma

YELLOWSTONE BRIGADE

This novel is a work of fiction. Names, characters, places, and incidents are either the product of the author's imagination or are used fictitiously. Any resemblance to actual events, locales, organizations, or persons, living or dead, is entirely coincidental and beyond the intent of either the author or the publisher.

ISBN: 978-1-942869-14-6
Second Edition Revised, Paperback
Published 2016 by Walnut Creek Publishing
10 9 8 7 6 5 4 3 2
Library of Congress Control Number: 2013903742
1. Native American Fiction 2. Action/Adventure 3. Historical Fiction

Any people depicted in stock imagery provided by Thinkstock are models, and such images are being used for illustrative purposes only.
Cover image, Certain stock imagery © Thinkstock.

Books may be purchased in quantity and/or special sales by contacting the publisher;
Walnut Creek Publishing
PO Box 820
Talihina, OK 74571
www.wc-books.com

This book is dedicated to my sister, Betty Solomon, and her husband, Rick Solomon. Many thanks for standing behind me Sis, and for giving me your support, and help through the years.

Introduction

The eighteen twenties and thirties were the shining times of the Rocky Mountain hunting Brigades that penetrated deep into the high lonely mountains. The mountain men were men of adventure, courage, and they had a deep yearning to roam the vast and wild Rocky Mountains. They searched for beaver and other fur bearing animals as they ventured into the far reaches of this wild land.

Pinto Stade was such a man, a giant of a man, one of the earliest adventurers that dared to enter the hunting grounds of the mighty, warlike tribes of the North Country. The Sioux, Cheyenne, Arapaho, Crow, and Blackfoot Nations, all claimed the Rocky Mountains as their own, defending the hunting grounds with their lives. Death rode every moment with the white hunters who roamed the mountains. They were looking to make their fortune, not in gold or silver, but in the hides of the animals in their traps.

Stade was a loner, an independent trapper and hunter. He kept to himself, not needing the companionship or safety of the heavily armed Brigades that employed up to fifty men in a party. Sometimes, a partner accompanied him as he slipped silently into the deep canyons of the Rockies, where the flat-tail beaver were thicker than fleas on a hound's back.

Protected only by his sharp wits and knowledge of the mountains, Stade trapped the many small lakes and streams that dotted the landscape. The last trapping season finished, Danny Sutton, his longtime hunting companion, decided he would quit the wild life of the mountains and marry. Selling their winter cache of furs at Cloud's Trading Post, Stade and Sutton said their goodbyes on the banks of the mighty Missouri.

Stade turned back to the trading post, his eyes focused on the sign over Carter's Inn. He always enjoyed washing away the long winter campfires with a drink at the Post's Inn, before returning to the mountains.

Sutton, knew Stades' habits, and warned him not to stay long at the Trading Post and not to drink too much. The same advice came from the serving girl at Carter's Inn as he drank a cup of ale. Knowing the girl spoke to the huge trapper, Martin Carter slapped the waitress, only to have a confrontation with the youngster Jehu Wolf, who also worked for Carter.

After the fight with Carter, Jehu Wolf knew he had worn out his welcome at Carter's Inn. Helping the lad escape the inn, Stade invited the young man to venture forth into the high mountains with him to learn to be a mountain man.

In the years he trapped and followed Pinto Stade through the mountains, Jehu Wolf, whom the tribes named White Wolf, earned his reputation as a fighter. His loyalty to Pinto Stade and his friendship with the Crow People, gained him great respect. His courage and strength became legendary in the lodges of the native tribes, trappers, and hunters of the Rocky Mountains.

Chapter 1

Misty fog lay thick and heavy across the wide Missouri as the large birch-bark canoe slipped silently along the sandy banks of the great river, known as the Big Muddy. Two buckskin-clad men pulled heavily on the hand carved, wooden paddles. Their eyes and ears trained vigilantly on the near and far bank. Neither spoke, their bearded faces were blank of any expression, only the sharp eyes betrayed any movement on the strong, solemn faces of the two trappers.

The bigger man, in the rear of the heavy-laden canoe, scanned the riverbank, while the trapper in front watched the muddy water. He looked for any driftwood or floating logs that might punch a hole and sink the already overburdened craft. Laden down with their winter's cache of furs, the hunters headed for the settlements to sell their pelts, trade for fresh supplies, and wash off the burdens and camp smoke of many lonely winter fires.

Casting his sharp, blue eyes westward, the bigger man gazed at the tall trees as they slowly blocked the setting sun. They were close to the settlements, but this was still the wild upper Missouri. Only a few miles ahead, they intersected the great Mississippi. Any man becoming careless along these shores could quickly find himself separated from his scalp and furs. Hostile warriors and renegade whites stalked the heavily forested banks of the great river in hopes of finding a lone hunter, returning with a winter's catch of prime plews, exactly as they were doing now. Whistling softly, the bigger man motioned toward the near bank, as he felt the current rise against the boat. The smaller and younger of the two men nodded, then steered the canoe to the shore.

Stepping lightly from the canoe, as it rubbed softly on the sandy bottom, the smaller man pulled the heavy craft further onto the shore. Retrieving his Hawken rifle from the floor of the craft, the hunter slipped quietly into the surrounding forest, then disappeared. The other man waited, his rifle resting lightly in the powerful grasp of his huge hands. Five minutes passed before the hunter finished scouting the small inlet and reappeared along the tree line, walking toward the river's edge.

Giving the bigger man, the thumbs up signal, the smaller man trotted easily back to the canoe. "Clean as a wolf's tooth, Pinto."

"Good, but we'll keep a sharp eye out anyway." Pinto studied the heavy forest along the river. "From here on in, Danny my boy, is the most dangerous part of the trip."

Danny Sutton looked over at the big man with a slipshod smile spreading across his handsome face. "It's to be my last. You want me to start a fire?"

Pinto Stade rose slowly from the canoe and stepped onto dry ground. Six feet tall in moccasin feet, but it wasn't his height that made him so big, it was the broadness of the hunter. Tipping the scales at two hundred and twenty pounds, the man didn't know his own strength. Shoulders broader than an axe handle, with powerful arms and hands the size of skillets, hands that could squeeze the life easily from a man, Stade was a mountain of a man.

"No, Danny my boy, no fire." The voice was deep. A faint touch of Irish brogue betrayed the man's heritage. "Not tonight, we're almost home safe."

Sutton laughed good-naturedly. "Now you know you're too dang old to be sleeping on the cold ground with no fire."

The sharp, blue eyes looked off toward the heavy woods. "Never mind my age, you young whippersnapper. Help me unload our furs."

The furs were bundled into bales, each weighing close to two hundred pounds. Both men handled the heavy bundles easily as if they were feather pillows. Stacking the bundles, the two hunters retreated to find themselves a smooth place against a drift-log. Scooping out a soft place in the sand for their tired backsides, the two sat with their backs almost together, permitting them to have a good view in both directions of the forest and riverbank.

"How far, you reckon, is it to Cloud's Trading Post?" Pinto pulled off a chunk of jerked meat and handed it to Sutton.

"Midmorning will see us there, I reckon."

"Thank ye, kindly." Danny eyed the coarse meat. "I'll tell you for a fact; this is the last jerky I aim to eat the rest of my life."

Pinto looked at the chunk of dried meat and nodded. "You're really quitting for good, are you?"

"I am. My Arabella is waiting for me in St. Louis. With my share of the money from this season's catch, I'm gonna buy us a small farm." The young hunter looked over where the bales of plews rested near the bank. "Yes, sir Pinto, I'm through with this life for good."

Pinto smiled. "We've fought Injuns, grizzly bears, and had the hair of the wildcat in our teeth for three seasons now, Danny. You sure you're gonna be able to settle into the quiet life of a farmer?"

"I'm sure, Pinto." Sutton leaned back and smiled knowingly. "I'll have Arabella. She'll keep me happy."

"Uh huh," Pinto smiled. "She must be quite a woman."

"She is that. You should come to St Louis and meet her, before you head out again."

"Wish I could at that, but we're running really late this spring. I told old Taff Lowrie, I'd meet him at the rendezvous, come late summer."

"You're really planning on hooking up with his Brigade and hunting with them this fall?" Sutton couldn't believe Pinto would do it.

"Thought I'd give it a whirl."

"But dang it, Pinto, we've always been independent hunters, not company men."

"We? You're fixing to get hitched," Pinto laughed. "No boy, I'm getting a mite old to be traipsing around the Rocky Mountains alone forever."

"Old, pssh, you ain't old, Pinto," Sutton scoffed. He's never seen a day Pinto Stade was scared of anything, man or beast. The worse or scarier things became, the calmer, old Pinto would get. No three men could pin him to the ground in the rough and tumble matches held each summer at rendezvous. Men walked around him with respect and women eyed him with awe.

"I feel old, boy. This Pawnee arrow in my back hurts more every season." Pinto stretched his back slowly.

Sutton nodded slowly. "How you know it's a Pawnee arrow? You done told me yourself you didn't see what kind of varmint shot you."

"Feels like a Pawnee arrow to me, that's how." The big man raised his right arm and winced. "Yep, she's Pawnee alright."

"Why don't you come to St Louis with me, sell your plews, and have a real sawbones take a look-see at your back?"

"Done told you why," Pinto shook his head. "Taff will be waiting for me at the Judith with his Yellowstone Brigade."

"We're independent trappers, by golly." Sutton growled between bites. "Independent."

"We were maybe, we ain't no more. Them big set-ups have done away with us little fellers."

"We got plews this year ain't we?"

"For a fact, Danny boy, we do." Pinto shook his shaggy head. "You better wait until we get the cash in our hands before you go to crowing a whole lot young'un."

"You a thinking we're gonna have trouble at the post?"

"I heard we might."

"And you're just now telling me?"

"Didn't want to worry you none." Pinto laughed quietly. "You're fixing to marry, and get yourself a piece of ground."

"This Hawken will guarantee a fair price for my furs." Sutton rubbed his hand along the smooth finish of the rifle. "I'll be having Arabella and my land."

"I hope ye the best, lad, the best."

"Thank you, Pinto. I know you mean it." Sutton studied the river bank. "Tell me, old hoss, why didn't we just sell our plews to David Miles, instead of toting them to Clouds, if'n you're worried about us being cheated?"

"I would have liked to sell to David, but with you needing the money and all, he just ain't big enough yet to pay top money." Pinto moved about, removing a small stone from under him. "Next year, maybe."

The two hunters snuggled up comfortably on the soft sand, but both men were alert, listening as frogs croaked out their love songs along the water's edge. The dark night's gloom and heavy fog carried the far-off call of an owl or the near whippoorwill. The splash of a catfish sounded on the river as it cleared the water, reaching for a low flying insect.

Pinto felt his scalp tingle as Sutton, without muttering a word, slipped suddenly from his sandy bed, disappearing into the darkness. Retreating quickly to where the canoe rested, the big hunter quietly reloaded the bundles of furs, careful not to make any noise. He knew here, along the huge river's banks, the slightest sound could carry far out into the night, across the water.

Sutton vaporized out of the gloom as silent as a ghost. "We got ourselves some company."

"How many?" Pinto whispered, stepping close to the boat.

"Too many." Grabbing the canoe, the two hunters backed it into the river until it floated on the current, then they climbed quietly into the craft.

Only the water, running from their moccasins, made a sound. The men settled easily into the canoe, rowing and slipping silently away from the sandy banks. Stroking powerfully, Pinto and Sutton have the heavy canoe several hundred yards downriver when gunfire exploded out of the night.

"They dang sure had us located 'fore they came in," Sutton whispers. "We sure let one of them slip up on us too close. Maybe we're getting a mite old."

"Pawnee scout," Pinto grunts, as he dipped his oar mightily into the muddy water. "Only one of them red devils could have slipped in on us that close, without our knowing it."

"Pawnee?" Sutton whispered back over his shoulder. "Ain't a Pawnee scalp within three hundred miles of here. 'Sides, a Pawnee ain't near as slippery as a Cheyenne."

"It was Pawnee. I'm telling you. A Cheyenne can't hold them Pawnee varmints a light to go by, when it comes to sneakiness."

The smaller hunter shook his head and smiled. If an Indian was involved, Pinto swore it was always a Pawnee. The big hunter hated the whole tribe. Man, woman, or papoose, it didn't matter. Shoot, he wasn't even sure the arrowhead he carried under his shoulder blade was Pawnee, but that didn't matter either. He despised the Pawnee Nation with a passion. On several occasions, Sutton questioned the old hunter how he came by it, but only received a sullen look for an answer. It was sure enough a curiosity, but Pinto wouldn't say a thing, only that it was Pawnee. On that score, he was plumb, sure enough certain.

The gunfire stopped as suddenly as it started, along the river's edge. Sutton nodded. Again, they barely escaped harm as they have so many times the last three years. He thought of the beautiful woman he has waiting, and the peaceful farm that he will buy with the money, the furs bring. He is ready to settle down to a quiet life. He wants to sleep soundly, eat hot meals at a table, and hopefully raise a batch of young'uns. No, sir, no more cold camps, cold coffee, or Indians trying to lift their scalps.

Following Pinto into the Rockies, these last three years have been an experience he wouldn't have missed, but one he was ready to leave behind. Danger, even death, lurks behind every tree, springing up every morning with the new sun, and going to bed with you every night. He was ready for the simple life of a farmer. He was ready to wake up with Arabella, who he met the previous summer and fell in love with, in his arms, instead of his Hawken Rifle. Too many of his friends were killed or simply disappeared somewhere in the rugged mountains, never seen or heard from again. A hunter must be alert, cautious, and wary as a wild animal, to survive in the vast reaches of the Rockies.

Mandan's, Nez Perce, Sioux, Cheyenne, even grizzly bears and rattlesnakes whispered the kiss of death and rode with them every day along the wild mountainous trails. No, sir, Sutton shook his head. He has cheated death. He left his tracks through the Rockies, along the Madison River, the Gallatin, the Jefferson, and many others. Now, he wanted to live the gentle, quiet life, away from danger. He has become fond of the big hunter behind him, but he knew Pinto would always return to the mountains. It was in his blood.

After a few days of carousing and drinking in the settlements, the big hunter disappeared back into the vast reaches of the mountains as silently as he came. Somewhere along the steep, rocky trail, the old trapper would one day disappear, just like so many before him, but it's the big hunter's way. He preferred the lonely and silent life of the mountains. He would never change. He didn't want to change. He was as wild, maybe even wilder, than the Indians or varmints that made the Rockies their home.

Sutton knew he wouldn't be with the big hunter this time, and it worried him immensely. He looked to the man as his own father, but it was time for them to go their separate ways.

Pinto said he would ride with Taff Lowrie into the Yellowstone Country. There they would trap the valleys and streams of the upper mountains. Lowrie led a Brigade of men, maybe thirty hunters with skinners, cooks, and wranglers. They were all rough and rugged men, but the upper Yellowstone was Sioux Country. The Sioux and their Cheyenne cousins didn't cotton to intruders in their hunting grounds. Further west was the terrible Blackfoot Tribe, possibly more ferocious than even the Sioux.

Riding alongside Pinto, into the rugged wilds of the mountains, Sutton had learned firsthand about Indians, their cruelty, and moodiness. Even with the many rifles and brave men, Lowrie had with his Brigade, it would be a long dangerous hunting season for his friend.

Setting up a base camp, the trappers separated into pairs, to set and work their trap lines, the most dangerous time. Alone, they would be vulnerable, and the hostile warriors knew it. Many times, Sutton had luckily avoided the war parties that set a trap, lying in wait for him and Pinto.

"You dead set on going with Lowrie this year?" Sutton whispered quietly.

"Yep, gave him my word." Pinto pulled mightily on the oars. "Me and Taff go back a long way. We came out here together, you know."

The younger man shook his head. "Alone, you've got a chance they won't discover you. With a whole Brigade, them heathens will know exactly when you ride into their hunting grounds."

"When I cash in my chips, Danny boy, I want someone to throw some sod over me," Pinto smiles. "You know how it is, but if it's not to be, so be it."

Sutton didn't bother to answer or even turn his head. He knew Pinto was starting to show his years. The years spent shadowing death in the hard mountains put uncertainty in the bravest and aged a man beyond his years. The wildness of the Rockies placed its heavy hand on many brave souls, and he knew what Pinto was thinking.

Each man wanted a burial, put in the ground, proper, with words read over him when he goes under. Nevertheless, these old, hard-crusted trappers turned their faces into the high lonesome when the leaves started to turn colors and the air started to have a bite to her. Sutton followed Pinto west, into the Rockies to trap and hunt, but it's for the money he would earn for a farm, not for the adventure and wildness Pinto craved. He smiled, Pinto would swear he wasn't going back, but the call of the mountains was just too strong.

Chapter 2

Cloud's small settlement and trading post came into view as the canoe rounded a broad bend. The tall stockade fence loomed high in the distance, surrounded by tepees, tents, and rough-hewn lumber shacks. Pinto and Sutton had traded last year with the trader, but the settlement had changed. The flat ground along the river, had plenty of horses, cattle, and people. They couldn't believe their eyes, as the trading post had grown three times the size it was last spring.

"Fort's grown some."

"Some?" Pinto swore quietly. "I've seen less people in St. Louis."

Sutton laughed. "Yeah, but that was maybe twenty years ago."

"Didn't say when." Pinto spit disgustedly into the water. One thing he hated was big cities or large gatherings of people. To him, any bunch of city pilgrims counting over twenty, was way too many.

The canoe slipped easily into shore, alongside one of the many wharfs holding boats, barges, and rafts of different shapes and sizes. Several black men stepped forward, ready to help unload the furs. The blacks were Charlie Cloud's slaves, waiting there to make sure he had first bid on the hides the trappers brought into his trading post. Cloud controlled most of the fort's fur trading and was the biggest buyer of pelts. There were other buyers in the settlement, and Cloud did not want to lose any business he didn't have to.

One of the huge black men reached for a bundle of heavy plews, his hand stopped in midair, as the hammer of Pinto's Hawken rifle cocked loudly in the morning air.

"Sorry boss, just figuring on helping y'all unload is all." The black's hand fell away as its owner backed off from the boat, his dark eyes staring at the huge bore of the Hawken. "Sorry."

"I'll tell you when to unload my boat, now git back." Pinto stood to his full height, stepping out of the boat. "Danny boy, you guard our plews whilst I go talk business with Cloud."

Sutton fingered the trigger of his Hawken as he pointed it aimlessly toward the scowling black men. He watched sharply as Pinto walked proudly through the gates of the trading post, his rifle resting easily across his arm.

The slaves retreated to their seats beside the wharf. They were far enough away from the boat so Sutton relaxed his attention on them, but remained near enough to dissuade any other buyers from encroaching on their owner's business. Some furs, Cloud didn't want at any price. The trappers bringing them in, were incompetent, a shiftless bunch. Their furs were cured out bad or skinned wrong.

The blacks knew which trappers Cloud would buy from. Pinto Stade was one that always had prime beaver and other plews.

Several minutes passed before Pinto, with a smaller, dark skinned man, dressed in the suit of a city dude, passed through the stockade gate and approached the canoe. The man seemed disgusted as he tried his best to keep from stepping into the muddy hog wallows lining the river.

"Why didn't you just have my boys bring your furs to the post?" Sutton heard Cloud questioning Pinto. "I don't need to walk all the way down here every time you come in."

"Been hearing things, Charlie."

"What things?" Cloud wiped a lace kerchief across his frowning forehead and looked down at his mud-covered shoes in disgust. He hated the name Charlie. Only Pinto Stade used it when he addressed his one-time pupil.

Pinto stepped beside the canoe and looked at the man. "I want your bid before I unload."

"You don't trust me, old friend?" The trader stared up at the tall trapper. "We used to ride the river together, remember?"

"Yeah, I remember, but those days are long gone." Pinto thought back to the day when Cloud's uncle rode into his camp and unceremoniously dumped a young, worthless Charlie Cloud from his horse. After tossing Pinto a pouch of money, Claremont Cloud rode out with just a few parting words. "Make a man of my nephew, or don't bring him back."

"I ain't changed any, old pard."

"You've changed, and I'm no longer your pard, Charlie Cloud." Pinto cut a leather strap and laid a bundle of beaver pelts out for the trader to examine. "Price 'em, and give me your best price the first time."

"You in a hurry, Pinto?"

"No, but my friend is."

Cloud cut his dark eyes to where Sutton sat with his rifle across his knees. The look reminded Sutton of a ferret's slanted eyes.

"I see he is." Cloud fingered the pelts gently. "They're the best I've seen this season."

"They're the best you'll see any season." Pinto spit. "How much you offering?"

Sutton had to admit, Pinto didn't mince words so he got straight to the business at hand. Most of the time, the old trapper was genuinely friendly and affable, but not with this trader. Last year he was stern, but not this straight forward and hard with Cloud, when they had dickered the price of their pelts.

"Six dollars for the beaver, six for the fox, eight for the silver fox, and eight for the martin."

"And the smaller pelts?"

"Forty dollars for the lot."

Pinto looked to where Sutton was waiting. Nodding slightly, he reached out his hand. "Done."

Cloud refused the handshake, pointed to the blacks, then to the furs. He turned toward the trading post with Pinto and Sutton following.

"Reckon you done made him mad, Pinto," Sutton laughed lightly.

Pinto nodded in agreement. "That man was born mad, Danny boy. Now, you keep your eyes open. He was mighty eager to buy."

The big trapper studied the retreating back of his one-time pupil and partner. They rode and trapped together four seasons, and then Claremont Cloud sent word for him to come back to St. Louis. The older

Cloud was sick, and Pinto heard he had gone under. The younger Cloud took over his uncle's trading business and moved the whole shebang further up the big river. Building the fort and trading post away from the bigger city competition, he did well and the business prospered.

Pinto trained him and was paid well for teaching the young Cloud the fur trade. The boy was an apt pupil, and now it was all paying off. The boy had a keen eye for good pelts, and he could trade with anyone, white or Indian. However, the younger Cloud was mean, even cruel, something Pinto couldn't break him from. In the years they traveled together, he saw the smaller Cloud fight many times with older and larger men. Some fights were friendly and just mere wrestling matches, while others were to the death. He never saw Charlie Cloud beaten; maybe a draw now and then in their rough and tumble wrestling matches. However, when the fight was serious, the small man became as deadly as a mountain cat.

Charlie Cloud had grown, not in stature but in reputation, and that wasn't always good. Now, he ran Cloud's Trading Post with an iron hand, always outbidding the other fur buyers and paying the best prices for pelts, cash money paid in gold. Pinto heard rumors how the gold sometimes separated from the trappers before it got warm in their pockets. In addition, there were stories of knife fights. Several men were killed; some called them duels, and usually right after they were paid for their furs.

Knife fights among the wild mountain trappers was commonplace, but Pinto knew, up against Charlie Cloud, it's murder.

All along the mountain trails and lonely camps, Pinto had heard rumors, but they were only whispers. He didn't believe Cloud would kill or drive off the trappers who brought their plews into the post to trade. It would be like killing the golden goose, but the rumors persisted.

Cloud wasn't a big man in size, but he was in heart. The man had grit. He would fight a grizzly bear with a switch. Several men met their fate after calling the man a cheat, then stood to face Cloud in a duel. Yes, the man was a fighter, and he was tough. His mother was a Creole from New Orleans. His father was a Cloud, brother to Claremont Cloud, who started the fur business Charlie Cloud now owned. Rumor had it, Claremont Cloud had a daughter somewhere back east, she owned the business, and pulled the strings, but this too was only a rumor. Cloud was also a businessman. Pinto didn't figure he would rob or kill trappers bringing in pelts, which was his livelihood.

The two hunters looked out across the wide Mississippi, as they try to form the farewell words they both dreaded. They only traveled together three years, but it seemed like a lifetime with all the dangers they encountered. Pinto traded the larger canoe for two smaller ones that would be easier for a single man to handle.

Pinto cleared his throat. "Well, Danny boy, Arabella is waiting for you."

"You gonna be alright here by yourself?" Sutton looked toward the trading post. "Cloud was frothing at the mouth to get our pelts, but he sure wasn't too happy with the way you spoke to him."

"I'll be fine. Old Pinto is gonna wet his whistle and head this boat toward the Yellowstone," Pinto smiled. "Cloud and me go back a ways. He won't bother me none."

"You should go now, old friend," Sutton looked up at the stockade gate, "now, Pinto."

Pinto slapped the smaller man on the back. "Cloud ain't exactly friendly, but then again, he ain't stupid. He wants more pelts so he ain't gonna do me no harm."

"I've heard he's killed men for a lot less than what you said to him."

"I ain't men, laddie."

Sutton touched his possible pouch and nodded. "Alright then, I'll be heading along."

"Don't drift too near the banks, Danny." Pinto gave the small canoe a shove. "Keep your eyes open, front and back."

"I'll be watchful, Pinto. I've got my farm money. You helped me get it the last three seasons. I'm a thanking you for everything. I ain't the green lad, you took under your wing." Sutton dipped his paddle deep, his forearms rippling with the strain. "You've always got a place to throw your blankets, when you're ready, anytime you're a mind to quit the mountains."

Pinto nodded and looked down at the younger man. "I'm obliged to you, Danny boy."

"When Arabella and me get settled, you come for a spell and visit."

"I'll do just that."

Pinto stood, leaning heavily on his rifle, watching as Sutton slowly became smaller and smaller, finally disappearing downstream in the distance.

He could feel the bag of gold coins hanging heavily from a rawhide bag around his neck. Raising his heavy arm, he waved across the water. Pinto knew Sutton couldn't see him, as he was too far, but he waved anyway. He's gonna miss the young man, as he already did. Hunting and trapping the mountains and isolated valleys of the Rockies was a lonely life.

Wiping his mouth, he walked toward a rough shack shanty that proclaimed drinks and food. Shoving inside, he studied the dark room, pulled back a chair, and settled into it. Four men sat at a table, talking in low tones, and two more stood at the other end of a rough wooden bar. Pinto laid a twenty-dollar gold piece in front of him and motioned a serving girl who was standing at the bar.

"Whiskey, girl, and keep it coming." Pinto pushed the coin forward. "Until you get this old hoss' thirst slaked."

A slender lad, even taller than Pinto, carried a keg of whiskey from the backroom, setting it gently on the bar. Pinto was impressed, as the boy didn't look that strong, but Pinto knew, by the way the bar groaned under the keg's weight, the whiskey barrel was heavy. Taking a closer look at the youngster, Pinto nodded. Wide blue eyes looked out from under a shuck of brown hair that framed a broad lean face. In itself, the face was friendly enough, yet there was a cold hardness about the lad. Long muscular arms unwrapped themselves from the barrel as the youth released his grip and straightened his broad shoulders. Pinto noticed the heavy handled skinning knife protruding from the youngster's boot top.

In time, this young man was gonna make a real hoss, with the promise of plenty more size and strength to come as he matured. The blue eyes glanced briefly his way, then looked over at the four men at the table.

"Wolf," the coarse voice came from the back. "Get your tail in here."

Pinto watched as the lad walked lightly across the dirt floor and exited the room. Downing another glass of the rotgut brew that passed for whiskey, the tall trapper wiped his face and motioned to the girl. Nervously, she set another full glass in front of him. An hour later, Pinto was beginning to feel the effects of the raw whiskey, but he still had his faculties, enough to see her hand shaking.

"What is it, gal?" Pinto glanced up at her worried face as it turned toward the opening door. "You seem worried about something."

Shaking her head, the fair-skinned girl quickly averted her eyes from a pair of buckskin-clad men that darkened the doorway of the room. Picking up his change, she turned hurriedly from the table. "Don't get drunk in here, mister." She whispered as she turned toward the bar. "You best leave now."

Pinto stared at her back as she walked toward the rough-hewn counter, angling away from the open door and the newcomers. He watched as the shorter of the men stepped in front of her as she turned to go behind the long bar. The buckskin-clad arm snaked out, grabbing the girl's wrist, causing her to drop the empty glass noisily onto the bar.

"What'd you just say to him, gal? What?"

"Nothing Martin, nothing."

The girl jerked her wrist sharply, trying to rip free from the man. "Just took his money is all."

"You're lying to me, gal. I seen the way you were looking at him." The man's dark eyes turned toward Pinto, who sat quietly sipping his drink, but taking in the unfolding drama before him. "You been making small talk with him, gal?"

"No!" The girl pulled from the jealous man's grasp then went behind the bar. "Leave me be."

The man's dark eyes looked wildly around the room then turned on the frightened girl. "Bull, I seen you making eyes at him."

From across the room, the voices were barely a whisper. The words coming forth from the girl were indiscernible, too quiet to understand. Pinto could tell by the way the man and the girl kept looking in his direction, he was still the focal point of their conversation, even though they lowered their voices.

Tossing off his drink, he motioned over at the barkeep, standing behind the bar. "I'll have another."

Turning to look closely at the big trapper, the swarthy hunter shoved the girl bodily from the bar. "Serve him, but keep your mouth shut, girl. You hear me?"

"I hear you, Martin."

"You okay, young'un?" Pinto spoke loud enough for the men at the bar to hear his words as the girl set the glass before him. "That fellow bothering you?"

Placing the glass full of brownish liquid on the rough plank table, the girl picked up his money and turned toward the buckskin-clad hunter, who was watching her closely. "Go, mister, please." The words again were barely audible. "You'll get me beaten bad, and you killed for sure if you keep talking to me."

Pinto's eyes followed the girl as she returned slowly to where two hunters stood beside the bar. Suddenly, the sickening thud of a fist, landing flush against something, sounded. He watched as the slender girl landed in a heap at the tall youth's feet as he reappeared from the backroom.

"Leave her where she is, Wolf." The hunter stepped away from the bar, his battle-axe gripped firmly in his hands as the lad reached down to help the girl.

Stopping in mid-stride, the youth looked over at the man. "What'd she do, Mister Carter?"

"Never mind that, boy." The hunter smiled, his white teeth showed smugly from his bearded face. "She's my bound woman. You just get back to your work, and be a minding your own business."

"She's your brother Luke's bound servant, not yours." The youth didn't back down. "What you aiming on doing to her?"

"I told you boy, get back to work." The man stepped forward as he raised a hickory handle. "She's my woman; I'll treat her as I want."

"Martin!" A loud voice came from the backroom of the building, as another man appeared in the doorway. "What's going on out here?"

The girl's eyes opened in fear as the storeowner and the one called Martin both stood over her.

"Your hired hand here is interfering with your bound girl and me, Brother Luke."

"Is he now?" The barman looked down at the prone girl then over at the tall youth and shook his head. "What'd she do this time?"

"Me and Brother Tate came in and caught her carrying on with that feller there." Martin threw out his chin, and motioned toward Pinto. "Wouldn't heed me when I told her to get back to work and keep her yap shut."

The girl crawled slowly toward the tall youth, trying to grab at his legs. "Help me, Jehu."

"Help me, Jehu." Martin mimicked the frightened girl. "I'll help you, girl."

The axe handle made a swishing sound as the hunter swung it cruelly, down toward the prone girl. Pinto watched as the handle was plucked, seemingly from the air, as the youngster wrenched it from the swarthy man's hands.

"I'll kill you for that, Wolf." The words were sharp, like the crack of a whip, as a sharp skinning knife appeared as if by magic, in the man's right hand. "Told you plainly to stay out of it. She's my woman. I'm gonna cut you bad, boy."

Bending slightly, the youth pulled his knife, slipping it smoothly from the boot top. Circling slowly, the two combatants parried several times, then came together in a rush. Pinto watched, nodding slowly. The boy was young, but he showed plenty of grit and no fear, as he faced the older man. He watched the other men inside the room closely, making sure no one interfered, as the fighters circled each other slowly. Lunging together, muscles bunched in knots, both men forced each other back and forth across the dirt floor. The hunter, Martin, was older and heavier, but the big trapper could tell the youth was stronger and faster.

Forearms bulge as each man strained against the strong grasp of the other's hand. Suddenly, Martin's eyes flew open wide, his mouth opened slightly, and he slumped against the bar. Pinto watched as the trapper's knife fell from his open hand and the red stain came in a rush as the youngster pulled his knife from the man's side. Two bystanders started forward but stopped as they heard the hammer cocked back on Pinto's rifle.

"Now boys, it appears to be all over. Me and the youngster will be backing out of here. Stand away from the door."

Pulling the girl from the floor, the tall youth lifted her bodily over his shoulder, started toward the open door where Pinto waited. Nodding his thanks, he disappeared quickly through the rough doorway.

Pinto looked over to where the one called Martin leaned against the bar, holding his side, then across at the rest of the men. "You boys sit back down and enjoy your drinks, and see to your friend there. He seems to be bleeding a mite."

Stepping outside the inn, Pinto found the youngster standing alone, beside the building. Motioning for the tall lad to follow him, he started toward the river and the landing where his small boat was moored. "You best come with me, boy."

"Where we headed?" The youth's legs were longer than Pinto's, making his stride carry him easily beside the older man. Pinto motioned toward the river where boats were rocking in the water's easy current. "I've got me a boat tied up down there."

"And me?"

"Boy, peers to me like you done up and wore out your welcome back there." Pinto flipped his finger toward the Inn. "I doubt them folks will let bygones be bygones, and welcome you back with open arms."

The youngster nodded. "You're probably right about that. Them Carters ain't exactly the forgiving type."

"Where's the girl?"

"Can't say." The tall youth shook his head. "Soon as we cleared the door, I set her down and she skedaddled out of there."

"Well, I reckon she's got somewhere to head for or she wouldn't have disappeared like she did." Pinto looked over at the lad. "You best come with me for a ways."

"What happened back there?" Cloud called from the trading post porch as the two men hurried past. He could hear the sound of angry voices coming from the inn.

The Hawken swung around and covered the trader, causing Cloud to take a step backward on the porch. "Little disagreement is all."

"Over Luke Carter's bound girl, I'll bet!" Cloud looked over to where several men had exited the inn and were looking in their direction.

"Yeah, reckon it were," Pinto nodded. "Tweren't her fault though."

"It never is her fault, but there's always plenty of trouble whenever she's around."

"Charlie Cloud," Pinto glanced again at the men then over at the porch. "We're leaving this place right now, unless you've got any objections?"

"Good idea." Cloud glanced again over at the men. "Sooner the better, I reckon. That is if you want to keep your hides in one piece. Them Carters ain't folks to fool around with."

Pinto started toward the wharf with the youth in tow. "I'll take your word for it. We're going."

"You taking Mister Wolf with you, Pinto?"

Nodding, the big hunter looked over at the youth. "Reckon I am, if he's a mind to trail with me."

"You'd best stay here boy and take your medicine from the Carters." Cloud grinned coldly. "Here, you might be beaten half to death, but out in the mountains with Pinto, will probably be the death of you. Almost was for me on several occasions."

The tall youth studied the trader then stepped beside Pinto. "Reckon if he'll have me, I'll travel along with this man, Mister Cloud."

"It's your funeral, Jehu Wolf." Cloud watched as the two men strolled casually toward the river and the waiting canoe as if they didn't have a care in the world.

One of the blacks, an immense man of stature, rushed up beside Cloud and studied their departing backs. "Them men should hurry from here, Mister Cloud."

"Are the Carters coming?"

The massive black head nodded. "Yes suh, Masta Cloud, them Carters are mad. They say the young white done stuck Mister Martin in the belly with his pigsticker, and you know how mean they can be."

"Well Benje, don't underestimate that man going there," Cloud smiled as he nodded in Pinto's direction. "He's the mean one, a real bad man. I know him quite well."

"Yes, suh."

Cloud turned his attention to the Carters, stopping them with his hand as they started after Pinto and Jehu. Martin Carter held a bloody towel against his side, stemming the flow of blood that was spreading across his leather shirt.

"You hurt bad, Martin?"

Raising the towel, Martin shook his head. "Nah, just nicked me is all. Sure bled like the dickens for a minute though."

"The kid could have done him in easy enough." Tate Martin spoke up as he looked toward the river at the two men's departing backs. "Who would have thought it, a mere lad getting the best of Martin Carter."

Martin growled then spit tobacco on the ground. "He got lucky was all. I aim to kill that boy for taking my woman."

Cloud shook his head. "Chauncy wasn't with them when they left here."

"She wasn't?"

"Nope, just Pinto Stade and the Wolf boy."

The older Carter craned his head and looked sharply toward the river. "That was Pinto Stade?"

Cloud nodded. "It was for a fact, Luke, Pinto Stade in the flesh."

"Don't know him personal, but I've heard he's a rough customer."

"That he is. I'll vouch for one thing. He's nobody to fool with."

Martin whirled, looking back toward the bar and trading post. "Where'd she get to you suppose?"

"Couldn't say, but she'll have to show up for work later," Cloud smiled slightly. "The girl ain't got anywhere to go, and she needs the money."

"When I get through wailing the tar out of her, I'm a going after that boy and Stade, and kill them both."

Cloud shook his head. "No you ain't, Martin. I got use for them two."

"What use?" Martin Carter was fuming. Not only did his side hurt, but his pride too. "I'm gonna kill him."

Cloud wasn't a big man, but the city clothes he wore made him look even more frail and small. Nevertheless, the hard life and free for all fighting, he was involved in while riding with Pinto, put grit in his craw. Everyone knew he ran the trading post fort and everything inside its walls with an iron fist.

Whirling on the surprised Martin, a stiletto-style knife, sharp as a razor, materialized and pressed lightly across the man's throat. "You heard me, keep away from the boy."

"You heard Mister Cloud, Martin." Luke Carter stepped between the men. "I should think you had enough of playing with knives already today."

Nodding slightly, Martin glared and stepped back, away from the flashing eyes of the trader. "Yes, sir. Mister Cloud."

"That's better. You lads can have him after they bring in their next supply of pelts." Cloud slipped the knife back in his belt scabbard.

"And the girl?" Martin Carter spoke up.

"She's yours; do with her as you please. Just keep her from stirring up trouble. It's bad for business. You know what I mean?"

Martin felt his throat where the knife had pressed. "Yeah, I'll do that."

CHAPTER 3

Brown hair floated to the surface of the muddy water as a head bobbed up from behind a partially submerged log on the riverbank. Jehu Wolf pulled on the oak paddle hard, as Pinto guided the small craft over to the girl as she waved at them in waist-deep water. Pulling the dripping girl bodily into the canoe, Jehu dipped his paddle and started back into the river's faster current.

Looking down at the girl, Pinto smiled and shook his head. "Where you headed, girl?"

Her blue eyes studied the big man's face closely before answering. "Just away from the Carters is all."

"Well gal, it's a big piece of land out here to get lost in." The big man pulled heavily on the paddle. "You got any kin, or any place to go?"

"Mister, if I did, I sure wouldn't be working for the Carters." The girl pushed dripping wet hair from her eyes and looked over at Jehu. "They're meaner than a riled up pile of rattlesnakes."

"Uh huh," Pinto grinned slightly. "I know a place upriver, I think we'll take you in, that is if you're willing to work for your keep."

"What do you think I was doing back there?" The girl tried to straighten herself. "Those people worked me like a dog, and fed me table scraps."

"Chauncy's a worker," Jehu looked over his shoulder, "I'll testify to that, Mister Pinto."

"What about you lad, are you a worker?" Pinto was curious why the boy continued to defend the Carter's hired girl.

"I'll hold up my end."

Pinto nodded. "You ever done any trapping?"

"No, sir, not like you. Just small stuff like rabbit snares, chipmunks, and such around my papa's farm."

"Cooking, wrangling?"

"Nope."

"You ever skin anything bigger than a squirrel?"

"No, sir. Can't say I have." Jehu shook his head. "Not unless you count a coon or possum as being bigger?"

"Well, I reckon they're a mite bigger," Pinto smiled slowly. "Tell me boy, just what can you do?"

The steady pull of the paddle slowed momentarily as the tall youth looked back over his shoulder at the trapper. "I reckon I can do anything you can do, that is after you show me how to do it."

Pinto laughed lightly. "Fair enough. We'll talk some more about it at the store."

"What store?" Jehu was curious.

Motioning with his chin, Pinto pointed ahead. "Few miles upriver, David Miles has a small trading post."

"How come you didn't trade your pelts with him?" Jehu looked down at the girl. "Sure would have saved you considerable trouble going all the way downriver to Cloud's Post."

"What's wrong with Cloud?"

"Everyone knows many a trapper has been separated from their furs and money when they stayed too long and got liquored up around Cloud's Post." Jehu nodded at the girl. "That's why she was trying to warn you not to get drunk."

Pinto looked down at the wet girl. "I'm a thanking you, gal. You tried."

"You don't listen so well, mister."

"Didn't have time to listen, thanks to my young friend there," Pinto nodded at Jehu. "Sides, I had me a big thirst to quench."

"He's cheated many a trapper," Jehu insisted. "I've seen it myself."

"He didn't cheat me. Sides, he pays better than Miles does." Pinto scanned the riverbank. "Not that David don't want to pay more; he can't."

"Small-time outfit, huh?"

"You might say that, but he'll grow soon enough."

"If he grows too much, Cloud will send his blacks, or the Carters to pay him a night visit."

Pinto looked sharply at the lad. "You believe that?"

"I do," Jehu nodded firmly. "Seen it happen already. Cloud is a cold-blooded scoundrel, and that's saying it nicely. Course, he don't bother everyone. He needs furs brought in, so he allows most of the trappers to leave with their money and lives."

"Can I get up now?" The girl moved her back slowly. "This piece of wood I'm lying across ain't exactly soft."

Pinto scanned the river again and nodded. "I reckon it's safe enough."

"Is the Miles' place where you're fixing to leave me?"

"It crossed my mind, gal." Pinto pulled easily on the paddle. "His missus will treat you kindly."

"Yeah, she will if I work myself to death." Chauncy rubbed her back. "Ain't I got anything to say about where I go?"

"You do at that." Pinto stopped rowing. "We'll leave you up ahead where we make camp, if you're a wanting off."

"Out here?" The girl looked over at the near bank of the river. Brush and dead driftwood dotted the sandy shore, then small green shrubbery picked up, leading back toward the tall timber lining the river. Nothing moved out there, only mile after mile of timber, and then open wind-blown prairie.

"Where would I go?"

"You climb out of this canoe and that'll be your concern, I reckon." Pinto studied the girl.

"Ssh, Chauncy," Jehu warned the girl, causing Pinto to look curiously at both of them again.

Chauncy shrugged her shoulders, smiling at Pinto. "Well, sir, since you put it that way, I reckon I'll go with you to the trading post."

Picking up the paddle, Pinto guided the canoe forward as he dipped the flat oak paddle deep into the brown water, making the canoe shoot forward. "Right glad that's settled gal, cause you wouldn't be lasting the night out here by yourself with all these night varmints. Now, we'll make camp for the night and dry you out before you catch cold."

"You're a cold-hearted old goat." The girl frowned.

"That I am; that I am." Pinto laughed, pulling on the paddle. "Leastways, I've been told that."

The newly constructed trading post, built by David Miles, was small, but it's sturdy with a stockade of tall cedar posts standing guard around the buildings. Chickens pecked and scratched the ground around the open gates. As Pinto beached the small canoe and stepped ashore, a pack of hounds bounded from the post gates, barking their heads off. Pinto watched as the pack raced out to them. Miles sure didn't need a sentry, that's certain. The huge hounds really made a racket.

With his rifle across his shoulder, plus Jehu and Chauncy trailing him, Pinto strode toward the trading post. The place was new; the smell of fresh cut timber filled the air, and the axe cuts still showed white from the green timbers pointing toward the sky. Twin gates hung from wide rawhide makeshift hinges. A tall scaffold was built, giving an alert guard, a bird's-eye view of the river and surrounding woods.

Dozens of deer and elk horns hung along the outside walls of the trading post. Several dark skinned warriors stood off in a cluster at the end of the covered porch, their half lidded eyes watched the newcomers as they approached. Squaws and babies came and went through the post doors.

Pinto nodded in their general direction, but did not make serious eye contact. Few warriors would hold eye contact with a stranger they did not know, especially if he was white.

"Pawnee." Pinto looked over at the warriors and cussed. He hated the whole Pawnee tribe because of the arrowhead imbedded in his back.

Jehu looked at the dark skinned men, noticing the many scars on the arms and chests of the men. "How you know they're Pawnee?"

"Shaved heads, lizard thin faces, and their slanted eyes, that's how I know, lad." Pinto took another look their way as he stepped through the doorway. "Sneakiest red boogers that ever walked these woods."

Jehu pushed Chauncy ahead, while taking one last look at one of the warriors before entering the post. "I take it you don't like 'em much."

"You're right about that, lad." Pinto stared hard at the warriors. "I don't."

A thin, lanky young man, dressed in homespun cloth, stepped from behind the long table and shook hands with Pinto. "Old friend, it's good to see you again."

"David, my friend, it's good to see you." Pinto grasped the man's hand. "How is the wife?"

"She's just fine, and y'all are just in time. She's in the back, getting supper ready." Miles looked over at Chauncy and Jehu. "These folks with you?"

"They are," Pinto nodded, "Jehu Wolf and Chauncy," Pinto hesitated momentarily, staring at the girl. "Don't reckon I know your last name, lass."

"Lee, my name's Chauncy Lee, Mister Pinto." The girl hesitated.

"Uh huh, Chauncy Lee, Jehu, this is David Miles. He owns and runs this place." Pinto studied the girl and looked over at Jehu. Something was mighty funny about the two, but the trapper couldn't figure it out.

Miles stepped forward and shook hands with Jehu then nodded at the girl. "You're welcome, both of you. Bet you're hungry."

"We're starved. Pinto doesn't slow down long enough to cook," Jehu laughed.

"Well, we'll fix that pretty quick. Supper will be ready in a jiffy."

"Your woman, Sarah, is a fine cook." Pinto tapped tobacco into his corncob pipe and leaned back against the post wall, patting his stomach.

"Thank you, Pinto. I'll tell her you were bragging on her vittles." Miles looked across at the trapper. "You get a fair price for your pelts?"

"Fair enough, I reckon."

"I've been buying a few. Maybe next year, I can afford to buy yours."

Pinto blew smoke into the air and looked around the post. "I'm sure you will. You've got a good spot here, David. You'll do a good business."

"I hope so."

"If my partner didn't need the money for his farm, I would have sold my furs to you this year."

"I know that, Pinto. I'll sure be ready to buy them next year." Miles smiled. "Did Danny Sutton head downriver to St. Louis?"

"Yep," Pinto nodded. "St. Louis, his farm, and Arabella."

"His betrothed?" Miles laughed.

"That's her."

"Well, I can't blame him a bit for that."

Pinto watched as Jehu walked over to where they were sitting. "Nor I, she's sure bound to be better company than this old hoss."

A dark warrior, one of the ones standing on the porch earlier, crouched in the darkness of the post walls and listened to the words of the white men on the porch.

"You pulling out tomorrow, Pinto?"

Pinto drew on his pipe. "Reckon tomorrow or the next, providing you can make the girl a place here."

"She's welcome, but I can only give her food and a place out of the weather."

"That'll do until she can do better, I reckon."

Miles looked over at Jehu. "What about you, Jehu? I can offer you the same deal. Wish it were more lad, but money's kinda short around here."

"I'm a thanking you, Mister Miles, but Pinto wants me to trap with him this year." Jehu glanced over at the darkened stockade yard. "If he's willing to teach me the fur trade, I'm willing to learn."

"Good, good, that's a better deal for a young man, even if it's a rough and dangerous life," Miles smiled. "Just watch your topknot."

"He'll do that," Pinto chimed in. "Reckon he'll have to have possibles; rifle and such. That is, if you can fix him up?"

"I could do that."

Pinto looked over at the lad. "I'll stake him until he gets through this year's trapping and earns his own money."

"Good enough," Miles nodded. "Where you be headed?"

"Taff Lowrie is taking a Brigade into the Yellowstone Country this year. I reckon we'll join up with him, come late summer."

Miles frowned, looking down at the rough porch. "Yellowstone Country!"

"Yep."

"That's rough country, old hoss. Sioux, Arapaho, Cheyenne, Crow, and they're all a rough bunch of boys."

Pinto nodded. "That they are, but the beaver are thick as fleas on a hound's back."

"Jehu, on second thought, maybe you should stay here with me," Miles smiled and looked over at Pinto. "Ain't no sense talking to this hardhead, but you're young. You better listen, that's a dangerous country."

"Thank you, sir, but I guess I'll try my luck, that is, if you'll outfit me?"

"Where you fixing to get horses, Pinto?" Miles asked. "If you're headed for the Judith, that canoe won't make it."

"I left my horses with the Flatheads, Yellow Horn's Village."

Miles motioned to where a fat Indian woman was folding blankets and spoke a few words. "Go with her, Jehu. She'll outfit you."

"Thank you." Jehu started to rise, but then sat back down. "One thing, Mister Miles, that tall, muscled-up warrior I saw when I walked up, ain't Pawnee."

"I know." Miles looked over at the youth curiously.

"Why, is there a problem?"

"He's Delaware."

Pinto blew smoke, "Bull, laddie, he's Pawnee."

"Mister Miles, the warrior is Delaware." Jehu looked again into the darkness. "Pinto didn't look close at this one. His name is Murdock-kinn. He's a quarter white, a quarter black, and the rest is Delaware."

"How do you know, lad?"

"I've seen him at Clouds. He works for the man from time to time, and he works for the Carters sometimes," Jehu warned. "He's a mean one, and I just saw him slinking around out there in the dark, trying to hear what you were saying."

Pinto hissed, "You sure, lad?"

"I'm sure." Jehu stood looking down at Miles. "You start taking Cloud's fur business, you better be ready, cause he'll sure send his brigands down on you."

Miles paled slightly. "Well, thank you, Jehu. I'm obliged for the warning."

"This Murdockkinn, is he some kind of a spy for Cloud?" Pinto looked up at the tall lad.

"He is."

Miles watched as Jehu followed the Indian woman into the trading post. "I don't have much help here, Pinto. It's just me and the missus."

"You gonna be alright, David?"

"I'll have to be. I sure can't rebuild anywhere else." Miles shrugged. "Can't afford to."

"I reckon not. Wish we could stay and help you look out after the place, but we can't." Pinto tapped the tobacco from his pipe. "But, we'll sure keep a sharp eye out, and we'll come on the run if you need us."

"We'll make out," Miles smiled in the dark. "I'll be right here to buy your plews next year, at a fair price."

Chauncy stood near the loaded boat and watched as Jehu finished adjusting the load so it would balance the boat. She could hardly believe the change in his appearance. The fringed buckskins and moccasins, with the long knife and hatchet, hanging from his waist, matured the lad, making him appear older, wiser, and she thought, very handsome.

Turning to her, Jehu pulled off the flat hat covering his eyes. "Well Chauncy, I reckon you'll be alright here with these folks."

"I'll be alright."

"I'll be back in the spring," Jehu hesitated. "You take care."

"I'll be here, waiting." She waved as he stepped into the front of the boat as Pinto shoved them off into the deeper water. "I'll be okay, don't worry."

CHAPTER 4

The canoe grated softly on the rocky bottom of the small creek that fed into the Musselshell River as Pinto brought it ashore. Skin lodges and tepees lined the banks of the clear creek. The finely decorated lodges showed the pride of their owners. Fat, fine muscled horses, of every color, roamed through the village, and along the grassy banks of the creek.

Men, women, and children hurried toward the beached canoe as Pinto and Jehu stepped ashore. The smaller children hung back in fright, but the older children, recognizing Pinto, rushed forward, eager to see what gifts or bits of sweets he had for them. The white-skinned trader never failed to bring them some gifts when he returned from the east.

"Flatheads, lad, they're my friends." Pinto looked over to where Jehu stood beside the canoe, staring at the villagers. The change that took place with his new buckskin clothes and moccasins completely erased the city look of the youth. Three weeks in the sun while paddling up the wide Missouri, then following the Musselshell to the Flathead Village, not only darkened the youth, but also hardened muscles that never held an oar before.

Jehu watched as the villagers pushed in and surrounded them. "Hope they're friendly, Pinto."

"They are friendly and probably more Christian than your own folks." Pinto patted the children on their dark heads.

"Glad to hear that." Jehu felt the youngsters pulling at his buckskins. "We're kinda outnumbered if you haven't noticed."

A tall, straight warrior stopped in front of Pinto and smiled broadly. "My friend, Pawnee Killer, has come back to his friends."

"Yellow Horn, my friend," Pinto shook hands with the Flathead Chief. "It is good to be back with my people, the Flathead."

"It is good you come now." The large warrior looked about. "The village move soon. Our horses need fresh grass, and the game disappear."

"Where do you move?"

"Further toward the big mountains, the one you call the Rockies."

Pinto nodded. "It is good then, I came in time. I will need my horses."

"They are ready, very fat and lazy." Yellow Horn pointed toward the creek. "Where will you make your camp this year?"

"Yellowstone Country."

The warrior nodded. "We have seen many white hunters going to the north, toward the Yellowstone Country."

"Good, our Chief Lowrie will not be far ahead." Pinto nodded.

"No good." Yellow Horn spread his dark hands. "Many Cheyenne make their summer camps this season in the Yellowstone Country."

"The Sioux will be with them?"

"You should not hunt this place, my friend." Yellow Horn looked over at Jehu. "Not if you want this one to grow old and keep his hair."

"This is Jehu Wolf. He is new to this country." Pinto looked over at the lad. "We must teach him its ways, and how to hunt and trap."

"And fight maybe." The warrior nodded. "It is early summer yet. Stay here with the Flathead People and hunt the big shaggies with us."

"Can't, we've got to swing by the Judith to pick up my cache of traps and some more gear, that me and Danny Sutton hid last spring at breakup."

Yellow Horn nodded. "When do you leave?"

"Sunup."

"It is not good that you go, but tonight we will have a feast in your honor, my friend."

Later that night, Jehu watched as the younger women of the village danced around the large fire, smiling shyly in his direction. Buffalo tongue and haunch, with herbs, pounded berries and onions, made up the fare of the feast. Older squaws served the youth until he felt as if he would burst from eating. Finally, he threw his hands up in friendly protest.

Pinto danced several dances and finally collapsed on a pile of buffalo robes beside Yellow Horn and Jehu. "Get up and dance, lad."

"I can't dance, Pinto. I never learned how and besides, I'm too full."

"It ain't a request, laddie. You have to." Pinto winked at Yellow Horn. "Them gals will take offense if you don't."

"Uh huh, well my stomach will take offense if I do." Jehu protested, but with urging from Pinto, finally he joined the line of young warriors shuffling slowly around the huge fire.

"If he lives, he will be a great warrior among the white trappers someday," Yellow Horn speaks as he watches the young white laugh with the younger men. "He shows no fear, and already he makes friends."

"There is no fear in him, and he is friendly enough." Pinto acknowledged.

A slender, young maiden danced in front of Jehu, and looked up, staring closely into his eyes. Tall for a woman, she reached almost to his shoulders. Dark eyes encased in an olive face, stared curiously, studying his features. Black, thick hair, reaching almost to her knees, swayed slowly as she danced in time to the beating drums. Jehu's face turned red as she continued to stare unabashedly at him.

Sensing his embarrassment, the girl laughed softly, her straight, snow-white teeth shining from the glowing fire. Laughing once more, she whirled and shuffled away, keeping time with the rhythm of the drums. Jehu's eyes followed the willowy girl as she danced around the fire.

Jehu retreated quickly to where Pinto was smoking his pipe. "Did you see her, Pinto?"

"I saw her alright."

"What was that all about?" Jehu looked toward the dancers, trying to find the beautiful woman. "I never had a woman stare at me like that before."

Pinto shrugged. "You never can tell about these people, laddie. Maybe she was curious, maybe something more."

"Something more?"

"She may be looking you over for a husband, Mister Wolf," Pinto laughed.

"What!" Jehu gulped, looking sharply at Pinto. "You're joshing!"

"Yep, these Flatheads are funny folks." Pinto puffed on the pipe. "If they're a mind to, they can pick a husband of their own choosing, providing they're the daughter of a chief or of an influential warrior, which by the way, she is."

"Not me, she ain't," Jehu shook his head. "I ain't ready to get hitched to anyone, not even a chief's daughter."

"Big advantage that one," Pinto grinned. "Her pa's Yellow Horn here, big medicine for you."

"I don't need me no advantage, no sir." Jehu watched the circling dancers for signs of the girl. "Thought you said these people were very religious?"

Pinto grinned. "They are, for a fact, but sometimes they get their religion a little mixed up. Not quite what the priests taught them years ago."

"I believe that."

"Well, laddie, don't get worked into a fever. We'll be leaving at first light and even these folks' courtships last longer than that," Pinto laughed.

"Good." Jehu's eyes found the girl. "I'm ready to leave right now if you are."

Pinto followed the youth's gaze. "Mighty handsome filly, don't you think?"

"I don't think, period."

The evening fires still smoldered as Jehu and Pinto watched as the Flathead Village slowly awakened with the morning sun. The horses and mules were rounded up, and then brought in by the young boys of the village. Two horses and four mules stood tied to cottonwood trees while Pinto went from one animal to the next, checking them for soundness. He turned only one lame mule back into the herd. The mule would recover from a split front hoof, but it would take at least six months for the hoof to grow out. Saddles and packsaddles were unwrapped from their hide bundles where they had been placed in Yellow Horn's lodge.

A fine Appaloosa stood ground tied with the others. Pinto studied the horse closely, but he did not know the animal. The Appaloosa was not one of the horses he left with Yellow Horn last fall. This horse was a thing of good breeding. The young boys that led the animals into camp insisted the animal belonged to Pinto even though the trapper told them the horse was not one of his. Shaking their heads, they dropped the horse's lead rope and sauntered away.

The horses stood quietly while they were saddled, but the mules, not used for almost six months, had become wild and skittish. The mules had to be wrestled and hobbled before they would stand to have the packsaddles cinched snugly on their backs. Several times, Jehu ducked as a mule kicked and missed him by only inches.

Pinto looked at the two horses and three pack mules, then nodded his head. "They'll have to do for now. We'll bring along the other packsaddle and try to trade for a mule from Lowrie before we start for home. You did a right good job handling them mules."

"My pap always kept mules."

"I figured you learned somewhere."

"What about the App?" Jehu looked over at the spotted gelding.

"He ain't mine."

Jehu breathed deeply, still catching his wind from the fight the mules had put up. "I thought we were trapping for Lowrie?"

"We are that, but he pays off in pelts," Pinto shrugged. "We supply our own animals and trappings."

"You mean we get a percentage of what we take?"

"Something like that, lad."

"Then why do we need Lowrie?" Jehu was confused. "Why not trap by ourselves and keep all we catch?"

"Simple, it's called protection."

"You mean in numbers?"

Pinto nodded, "Exactly. Where we're headed, the beaver are thick as fleas, but we can't just ride into Sioux and Cheyenne country alone and start trapping. Those old boys are thick as fleas too, and they bite a whole lot harder."

Jehu agreed. "I see what you mean."

Pinto motioned at Jehu, and then smiled. "Looks like you've got a visitor, lad."

Yellow Horn, accompanied by the willowy young woman from the previous night's dancing, walked over to Jehu and Pinto. Yellow Horn shook hands with both white men. Several older squaws and warriors stood about, watching the proceedings with anticipation and curiosity.

"Why you no saddle the Nez Perce horse?" Yellow Horn looked at Pinto then motioned at the Appaloosa. "Him, fine horse."

"He's not one of mine." Pinto shook his head.

Yellow Horn smiled with a glint of mischief in his eyes. "He is yours. I give horse to my friend, Pawnee Killer."

Pinto was suspicious. "Why would Yellow Horn give me such a valuable gift?"

"You are my good friend, and you bring the little ones many sweets, and the women pieces of cloth."

"Then, I thank my friend for the horse."

"Tall one, this is my daughter, Alamette." Yellow Horn spoke to Jehu through Pinto, who interpreted the broken words of English, French, and Flathead. "She wishes to give you a gift. Also, she hopes you have good medicine in your hunt and will return to us safely."

Pinto smiled broadly and nodded, as the girl stepped forward and presented Jehu with a beautiful bone necklace, decorated in many colors. Taking the necklace in his hands, Jehu smiled politely, not knowing what to say to the girl.

"Tell her I thank her, but I don't have anything to give her in return, so I cannot accept her gift." Jehu tried to give the necklace back, but the girl stepped back and shook her head.

"Careful, lad, you sure don't want to insult her or Yellow Horn; might not be healthy." Pinto whispered to Jehu. Smiling broadly, he nodded to the girl. "Give her something, anything."

Jehu reached into his possible bag, brought forth a sharp folding knife, and gave it to the girl. Smiling, she spoke something he didn't understand and hurried away. Yellow Horn smiled happily and shook Jehu's hand vigorously.

"These people are sure easy to please. That little old knife isn't worth much, but it sure made them happy." Jehu grinned.

Pinto shook his head. The gift exchange happened so fast, he didn't have time to explain to Jehu. "Laddie, my boy, I don't think you understand."

"Understand what, Pinto?"

"The Flathead People are friendly alright, but they're still primitive, unused to our ways."

"So?"

Pinto grinned. "Well, me boy, a Flathead girl, with the high status of this one, doesn't normally speak to strangers or hardly to anyone outside her immediate family, especially a white man."

"Pinto, will you get to the point." Jehu asked in exasperation.

"I will. The girl took a liking to you, a real liking. When you two exchanged gifts, she just promised to wait for you."

"She did what?" Jehu almost choked and offered Pinto the necklace. "Why, I hardly know her, for Pete's sake. Give her the thing back."

Pinto held up his hand, refusing the offered necklace. "You hold on now, boy. I know you don't understand their customs, but the fat's in the fire now. You gave your word when you shook hands with Yellow Horn. You give him back that necklace and you'll be insulting him, her, and the whole tribe. Laddie boy, I'll guarantee you don't want to do that."

"Why not?" Jehu offered the necklace again. "I ain't marrying her, that's for sure."

"I'll tell you why not. These people are friendly, Christian Injuns, but you insult one of their women and they're fixing to come unfriendly real quick."

"That bad, huh?" Jehu looked over where the girl stood, showing off the knife.

"That bad." Pinto handed Jehu the reins to one of the horses. "We'll be leaving now. When we come back this way, you just keep right on a going and don't stop."

Jehu shook his head. "Maybe she'll forget and marry somebody else."

"I doubt that very much." Pinto laughed. "She looks smitten to me."

"How? For crying out loud, Pinto, we just met yesterday."

"She's smitten, laddie," Pinto laughed again. "When an Indian girl is smitten, she's smitten, hook, line, and sinker."

"And I don't have anything to say about anything?"

"Nope, after you're married, then you'll be the boss, but for now, she's running the show," Pinto laughed. "Catch the App's lead rope and bring him along."

Yellow Horn waved as Pinto and Jehu turned their horses to the northwest, toward the towering Rocky Mountains. Jehu turned once in the saddle as they entered the cedar and pine trees covering the foothills. He thought he saw the girl, Alamette, standing out from the rest, waving her hands. He had to admit, to himself, she was a beautiful woman with her olive complexion and tall, willowy figure, but marriage, huh uh. He wanted to see the tall mountains and the wildcat before he settled down. Then there was Chauncy, working back at Miles Trading Post. He had to be certain she was okay.

"Women," Jehu whispers under his breath.

Pinto turned in his saddle. "You say something, laddie?"

Jehu swore, as he spoke louder than he thought. "No, nothing."

Ten days of steady traveling found Pinto and Jehu making camp on the banks of the Judith River. Hobbling and sidelining the animals, they turned them loose on the lush grass, setting about, making night camp. The weather was beautiful, with clear blue skies and clean fresh air. Only the constant swarming of horn flies caused them any discomfort.

Pinto applied bear grease and alum to his bare skin, offering the bent can to Jehu. Shaking his head, the youngster declined as the foul smelling mixture stunk to the heavens, and he wasn't fixing to put the foul concoction on his body. Pinto only shook his head and smiled, setting the can on a pack in plain sight. By morning, after the plentiful mosquitoes during the night, he knew the lad would be ready to try anything. The horn flies could be downright pesky, but the mosquitoes brought blood and they hurt.

The Judith wasn't a real big river by most standards, but it was beautiful with its clear, cold water running down from the mountains, and its beautiful, pebbly banks. Tall aspens, cottonwoods, and willows lined the banks, giving off an abundance of shade that enticed the deer and buffalo to bed down along its banks. The problem with the shade, as Pinto knew, if they spread a bedroll where a warm-blooded animal bedded down, they would probably awake covered with ticks and fleas.

Jehu piled up a good supply of firewood close to the base of a large cottonwood tree and started to assemble a fire. Late afternoon was upon them and the sun was beginning to settle slowly behind the mountains to the west.

"Why did we hobble and sideline the animals?" Jehu watched as Pinto squatted near his gear. "You afraid they're gonna run off?"

"Injuns, laddie, I spotted many signs on our way across the flats."

"Indians!" Jehu looked quickly about him.

"That's what I said, Injuns; probably Pawnee."

"I didn't see anything."

Ignoring the last remark, Pinto rummaged through his saddlebags, pulled out a ball of string, and held it up. "There you are."

"That gonna catch the Indians?"

Pinto shook his head. "No, laddie, it's gonna catch fish."

"Fish; you were talking about Indians."

"I'm going fishing, me boy, if I can dig me some worms." Pinto started for the river. "There's fish in these streams that'll make your mouth water.

"What's wrong with grubs or grasshoppers?" Jehu rolled over a decaying dead log and started examining the rotten bark.

"Nothing, catch me some and I'll fry you up a passel of pan fish that'll melt in your mouth."

"It's a deal," Jehu smiled.

With supper over, they watered the horses, then moved them to fresh grass for the night. Finally, the two hunters leaned back against their packsaddles and enjoyed the quiet of the evening. Far off, a wolf howled, sending out his lonely call across the vastness of the foothills and mountains. Jehu shivered; the lonely cry always sent chills up his spine. It wasn't fear; only the chilling lonesome sound of the howl made him shiver.

"Lonely cry, ain't it, lad?" Pinto noticed Jehu looking off toward the wolf's cry.

"Yes, but it's a call of freedom too."

Pinto blew smoke from his old pipe. "You're right there, they're free for sure."

"Are they dangerous, Pinto? Are they as dangerous as I've heard hunters talk about back at the post?"

"They could be, lad." Pinto looked across the small fire at the youth. "I've had them follow me for days, just waiting to see if I would make a kill, I reckon. They're smart and they will attack a man if they're hungry enough, or if the man is hurt and helpless."

"Kinda creepy ain't it?"

"Jehu, everything out here is dangerous." Pinto pulled a burning twig from the fire and relit his pipe. "A snakebite, infection, or bear attack, anything can kill you. Out here you're alone, and don't you forget that, lad."

"Yes, sir." Jehu stared hard into the fire. "Sounds like you're trying to scare me into returning to the trading post."

Pinto shook his head. "No, lad, just warning you is all. This country can be very dangerous. A man has to learn to stand on his own two feet."

A smoky haze covered the Judith Basin as the old trapper led Jehu along a game trail beside the Judith River. Pinto pulled in his bay gelding and studied the small flat valley on both sides of the river. Lodges and horse herds were scattered across the valley.

"Shoshone, I figure." Pinto looked back at Jehu. "Bad actors."

"Where are your traps cached?"

"A few miles further downriver," Pinto motioned with his head. "We got to get by this village to get there."

"That shouldn't be too hard."

"Could be, there's bound to be hunters out." Pinto nudged the gelding toward a stand of cedars. "We'll hold up here until dark, and then try to move past the village."

"Through the timber in the dark, that could be rough going."

Pinto dismounted and loosened his cinches. "We'll drop down into the valley floor and hope for the best."

An hour past sundown, Pinto led the gelding slowly down the game trail and stopped as they leveled out on the valley floor. Across the grass-covered flats, drums were beating a steady rhythm as villagers danced around a large bonfire, screaming out their valor in battle.

"We're in luck boy." Pinto stood still, listening to the drums. "They must have had a victory, 'cause they're sure celebrating loud."

"You mean they always celebrate a fight?"

"They do if they win." Pinto mounted the gelding. "And by the way, they're a yelling. This time they must have won big."

"The Appaloosa stands out like a sore thumb with his white color and all." Jehu looked into the darkness, toward the village.

Pinto glanced at the horse. "For a fact he does. That's why I always ride bays or sorrels here in the mountains. Smear some mud on him, that'll help."

Pinto led his gelding with two mules snubbed to his saddle horn. Jehu led the Appaloosa and the remaining mule. The moon wasn't full, but it spread enough light for the two men to follow a dim trail along the valley. The drums slowly faded as the trail led down to a shallow crossing on the Judith.

Several times, they passed through small groups of mares and colts as they made their way quietly away from the village. Pinto was thankful the horses didn't stampede or run away from them in fright. Occasionally, a mare would nicker at strangers or a stallion would come from the group to challenge them, but no alarm sounded from the lone horse guard.

Pinto let out a sigh of relief as they splashed ashore on the north side of the river. "Well, we made it."

Jehu looked back, across the river. "Them Shoshone dangerous?"

"They're Injuns ain't they?" Pinto looked confounded at the youth. "Any Injun is warlike and dangerous if they got you outnumbered and have no reason to be friendly."

"All of them?"

"All of them. It's just their nature." Pinto turned his gelding west, along the river. "It's their favorite pastime to steal horses and fight. They love it, and laddie, they're good at it."

Pinto winded his way through deep woods and pulled up in front of a tangle of shrubs just as the sun broke brightly across the mountains. Dismounting in the small clearing, he tied the animals to the small trees covering the ridgeback that followed the side of the mountain.

"We're here, laddie."

Jehu looked about the clearing, then over at Pinto before dismounting and tying his stock. "This is where your traps are cached?"

"Yep, me and Danny brought 'em up here instead of dragging them all the way back downriver when we packed out our plews in the spring. We were already overloaded as it was."

"You already knew you would trap with Lowrie this year?" Jehu was curious. "How did you know he was going into the Yellowstone?"

"I knew; word gets around even here in the mountains."

"How far is it to the Yellowstone Country where we're to meet him?"

"Maybe two, three weeks before we make contact with the Brigade." Pinto started unsaddling. "If we're lucky."

"Luck, what's luck got to do with it?"

Pinto shook his head, "Laddie, me boy, you ever heard of rain, floods, broken legs, crippled horses or sickness, not to mention Injuns?"

"Alright, I understand."

"Good, now make camp." Pinto pulled out his pipe and studied the lad. "Keep the fire small, very small."

A week later, Pinto sat his horse on a small hill and studied a large village sprawled up and down a wide valley. Kicking his gelding, he headed downhill, toward the encampment. Jehu studied the village, thinking he has never seen so many lodges in one place. Kicking his horse forward, Jehu fell in behind the trapper, following him straight into the middle of the encampment. Several times, over the last month, he has learned to rely on Pinto's good judgment. He is hundreds of miles deep in the Rockies, surrounded by warlike tribes, so he has no choice.

A mounted warrior sends a shrill whistle screaming across the valley as the two white men came into view at the end of the village. Children and women looked on in curiosity as the trappers rode easily into the center of the village.

Seeing Jehu, looking at him, Pinto smiled, "They're Crow, laddie, mostly friendly toward the whites."

"They look pretty rough to me."

"They can be, but these I know. They are my friends." Pinto pulled his horse to a stop in front of a large lodge and waited. "Their chief is Red Hawk. I trade with him every year."

"Uh huh, well, unless I miss my guess, you're fixing to meet with him real quick." Jehu noticed a tall, aristocratic warrior walking toward them, a red hawk feather attached to his topknot.

Pinto nodded, "You're learning laddie, you're learning."

"Pawnee Killer, it is good you are back among the people." The tall chief greeted Pinto and shook hands with him.

"It is good to be back with my friends and family."

"Your friend Lowrie and many white men wait in the small valley downriver for you, even now."

"That is good. I was afraid we would be late."

"And this young one?" Red Hawk looked over at Jehu. "He is tall, even for a white man."

"His name is Jehu Wolf. He will trap with me this season and hopefully many more to come."

Red Hawk looked Jehu up and down, shaking his head. "And the other, Sutton, what has become of him?"

Pinto laughed lightly since he knew Danny Sutton was popular among the Crow. "He has taken a wife to his lodge. He will no longer ride with me after the flat tailed ones."

"And you just got him trained. We will miss his laughter." Red Hawk turned to Jehu. "You are welcome into the Crow lodges, tall one."

Pinto translated the chief's words. Jehu nodded, "I thank Red Hawk."

"My friend will come with me and see his children." The chief turned. "My young men will show this one where to camp."

"We need to see Lowrie and let him know we are here."

"You will see your children first, besides Lowrie already knows you are here in the village." Pinto didn't bother to question the chief further. If Chief Red Hawk said Lowrie knew, then he knew. Telling Jehu to go with two young warriors and unsaddle, Pinto followed Red Hawk toward a lodge. An old squaw sat scraping on a deer hide as the two men walked up. Without turning, she spoke through the open doorway of the lodge. Two children appeared from inside and stared curiously at the tall white man.

A boy of about nine years pulled another of about six along beside him as he approached Pinto. Kneeling, he took the two boys in his strong arms and hugged them. The younger boy cried out in fright as the huge white man hugged him. The older boy laughed at his little brother and hugged Pinto.

"They look like their mother and grandmother." Pinto added, looking over at the old woman. "I thank you, Grandmother, for taking care of my children."

The old woman never turned as she spoke over her shoulder. "They need their father. They need his guidance. She would have wanted it so."

"I know, but they are safer here and much happier with you, Grandmother." Pinto knew he spoke the truth. Back east, with his folks, they would be considered half-breeds.

"And when I am no longer here for them?"

"You will be here longer than any of us, but if you decide to join your ancestors and abandon the children, then I would return for them."

"Bah." The old woman went back to scrapping the hide. "You should be here to teach them. They need a father's strength."

Pinto looked into the bright faces of his children. Straightening, he looked over at the old woman, then at Red Hawk. "I know, but since their mother is gone, it is hard to stay here in her lodge, with her people."

"You are here with them now, my brother." Red Hawk smiled, looking down at his mother who had turned her back on them.

"My sister would be proud of you and them if she lived."

Pinto looked down at the two small faces and smiled. The boys reminded him of her. They had her eyes and black shining hair. "I know she would."

Jehu was busy making camp when Pinto walked up with the two boys. He carried the smallest one in his huge arms, and the other boy walked proudly beside them. "I want you to meet my sons, Jehu."

"Your sons?" Jehu was genuinely shocked. "Well, I'll be."

Kneeling down, Pinto set the boy down, smiling into their dark faces. "Their mother is dead. I will speak no more of her."

"They are beautiful children."

"She was beautiful." Pinto looked at the two small faces. "They both take after their mother."

Kneeling before the two youngsters, Jehu smiled and presented them with some hard candy from his hunting bag. "What are their names?"

Pinto pushed the older one forward. "This is James Stade and this is Joshua Stade."

Jehu tussled the boy's dark hair, and smiled, "I am Jehu Wolf."

The youngsters looked up at the tall man, then back down at the candy sticks. Smelling it first, they finally, with Jehu's urging, ran their tongues over the smooth candy and smiled. "I reckon they've never tasted candy before." Jehu looked at Pinto.

Pinto smiled. "No, I s'pect they haven't."

Chapter 5

Taff Lowrie stepped out of his tent as Pinto and Jehu rode into the Brigade's camp. Not a particularly big man in stature, Lowrie commanded the respect of his men by his strong personality and iron will. Less than six feet in height, he weighed hardly more than one hundred fifty pounds, but his small frame, for some reason, demanded respect from his men.

Dismounting, Pinto shook hands with Lowrie, looking about the small camp. Several trappers, skinners, and camp workers walked up to greet the legendary trapper. Pinto counted less than twenty-five men.

"This is Jehu Wolf," Pinto introduced the youth.

Lowrie looked Jehu up and down. "Where's Sutton?"

"He stayed behind this season."

Lowrie rubbed his chin, as he looked Jehu over. "He's young, Pinto. You know, your life could be in the balance, if he partners with you."

"Um huh, he's got sand, Taff."

"He's young." Lowrie didn't hold back his thoughts. That's why his men admired him. "You sure, old hoss? I can use him as a cook or camp guard."

"Yep, he's young, but I'm sure. He'll partner with me this season." Pinto turned back and mounted his horse.

Lowrie stepped forward. "Where you be heading?"

"I've always been a free trapper. Reckon if you can't use him, then I'll stay that way."

"The lad can stay, Pinto." Lowrie shrugged his shoulders. He sure wasn't about to let Pinto leave on his own. "And he's welcome."

"That's better," Pinto dismounted again. "He'll pull his weight."

"He better," Lowrie looked over at his men.

A bearded trapper stepped forward and studied the Appaloosa horse Jehu was holding. Walking around the horse, he patted the animal softly. Looking over at Jehu, the man spit tobacco juice that splattered on the youth's feet.

"He's got sand alright, Lowrie." The man swaggered and stopped before Jehu. "Horse thieves normally do. He comes in here riding my horse like he doesn't have a care in the world."

Lowrie looked over at the horse, then over at Pinto. "What's Scott talking about Pinto?"

Pinto shrugged, "Can't say. Yellow Horn, the Flathead Chief, gave me this Appaloosa."

Scott cut off Pinto as he grabbed for the Appaloosa's reins. Quicker than a cat, Jehu grabbed the man's wrist and slung him bodily, into Lowrie's tent, causing it to collapse on one end.

Lowrie started to step in, but Pinto held him back with a look. "Let them be, but remember, Scott started it."

Fighting free from the tent, Scott rushed at the youth, only to find thin air awaiting his wild swings. Whirling, he pulled a skinning knife and advanced. Jehu backed slowly as the infuriated trapper creeped forward.

"I'm gonna show you, boy, what we do to horse thieves out here."

"I ain't a horse thief, mister. You show me anyhow." Jehu eyed the sharp knife. "I like being shown."

The knife flashed in the morning sunlight as Scott slashed repeatedly at the retreating youth. "Stand still, boy. I'm fixing to gut you like a deer."

"You got a big mouth, mister. Go ahead, gut me."

One minute, the men of the Brigade were watching in anticipation as the two men circled each other. Next, they watched in fascination as the tall youth dashed forward, grabbing Scott's knife hand, then with a mighty heave he lifted the trapper from the ground, heaving him bodily over Pinto's bay gelding.

Disappointed the fight ended so quickly, the men watched as the tall youth pressed his foot down, with all his weight, on Scott's exposed throat. Picking up the skinning knife, the trapper dropped when he hit the ground, Jehu slowly cut open the man's hunting shirt, revealing a hairy chest.

"Am I a horse thief, mister? Maybe you were mistaken." The knife hovered threateningly over the man's bare chest. "I've seen many a horse colored up like this one here."

The man's shaggy head nodded. "You're right, I was mistaken."

Jehu smiled and picked the man up bodily from the ground with one hand. "I thought so, my friend. Now, shake and let's be friends."

Ben Scott didn't like it, but he knew the awesome power in the youngster. He sure didn't want to take another chance at escaping death. Pushing out his hand, he shook, and then nodded curtly. "Friends it is."

Lowrie shook his head in disbelief as he watched one of his toughest men beaten soundly by a young pup of a lad, and with little difficulty. Looking over at Pinto, then at the horse Scott was thrown over; he nodded slowly and gave the flat hand sign of yes.

"What'd I tell you, Taff?" Pinto grinned and offered Lowrie a plug of tobacco.

"Well, Pinto, I don't know about sand, but that boy's as strong as a mule," Lowrie laughed. "He's hired."

Jehu led the horses down near the water to set up camp while Pinto looked over Lowrie's mules. They needed a replacement for the one that split his hoof and left behind in Yellow Horn's Village.

Pinto pointed out a big red mule, with a tan brownish muzzle, to Lowrie. "That horse mule broke?"

"Why, he's broke gentler than a dead pig under a gate." Lowrie swore, smiling real wide. "Yes, sir. Pinto, he's broke for the ladies and kids."

"Uh huh," Pinto walked closer to the grazing mule. "What's wrong with him Taff?"

"You know this pilgrim well, old hoss," Lowrie laughed. "He's a good mule Pinto, but he's a stump sucker is all."

"Can't use him."

"Shucks Pinto, him biting on a stump now and then ain't gonna hurt his packing abilities none. No, sir."

"Might not right now, but what about when he wears his teeth down or pulls them out, what then?"

"I'll make you a real deal on him," Lowrie studied the mule. "Use him this season and trade him off down in the settlements."

"Ain't interested," Pinto shook his head. "Ain't ruining my reputation trying to sell a stump sucker."

"Alright, tell you what; I'll bring you that little bay mule standing over there."

"He's sound?"

"I'll guarantee your money back anytime you say." Lowrie looked toward the bustling camp. "What do you say? I gotta get this camp ready to head for the Yellowstone."

Pinto frowned; the bay mule is smaller, but square built and stout. "Alright, have Abner catch him and bring him over."

"For a hundred dollars, I'll do just that."

"Fifty," Pinto fired back.

"Seventy five dollars and no less."

"Bring him."

"You're a hard man to please, Pinto Stade."

"No, I ain't Taff Lowrie, or I wouldn't be trapping for you."

Lowrie smiled, shaking his head as Pinto turned back to the river to find Jehu and his camp. He always enjoyed a good horse or mule swap, and he enjoyed it the most when Pinto was involved. If he had traded the red mule to his old friend, he would have something up on the big trapper the whole winter. Taking the lead rope, as Abner the horse wrangler led the little mule; he shook his head and started for the river.

"Where you hail from, lad?"

Jehu looked around his camp and found Taff Lowrie standing behind him, holding a mule. "Didn't hear you come up, Mister Lowrie."

"Out here, young man, you learn to walk quiet, or maybe not walk at all."

"Yes, sir. I'll remember that," Jehu nodded. "To answer your question, my folks have a small farm in western Kentucky."

"Good farmland around there."

"Yes, sir, it is. Have you been there?"

Lowrie nodded thoughtfully. "I have, but it's been quite a spell."

"What about Pinto? He don't say much about himself. You know, he kinda clams up when I question him about his past."

Lowrie looked over to where Pinto was sitting and smoking with a group of his old acquaintances. "He's an odd one that way. Doesn't say much about himself, but he came from Virginia. We rode together, off and on, for many a year. Fact is, when we were just little shavers, we followed old Andy Jackson to New Orleans."

"You must have been young, real young?"

"We were; it was kinda funny." Lowrie tied the mule on the picket line and pulled up a pack to sit on. "Have a seat Jehu, and for that show you put on today with Ben Scott, I'll tell you all about Mister Pinto Stade."

Jehu quickly pulled him up a pack, knowing he was fixing to hear a good story. "I'm ready, Mister Lowrie."

"First, my name is Taff to all my men."

"Yes, sir."

"We were about fifteen or so, I reckon. Both of us got all het up over the British burning our capital, and doing general mischief everywhere they could. Shucks, everyone in the country was mad as hornets about them." Lowrie lit his pipe and stretched his legs out to get comfortable. "Both of us were runaways from our folks, so we kinda took up with each other, and here we are."

"You ever been back?"

"Tried to go back, but after all the fighting, then the Red Stick Wars and all, neither of us could settle down to civilization, so we just kept riding west. Reckon our folks were glad to be rid of us."

"You've been together all this time?"

"Off and on; most times, Pinto stayed alone or with a partner, but this year he agreed to hunt for me. Up north in Yellowstone Country, I'll need all the experienced men I can get."

"That's why you didn't want me to come along?"

"It was; out here a man has to depend on his partner. If he lets you down, chances are you're probably a dead man."

"I ain't aiming on letting him down."

"No, laddie, I seen that today; you'll stick."

"You ever get married?"

Lowrie smiled. "Tried it once, but she didn't like me sleeping in my buckskins and them long sleeping gowns made me feel, well, naked."

Jehu laughed, as he remembered his father and mother in the long sleeping gowns. Looking over at Lowrie, he laughed again. He just couldn't picture the boss trapper in a long gown. "What happened then?"

"Well, we joined up again and wound up out here with old Fitzimmons, a few years back." Lowrie reminisced. "Man we were green. Not to fighting and killing, but we sure weren't trappers, that showed plainly enough. Shucks, we didn't even know which end of a trap to bait. Poor old Rafe Fitzimmons had his hands full trying to make mountain men out of two fool kids."

"That bad, huh?"

"It was an ordeal," Lowrie grinned, as he remembered. "One time, I set a bear trap, and like a dang fool, stumbled and stepped in the dang thing myself. Couldn't get myself out."

"What happened?"

"Pinto found me around midnight, half froze and madder than a wet hen."

"You mad 'cause you stepped in your own trap?"

"Nah, I was mad because it ruined my last pair of knee-high leather boots and Pinto had something to laugh at me about all winter."

"Did it hurt you?"

"Smarted some, still got them teeth marks to remind me." Lowrie pulled up his pant leg to show Jehu the deep scars from the trap. "Ain't never owned me a pair of city shoes since."

"One more question?"

"Shoot."

"Yesterday, I met Pinto's two children. What happened to his wife?"

"Did you ask him?"

"No, didn't figure he would tell me if I had."

"He wouldn't, and I shouldn't." Lowrie looked over at Pinto. "Her name was Lintamine, or Flowing Wind in English."

"He said she was beautiful with long, black shining hair." Lowrie nodded, "Her skin was smooth as new churned butter, olive complexion, and she had the prettiest smile, snow-white teeth, and those curved lips. She was the daughter of a great chief and the sister of Red Hawk. Her and her father were killed by a Pawnee raiding party, while Red Hawk, Pinto, and the other young men were away hunting the shaggies for their winter meat. Yes, she was a beauty."

"That's why he hates all Pawnees?"

"It is," Lowrie puffed on his pipe. "That's also why they call him Pawnee Killer. He is their sworn enemy, as they are his."

"The Pawnee are further west aren't they?"

Lowrie shook his head. "The Pawnee are raiders. They're liable to be anywhere at any time."

"Pinto blames everything that happens, on them."

"Once, down on the Musselshell, about four years back, as we headed for the spring rendezvous, we met up with a bunch of Pawnee bucks and a subchief, named Bull Runner." Lowrie stabbed at the ground with a sharp stick. "Old Pinto was in the lead when we came upon them varmints. He didn't wait, as soon as he recognized them as Pawnee, he rode hell-bent for leather, right into them boys and killed old Bull Runner and two others before they could get away."

"All by himself?"

"All by himself," Lowrie smiled. "The rest of us were frozen in our tracks. We couldn't believe our eyes as he charged them alone. I reckon them red devils couldn't either. Poor souls thought the devil himself was after them, the way he went screaming and smashing into them."

"What'd they do?"

"The same thing I would have, if that crazy man came charging at me that way," Lowrie laughed. "Those bucks ran like Lucifer himself was among them."

"All by himself." Jehu shook his head in amazement.

"It was all we could do to keep him from pursuing them bucks, but he had an arrow sticking from his back when we got to him."

"So, it's a Pawnee arrowhead in his back?" Jehu laughed.

"Can't say for sure. It's still in him you know, but they were Pawnee," Lowrie nodded. "That fight made him a big man out here, a man with strong medicine."

Pinto walked over to where the two were sitting, looked at them curiously, then started saddling his gelding. "You two having a good visit?"

"We are." Lowrie watched as Pinto saddled his horse. "Where you heading?"

"Figured I'd go visit Red Hawk and the children, while I have time."

"That's good, Pinto."

"You stay here Jehu, get to know the men, but you stay away from Scott." Pinto looked over at the lad. "And watch your topknot, he's a bad one."

"I'll watch over Jehu for you, Pinto," Lowrie laughed, slapping the youngster on the back. "First thing you know, he'll be watching over us. We ain't exactly spring chickens, you know."

"We ain't? Shucks, I've never felt better." Pinto nodded at Jehu, then rode off, toward the crow Village.

"There goes a real hoss, Jehu." Lowrie watched Pinto ride away. "Be proud you have him for a friend."

"I am."

Lowrie watched his old friend ride out of sight. Shaking his head sadly, "He'll never be a real father to those kids, but he'll see after them."

"Is that why he leaves them with the old squaw?"

"Like I said, she's their grandmother and Chief Red Hawk's mother." Lowrie nodded. "That's why, alright. Pinto still has guilt over Lintamine, and he knows they're better off with their own people."

"He could take them back to Virginia."

"No, he couldn't. Back east, they would be half-breeds, cut off from their own people. No Jehu, those kids are better off where they are, and Pinto knows it."

"It's kinda sad."

Lowrie nodded in agreement. "She was a beautiful woman; prettiest I ever laid eyes on."

"Sounds like you were sweet on her too," Jehu grinned.

"I was; shoot we all were, but she had eyes only for Pinto, from the first day we rode into the Crow Village to trade." Lowrie turned and walked away.

Jehu watched the old trapper disappear down along the river, then turned back to make camp. He could only imagine the dangers and great adventures Lowrie and Pinto had been through in their younger days. He wanted to hear more tales. Jehu knew, as wild as it seemed out here now, it must have been far wilder back a few years. Straightening to his full height, the youth looked toward the tall Rocky Mountains, knowing, eventually, he too, would face danger. Indians, grizzly bears, and swollen rivers were somewhere ahead, just waiting to test his mettle.

Chapter 6

The late summer of eighteen thirty-two brought the time of the drying winds. Lowrie waited for three weeks, for the rest of his men to arrive, and then ordered the Brigade to pack their mules and saddle their horses. He lined the long column out then headed due north for the Yellowstone Country.

With hopes of counting coup and capturing many horses from the Sioux, three young Crow warriors accompanied the Brigade as scouts and hunters.

The Brigade presented quite a sight in the early morning light, wearing their colorful buckskins as they rode their frisky prancing horses. Their rifles rested lightly across their laps, eagle feathers adorned their hide headgear, and porcupine quills decorated their fringed buckskin shirts. Yes, they put on quite a show as they waved good-bye, passing the Crow People of Red Hawk. The villagers stood in lines, smiling and waving, bidding the Brigade farewell and wishing them good hunting.

Jehu rode the Appaloosa, who seemed to show off, prancing as he passed the young maidens, who were smiling broadly at him. Even Red Hawk raised his hand to salute the tall youth as he passed.

Pinto knelt beside his children, who were clinging tightly to him. Jehu was curious, no more time than he spent with the boys; he was surprised they were sad to see their father leave. Well, he heard somewhere that blood was thicker than water. He knew Indian children doted on their fathers.

Jehu looked across the mountains, never realizing the Rockies were so tall and steep. The game trails the Crow scouts led them over, as they made their way toward the Yellowstone Country, were narrow and rocky. Pinto said these trails were much harder than following the valleys, but they were faster and safer than the lower trails where they might encounter hunting parties of Sioux, Cheyenne, or Arapaho. In early fall with the air turning cold, the Indian tribes hunted so they would have buffalo meat for the coming winter. They prepared for the heavy snows that would soon fall, confining them during the cold times to their hide lodges.

The mountains were majestic as far as the eye could see. Early snows top the high peaks, where only a soaring eagle could traverse. Far above, a lone Hawk looked down in disdain and screamed out his call at the long column of men winding their way down into the valley.

Jehu breathed in the sweet air and smiled as he recalled the preacher's talk of heaven on earth. This place, with the many colored wild flowers, green rolling grass, and the wind blowing softly through the aspens, must be the place they preached about. The Rocky Mountains were as close to paradise as he could ever wish for. Jehu felt he was home; he belonged here. He already felt as one with this wild and unconquered land. He was elated, happy to be in this far-off place with his friends and men he knew he could depend on, men who may hold his life in their hands.

The Appaloosa walked surefooted, down the rocky trail, leveling out onto a flat valley where small streams of shallow water coursed through.

Lowrie raises his hand, then circles, making the motion to make camp.

On the long trek to the Yellowstone, where few words were spoken on the trail, Jehu learned the hand signals the Crow scouts used to relay their wishes. Where Taff Lowrie was friendly back on the Judith, here, he was all business, gruff and stern. Pinto already told him not to take it personally. It's just his nature out here where he wanted the men on alert. Here, danger lurked all around, and death waited behind every rock and tree.

"We'll make camp here for a few days, while the Crows find us a good place to squat for the season." Lowrie gathered the men about him.

"You boys, be ready and alert. I don't think we've been spotted yet, but it's coming sooner or later. Let's just hope it's later."

An old trapper, with a scraggly tobacco stained beard, smiled widely. "You getting worried, Taff?"

"Just being careful, Jethro." Lowrie nodded, looking about him. "Wouldn't want you to lose that fine beard of yours, now would we?"

"Well, sir, I wouldn't want to either. I've become kinda fond of it over the years."

Jehu grinned as he watched and listened to the old man. Jethro Loomis was the oldest of the trappers. He had been with Lowrie for several years, way back to when they both trapped for Fitzsimmons. The old trapper was arthritic, almost too old to face the hardships and chill of the cold water while setting traps. Still Jethro refused to give in to Lowrie, to become the camp cook and hide scraper. No, sir, he swore loud and long, never would he become a lowlife cook, never.

"I need two volunteers to get us some camp meat." Lowrie looked about before the men dispersed to make camp. "Who wants it?"

"I'll go," Jehu speaks up.

Lowrie studied the tall youth. "Alright Jehu, who else?"

"Me," Ben Scott called out. "I need to stretch my legs."

Lowrie looked over, where Scott stood beside his horse and then at Jehu. Uncertainty stood out on his face as he tried to decide. "You boys ain't gonna kill each other out there, are you?"

Scott laughed, "I'll get him back alright, Taff."

"See that you do," Pinto stepped forward with a warning sound in his voice, "Or answer to me. We'll need all the men we've got before this season is over."

Three miles from base camp, Jehu and Scott tied their horses, hiding them in a deep sheltered stand of cedars and small pine. Scott, with Jehu trailing silently behind him, slipped quietly along the small stream, their moccasins hardly making a sound on the soft grass.

Scott stopped abruptly, pointing to the ground and the moccasin tracks Jehu already left in the soft, sandy soil. "Boy, never leave a track if you can help it, even in camp." Scott wiped out the tracks with a branch. "You never know who might stumble on it."

"Yes, sir. Sorry."

"If we get discovered, some of us could go under." Scott nodded, "And I'm kinda fond of my hair."

"Yes, sir." Jehu looked over at the trapper. "Tell me Mister Scott, how we gonna stomp around in these valleys and set traps without being discovered?"

"Oh, there's no doubt we'll be discovered sooner or later, but these old mountains are high and vast, with some mighty deep canyons." Scott waved his hands. "When the snow flies, hopefully the Injuns will stay further down, closer to the grasslands. They're after buffalo, more than anything else."

A small noise along the creek startled a huge buck then he lifted his head from the soft grass he had been nibbling on. Scott froze in his tracks as he broke a twig beneath his foot. The buck's tail twitched nervously, but he made no attempt to move away. Scott waited until the buck dropped his head once more, and then stealthily started forward again. Jehu waited quietly as the trapper moved silently as a stalking cat, through the thick jumble of brush.

Watching, ever so slowly, Scott's fifty caliber lined up with the buck's shoulder then he heard the report of the discharging weapon. Powder smoke blew into the air, temporarily hiding the buck from Scott's view.

Quietly, Jehu stepped beside the hunter. "You got him, Mister Scott, dead center in the heart," Jehu whispered.

"We'll wait here a mite." The older hunter squatted under a cedar and surveyed everything in sight.

Jehu was curious. "Why, what's wrong?"

"Nothing boy, we'll just give that buck time to bleed out. We'll wait to see if any unwanted company heard that shot and come a snooping around."

"You do this every time you shoot?"

Scott bit off a chew of tobacco and offered the plug to Jehu. "You do if you want to keep your hair."

"No thanks, I never got the habit."

"You're learning. Just remember, patience out here is what will save your hide. It's your best ally." After twenty minutes, Scott stood up slowly. "Let's go find our deer."

Both hunters had a deer over their shoulder as they rode unannounced into camp. Lowrie walked over and nodded. Little Elmer, the camp cook, with the help of two young Crow warriors, had one of the deer skinned out and roasting hotly over a fire before Jehu could wash up.

Pinto walked over to the stream where Jehu was washing the dried blood from his hands. "Looks like you and Scott had a good hunt."

"The deer are plentiful around here."

"Reckon they are, means they haven't been hunted much, we're in luck." Pinto looked over to where Scott was sitting. "You have any trouble with him?"

"None, he taught me a lot today."

"Mostly, he's a good man." Pinto nodded. "But you keep alert, you never know."

"I'll do that."

"Had me a look around whilst you two were gone." Pinto sat down on the stream bank. "Beaver sign is plentiful, all along these valleys."

"Does that mean we'll do good this year?"

Pinto nodded. "We should trap plenty of flat tails, but we still got it to do, then get out of here with our hair in place."

"We'll get out, Pinto."

"You seem pretty sure, lad."

"I am, got me a hunch this is gonna be a good year." Jehu looked out across the beautiful mountains and forests. "I'm planning on being out here for a spell."

"Lowrie says we'll rendezvous down on the Green this year, sell our plews, buy supplies, and head back to the mountains."

"You mean we're not going back to Miles Post this spring?"

"Probably not."

Jehu sat down and studied the clear water. He didn't count on staying out two seasons. Would Chauncy be alright? What about the Carters? How long would they stay away from Miles' trading post? If they discovered Chauncy there, Martin Carter would probably drag her back to Cloud's Trading Post and put her to work at the Inn. Jehu knew, legally, she was an indentured servant that still owed the Carters money. "Didn't figure on staying so long."

"Me and Sutton stayed out three years in a row. We sent our plews in with Taff." Pinto looked at the lad. "You're worried about the girl, ain't you?"

"I told her I'd be back."

"She'll be fine. Miles is a good man. 'Sides, I thought you didn't want a woman."

"I don't, but I did give her my word I'd return."

"You will, just not this year." Pinto stood up. "But, if you're dead set on going, you can ride back with the men. Some of them will probably be heading home after rendezvous."

"We'll see," Jehu nodded. "Thank you, Pinto."

"You're welcome, lad." Pinto smelled the air. "Come on, smells like that venison is ready, and I'm starving."

The hardworking beaver damned up a small stream across the valley, turning it into a fair sized lake of water. Pinto and Jehu set their traps in the shallow backwater of the lake, taking many beaver from the spot. Pinto was beside himself with joy. Never had he seen beaver so plentiful or so fat. The cold water thickened their hides, making their fur prime. Many a night, Pinto would hold up a beaver and shake it at Jehu, laughing that booming laugh of his. "We're gonna be rich, lad, rich."

A hard winter was near and a month passed as the Brigade's luck held. The beaver were falling steadily into their traps, and so far, their presence in the mountains had not been discovered. Snow started falling steadily, forcing them to leave tracks upon the land, something they couldn't help, but the trappers knew the tracks left evidence of their presence in Sioux country.

The beaver had already been trapped out in the valleys around their base camp, so Lowrie ordered to move the camp deeper into the mountains, closer to the larger valleys. Again, they found a hidden valley, out of the path of wandering tribes, and again the beaver were plentiful. Lowrie was elated, as he has never seen the trapping so good. Fox, martin, bobcat, and wolf fought their way into the steel traps lying along the game trails.

"We're gonna be rich men this year." Lowrie smiled and puffed on his old pipe. "Rich men, I tell you."

Jethro spit into the fire, causing the coals to hiss. "I'll tell you, Taff, what we're gonna be. We're gonna be hip deep in snow before sundown tomorrow."

Lowrie looked up at the sky and the forming clouds. "What do you think, Running Dog?"

The Crow scout looked over at the white chief and nodded in agreement. "Snow big, soon."

Lowrie shook his head in disgust, and then looked over at the stretching frames covered in green pelts. "Well, we've had a good run so far. We may have to lie up a day or two, but it'll blow itself out, then we can get back to work."

"It's just an early storm coming in is all." Pinto added. "Won't last long."

"Well, we can make good use of the time we have, scraping and stretching the hides we've already taken." Lowrie shrugged and looked again at the darkening sky.

"What about our traps, Taff?" Jethro questioned. "We need to spring 'em, or chance losing some prime skins."

Lowrie nodded in agreement, "It'll only take one man on each trap line to bring the traps in. You boys, get to it. The rest of you, work on our plews."

Jehu stood up and picked up his rifle. "I'll go, Pinto."

"You sure, lad?"

"I'm sure."

Lowrie listened and stepped up beside Pinto. "If Jehu's going after the traps, you take Running Dog and go get us some extra camp meat."

Pinto nodded, "Okay, Taff."

Again, Lowrie looked above at the clouds. "A body never can tell about these mountains. It may blow out quick or last a week."

"You take care of your hair, boy." Pinto placed his hand on Jehu's shoulder. "It shouldn't take you, but a few hours to pull the traps. If we've caught anything, bring the carcasses to camp and we'll skin them here."

"Yes, sir. Pinto."

"Hurry, lad. I don't like the looks of the sky."

"I'll hurry."

Jehu rode the Appaloosa and led the gentlest one of the mules. He sure didn't have time to wrestle or fight with one of the more stubborn animals. The trap line started about two miles north of camp, in a small chain of lakes. Beaver signs had been plentiful when they scouted out the small lake, linked with others further north, earlier in the week.

The wind picked up and the temperature dropped considerably as Jehu arrived at the first small lake. Tying the animals off, he shrugged out of his coat and waded into the water. Pulling on a stake chain, he removed the first steel trap from the lake bottom. He was surprised, the water doesn't feel that cold, but he knew with the temperature dropping like it was, come morning, the lake's edges could form ice.

The next trap produced a beaver, which he quickly gutted and tossed on the shore. Halfway around the lake, Jehu had three beaver already. The wind died down, but now the snow began to fall in big flakes. Jehu hurried, as he didn't expect to find so many animals in the traps. Gutting them was taking time and he had many more to retrieve. He told Pinto he would hurry. He sure didn't want the embarrassment of Lowrie sending out a search party to look for him.

The sky was dark as evening approached and the temperature dropped. Jehu had almost all the traps hanging from the packsaddle on the old mule. Nine prime beaver hung across the saddle, a good day's work. Jehu was beginning to feel the cold, as he had been wet now for several hours, but he wasn't about to abandon valuable furs or let Pinto lose faith in him.

The last trap was empty as Jehu tugged at the chain stake and hung the wet trap across the mule. It was almost dark and he was at the end of the trap line, at least three miles from base camp. He was proud of himself, as he didn't quit or leave any of Pinto's traps behind. Leading the mule, he started back the way he came, following the shore of the lake, making his way back to where he left the Appaloosa tied.

It was snowing hard, coming down in huge flakes, already covering the heavy cedar limbs. Close ahead, he could see the shape of the gelding, but something else caught his attention. Chills ran up his spine as two warriors, not the Crow scouts from camp, but strange warriors, stepped out from behind the horse, unaware of his presence. The mule brayed when he smelled the Appaloosa, causing the warriors to whirl and draw their bows. Jehu cussed his foolishness. His rifle hung out of reach on the Appaloosa, and thankfully, the warriors obviously didn't see it or know what it is.

Throwing himself sideways, Jehu felt one of the arrows penetrate his side, causing a burning sensation. He watched as the old mule fell to the ground in its death throes, as another arrow missed him and buried itself in the mule. Rising from the snow-covered ground, he heard the warrior's scream of triumph as he charged across the open space that separated them.

Pulling his skinning knife, Jehu ducked under the first warrior's advance, driving the long blade through the man's stomach. The force of the thrust jerked the knife from his hand, leaving him defenseless as the second warrior raised his war axe to strike. Unarmed, he deflected the heavy war club with one arm while taking a deep cut to his other forearm from the warrior's sharp knife. Both combatants clashed together as the warrior tried to drive the sharp blade into Jehu's vitals.

Rolling on the ground, Jehu managed to get a strong grip on the warrior's knife hand and flipped the man over him, into the snow. The man was cat quick. He was back on his feet before Jehu could reach him. Both men circled in the deepening snow with Jehu retreating slowly before the warrior. Feeling for the protruding arrow, without taking his eyes from the Indian, he snapped the wooden shaft from his back and tossed it at the Indian.

The warrior crouched, ready to spring at the white, when suddenly, his eyes widen as he fell forward, a feathered arrow shaft was sticking out of his back. Jehu recognized Running Dog, and walked toward him cautiously.

"Well, me laddie, how are you feeling?" Pinto stood over the cot where Jehu had rested, inside Lowrie's tent."

"I've got a headache." Jehu touched his forehead. "Everything's kinda fuzzy."

"Probably from loss of blood. Jethro had to cut that arrowhead from your side." Pinto motioned over his back to where the old trapper sat smiling. "You lost yourself quite a bit."

Jethro walked up beside the cot. "You hungry, young'un?"

"Starved, it seems like I haven't eaten in a week. How long have I been here?"

"Running Dog brought you in last night."

"I don't remember too much, except it sure was cold." Jehu tried to sit up. "Last night, huh? Sure seems a lot longer."

"Lie back, lad, I'll feed you." Jethro started to sit down on the cot.

"I ain't dead, Jethro, I'll feed myself." Jehu pushed himself up stiffly and reached for the bowl Jethro was holding. "Man, my side's throbbing."

"It should be. Look what I took out of you." Lowrie held up a razor sharp flint arrowhead. "You break that wound open and I'll let you bleed to death."

Jehu looked down at the bandage across his side. "That came out of me?"

Pinto spoke up proudly. "Sure did, lad, just kinda pin cushioned you. I reckon you'll be sore enough for a few days."

"Stew's good Jethro, thank you."

Lowrie puffed on his pipe and studied Jehu. "Running Dog told us what happened as he saw it."

"Thank him for me, Pinto. I'm sorry about the mule." Jehu chewed slowly. "Old Molly took an arrow meant for me."

Lowrie stood up. "We're sure glad it wasn't you, lad. I can get another mule"

Jehu stopped chewing. "What Indians were they?"

"Cheyenne."

"Does that mean we're found out?" Jehu downed the stew hungrily.

Pinto shrugged. "Running Dog and his boys hid the bodies. They won't be found until spring, but the Cheyenne might come looking for them."

"Providing the tribe knows where they are, which they probably don't." Lowrie spoke up as he started for the flap of the small tent. "These young bucks hunt and steal horses everywhere. It was just your bad luck that they happened to pass through this valley."

Handing the bowl to Jethro, Jehu looked over at Pinto. "Help me out of the man's bed and into mine."

Lowrie shook his head. "You stay here tonight, lad. Tomorrow I'll kick you out."

"Sounds good to me." Jehu lay back on the pack that served as a pillow. "Sounds real good."

"Here," Lowrie handed Jehu the arrowhead. "Keep this for a souvenir."

Jethro snatched the arrowhead and grinned down at Jehu. "I'll fix a leather thong on it and you can wear it around your neck."

"Thank you, Jethro."

Pinto took one last look at Jehu then followed Lowrie and Jethro through the tent flap and out into the cold air. Running Dog sat outside before a glowing fire, wrapped snugly in a blanket. Large snowflakes floated into the fire, causing a hissing sound when they landed.

The warrior waited until the whites wrapped themselves in blankets and settled in beside the fire. "The tall one, will he live?"

"Thanks to you, he'll be fine." Lowrie replied to the warrior.

Running Dog nodded. "This is good. Him brave warrior. Him kill one and fight the other with arrow in his side."

"We thank Running Dog for bringing in the white horse and the traps with the lad."

The young Crow warrior looked over at the tent. "Him plenty brave warrior."

"Tell me, Jethro, how long will this storm keep up?" Lowrie asked the old trapper.

Shrugging, Jethro spit into the fire, and then nodded at Running Dog. "Can't say; ask him, he's the Indian here."

Running Dog looked at the old trapper and smiled. "Two day, it will be over."

"Good, soon as it passes, we'll move the camp further north, just in case."

"Cheyenne no come, this place too cold." Running Dog spread his hands to the fire. "Bad weather, warriors stay close to tepee and squaw. These two warriors young, out hunting, looking for horses to steal."

Pinto puffed on his pipe. "He's probably right, but maybe we should move our base camp further back in the mountains anyway."

Running Dog shrugged. "We bring five Cheyenne horses and two scalps here for the tall one."

Pinto spread his huge hands. "They're yours; he would want you to have them."

"Running Dog thanks the Pawnee Killer." The Crow smiled brightly. "Cheyenne steal horses from the Nez Perce people, I think."

Lowrie stiffened. "You mean the Cheyenne are out raiding and the Nez Perce could be following them here to this valley."

Running Dog shook his head. "Maybe split nose people follow. Cheyenne take three good horses from them."

"Now that's just what we need. Those Nez Perce warriors are a mean bunch when you get them riled." Jethro groaned, "Stealing their horses will do that just fine."

Lowrie swore, "Pinto, get some sentries out. Tell them if I catch them asleep it won't be good for their hides."

A week passed, and Jehu was up and about. The arrow wound was still sore to the touch as was the knife cut, but both were healing. The arrow entered his side, causing a lot of blood loss, but it only hit the muscle above his waist. The knife wound was superficial, deflected by his arm, so it was healing quickly.

Running Dog tried to persuade Jehu to take one of the Cheyenne scalps that he took from the two dead warriors, but he refused. The Crow only shook his head in surprise at the refusal. He didn't understand the white's ways, but he was proud to keep it himself.

Jehu took the arrowhead Jethro fixed with a leather thong, and presented it to the warrior.

Running Dog smiled and placed it around his neck. In return, Running Dog removed a shell bracelet from his arm and presented it to Jehu. "Wear this proudly Jehu Wolf, from your friend, Running Dog."

Jehu also bought a steel skinning knife from Lowrie and he presented it to Running Dog for saving his life.

The gift brought a gleam to the Crow's eyes, almost as much as the scalp and the arrowhead necklace. "Thank you, my friend. I will carry it with pride."

Three days later, the storm blew itself out and a warm Chinook wind started melting snow from the ground. The snowstorm came early this season and it didn't last, but the men knew there would be plenty more to come. Lowrie gave orders to break camp and be ready to move out at first light. The Brigade would travel to the north and west until the Crow scouts found a suitable place to make a permanent camp for the winter. Once the heavy snows started, they would set and run their traps and trap lines, but they wouldn't be able to move their camp so easily.

Jehu settled stiffly in his saddle when the Crow scouts came rushing excitedly into camp. Walking out to bring in their stolen Nez Perce horses, they found the horses gone from where they were staked out to graze. Fresh tracks show in the light snow, tracks made by a few horses heading back to the north. The Nez Perce tracked the Cheyenne horse raiders from where the horses were stolen, following the tracks doggedly into the small valley to the Brigade's camp. Patiently, they waited and watched, and then silently they stole their horses back after the white trappers turned in for the night.

Running Dog and the Crows were beside themselves with anger. Not only had they lost several horses, but they lost their reputations as being the best horse thieves on the plains. What was worse, the whites witnessed the theft and would laugh behind their backs. The Nez Perce came in right under the Crow's noses and took back their horses, but they had taken none of the Brigade's animals. Running Dog and the other two warriors want to give chase immediately, but Lowrie held up his hand, and stopped them.

"You would just ride into a trap, my friends." Lowrie stared at the warriors. "I need you to find us a camp for the winter."

"They shame us," Running Dog was beside himself. "They have stolen our horses. We must go after them."

"They weren't your horses." Jethro spit a brown stream into the snow. "I believe they were stolen from the Nez Perce first."

"They were ours."

"Then go, but my men will not ride with you." Lowrie stared about him. "The snow is too deep, and they have several hours head start on you. I promise you, I will give you many horses to replace the stolen ones when we are finished trapping."

Disgruntled, the warriors mounted the three horses they kept tied to their lodge and fell in line with the Brigade. Grim and hard faced, they felt they had been shamed, to go back to their village without the Nez Perce horses and knowing the white trappers would tell the story. To them, it was an act of cowardice.

CHAPTER 7

Lowrie moved the Brigade's camp two days march west, along the banks of the Yellowstone River, into a secluded valley the Crow Scouts found. The valley and surrounding country was covered with small lakes, waterways, and creeks that abounded with beaver dens, dams, and fallen trees. Several game trails were beaten down by an abundance of small game and deer crisscrossing the country. From the signs and tracks leading to the small creeks, Pinto guessed the valley had never been hunted or trapped hard. It was virtually a gold mine for the fur trappers.

One of the smaller valleys was a natural fortress, with only one way in and out; exactly what Lowrie was looking for to build his headquarters for the winter. Issuing orders, he had their camp backed up against a rock ledge that offered good cover if the Brigade should come under attack. Their stock had a natural supply of water, plenty of grass, and bark to eat on, when the deep snow came. Bark from the surrounding trees wasn't the best fodder for the horses, but if the snow became deep enough, it would see them through the harsh mountain winter. No sign of old villages or campfires was found, making the Crows feel the valley along the Yellowstone was seldom occupied. Most of the tribes preferred staying out on the open plains, closer to the buffalo herds.

Light snow still covered the valley floor, not deep yet, but the heavier winter snows were still to come. The weather hadn't been cold enough yet to freeze the streams and small waterways. They were still open and flowing, clear for the trappers to set their lines of steel traps. The Brigade went to work with axes, saws, and hard muscle. They hurried to get small cabins and tents up for protection against the cold days and heavy snows that they knew would come. The sooner they finished camp, the quicker they could get busy, trapping the beaver that would bring cash money at rendezvous.

Three days later, the camp was finished. The cabins were only roughed in shanties, nothing pretty, but they would hold back the deep snows and rains yet to come. Huge stacks of firewood for the winter laid piled against the cabin walls. Lowrie looked around the small stockade perimeter and nodded. The Brigade was as ready as it would ever be for the oncoming winter. Now they were ready to get down to the business of trapping beaver and other fur bearing animals.

Lowrie put out the order. He gave the men the okay to leave camp the next morning and start setting their trap lines. The trappers would pair off and lay their trap lines in teams of two. One would set and bait the traps, while the other stood guard for any unwanted company. Many a lone trapper forfeited their lives by becoming too careless while trapping alone. In the deep snow of winter, it is impossible to keep their tracks hidden from searching eyes. Many an unwary man had been killed while focusing his attention solely on his traps. Traps and bait were readied as the men sat around their campfires, laughing and joking, eager to get an early start.

Jehu walked slowly back, through the large camp, stopping in front of Pinto and Lowrie. "They're gone."

"Who's gone, Lad?" Lowrie pulled the smoking pipe from his mouth.

"Running Dog, Tall Grass, and Owl Man," Jehu eased down on a packsaddle. "Ain't nothing left where they camped, cepting horse droppings."

Lowrie swore under his breath, "They're your kinfolk Pinto. What are they up to?"

"I figured they'd go, leastways after they gave up without much of an argument." Pinto nodded. "They went after them horses; had to. Their pride was at stake."

"Great!" Lowrie threw his arms up. "The Nez Perce have a three day lead on them at least."

"Don't matter; Running Dog will follow them clear back to their village if he has to, but they'll get them horses back or get themselves killed trying."

"What is so important about them dang horses?" Lowrie growled.

Pinto looked over at the Brigade leader. "I told you, their pride, that's what, Taff. You know that, as well as I do. You ain't no greenhorn. They take them horses being stolen from under their noses very personal."

"That's a bunch of bull. Those horses belonged to the Nez Perce to start with." Lowrie was fuming. "Well, they're your relatives. What are we gonna do?"

"Nothing; I'm gonna set my traps come morning."

Lowrie shook his head. "We can't do that. I gave my word to Red Hawk that I'd see after them lads if he let me use them for hunting and scouting."

"So!"

"So nothing, if something happens to Running Dog, I doubt he'll do anymore trading with us, or even let us pass through Crow hunting grounds without a fight."

Pinto agreed. "Yeah, reckon you could be right. Red Hawk is partial to his nephew alright."

"You think you can bring them back?"

"I can give it a whirl." Pinto studied the flames. "But, mind you Taff Lowrie, I ain't promising anything."

"Who do you want to go with you?"

"I'm going," Jehu spoke up.

"You up to it, lad?" Lowrie looked over at Jehu. "You ain't had much time to heal up yet."

"I'm going." Jehu glanced at Pinto. "We're partners, ain't we? If we ain't, say so now. If we are, then I'm riding with you."

"It's your hide, and yes, we are partners."

"When will you be riding out?" Lowrie tapped out his pipe.

Pinto stood and looked up at the stars. "Come morning, soon as it's light enough to track them."

Lowrie stuck out his hand. "Good luck, old hoss."

"Thanks, we'll probably need it."

"Pinto, I gave my word to look out for them boys. I know this is dangerous business for you and Jehu. You know I wouldn't ask you to go unless I thought it was mighty important."

"Quit fretting, Taff. We ain't dead yet." Pinto looked over at Lowrie. "I know how serious this could be if something happens to them Crows."

"It could put a damper on all of our trapping operations." Lowrie shrugged. "We could be finished in the mountains without the furs of the Crow."

Pinto turned from the fire. "I doubt Red Hawk would get that upset. Once upon a time, he was a young hotblood. He knows how the young bucks can jump the gun at times."

"No matter, I gave him my word." Lowrie said as Pinto departed.

"Your word means that much, Taff?" Jehu questioned the Brigade leader.

Lowrie looked to where Jehu still sat. "Out here, among the savages, all a man has is his good word. Don't be forgetting that. Now you better turn in."

"Yes, sir."

"Jehu, I can get someone else to go with Pinto."

"He's my partner. I'm going."

"Good luck." Lowrie nodded. "Tell Pinto your traps will be set and run every day while you're gone. You have my word."

The snow was melting fast in the warm afternoon sunlight. Pinto had little trouble following the wide track left by the Nez Perce raiders and the Crow Scouts following them. Pushing their horses at a fast trot, Pinto was surprised the Nez Perce were in no hurry. They had stopped and made camp on their first night after stealing back their horses. Pinto was worried. Apparently, they were not afraid of the Crows following or catching up with them, which meant they were more than willing to fight. Arrogant, Pinto thought to himself, but he had heard the Nez Perce were great warriors. To run from only a few Crow warriors would make their leader lose respect.

As best he could figure, from the tracks that were left, there were at least seven of the Nez Perce. Pinto wasn't certain, but studying their back-trail, he was thinking the tracks showed where a lone horseman had remained back. If this was true, the Nez Perce knew the Crow were few in number, and how close they were. Somewhere ahead, they would lay a trap, waiting for Running Dog and his friends. Enemy scalps, Crow horses, and weapons would be a real prize for these warriors.

"How you doing?" Pinto could see the pinched face of the youth.

"I'm hurting some, sore as the dickens and tired, but I'm right behind you." Jehu pulled his fur cap down over his ears. "Don't you be looking around for me, Pinto Stade."

"You'll do, Jehu." Pinto grinned.

The slight murmur of distant voices, sounded ahead. Pinto pulled in and sat his gelding quietly, listening to the wind stirring through the trees. Again, the faint, but distinct sound of voices came from ahead. Dismounting, he checked his rifle and handed his reins to Jehu.

"Wait here, Lad. I want to take a look up ahead."

Jehu stared down the trail where Pinto disappeared among the tall Aspens and Box Elders. The horses pulled bark from the tree trunks, chewing the rough fodder hungrily. Jehu did not see any reason for stopping them. After three days of pursuit, he knew they were famished. If they didn't eat something soon, they would start to lose their strength.

Pinto came back down the trail at a dogtrot, pulling up beside Jehu. "You up to a fight, lad?"

"No, but I'll get that way after I loosen up a bit." Jehu dismounted slowly. "What's going on up there?"

"Check your rifle Lad, and get to loosening." Pinto checked his priming and started down the trail.

"Pinto, what's happening?"

Pinto laid his huge hand on Jehu's shoulder. "Like I figured, the Nez Perce laid themselves a trap. Our Crows rode right into it and now they're trapped under a rock outcropping just ahead. The Nez Perce can't get in, but our lads can't get out, so we'll have to lend them a hand."

Pinto led off, down the trail, cautiously making his way forward toward the ruckus ahead, where both sides were taunting and threatening one another. Jehu shook his head in awe as he watched Running Dog rise from behind a rock and jeer at the infuriated Nez Perce. He had to respect the young Crow. Only Running Dog, with his arrogance, could laugh in the faces of a superior number of the enemy, and sure death.

Their attention focused on the screeching Crow warriors. The Nez Perce were unaware there was another enemy closing in behind them. Dozens of arrows were stuck in the ground around both the Crow and Nez Perce warriors. Jehu couldn't believe there had been no real damage done to either side, but the rocks and brush made it difficult for an arrow to penetrate accurately before they were deflected.

"You ready, laddie boy?" Pinto cocked his rifle.

"We gonna shoot them without warning?" Jehu looked at the back of the buffalo robed warriors. "Seems kinda cold-blooded."

"S'pect it is, but there's seven of them varmints and only two of us, plus the fact you're hurt bad already. I would sure like to keep my hair."

"I reckon you're right," Jehu cocked back the hammer of his Hawkens, "but I don't have to like it."

"I agree, it's a sorry deal, but we ain't got much choice." Pinto braced his rifle against a tree. "You take the big one on the right and I'll get the one on the left."

"Then what?"

"Pray, 'cause they're either gonna run at us or away from us." Pinto waited for Jehu to take aim. "And them being Nez Perce, I don't see them leaving without their horses, which happen to be right behind us."

"Yeah, I seen 'em when we came in."

Jehu took a deep breath then sighted in on the broad back, only fifty yards distance. Pinto's rifle belched fire and lead, killing a warrior, as Jehu's shot sprawled the broad warrior he had taken aim at, face down into the muddy ground. Reloading as fast as he could, Jehu knocked one more warrior down before the others bowled into them.

Pulling his skinning knife, Jehu forgot how sore he was, or how the wounds hurt as he strained against the Nez Perce that grappled with him. Miraculously, Pinto killed one of the onrushing warriors with his tomahawk. However, now each of them was locked in mortal combat, wrestling around in the mud and snow with the remaining Nez Perce.

Jehu was still weak from his wounds and three days of hard riding. He was lucky the warrior, he struggles with, is one of the younger, less mature of the Nez Pearce warriors. Holding on to the man's knife arm as best he could, Jehu felt his strength draining from him. Suddenly, the warrior was pulled bodily, from him. Jehu watched as Pinto dispatched the young warrior with a thrust from his knife.

"You okay, Jehu?" Pinto helped him to his feet. "You ain't hurt?"

"I'm okay." Jehu sprawled onto the ground. "At least I think I am."

Running Dog, with Tall Grass and Owl Man following, raced across the ground just as the last Nez Perce breathed his last breath. "Aye, we are too late to help our friends."

"Not too late to gather up your horses." Pinto looked around at the blood-splattered ground. "Get 'em and let's get outta here."

"And these?" Running Dog looked at the dead Nez Perce.

"They're yours, my nephew." He knows Running Dog referred to the scalps of the dead warriors. "They paid for their carelessness, but they are still great warriors.

"But not as great as the Crow, my uncle." With one swipe, he wrenched the scalp from the biggest Nez Perce warrior.

Pinto smiled at the bewildered Jehu. "If we hadn't come, it would have been our Crow brothers here who would be bald-headed."

"They act like they were the ones that killed them warriors." Jehu watched the Crows dancing and screaming around the dead warriors.

"Well Jehu, they figure there's no use letting them scalps go to waste," Pinto laughed as Jehu turned away, shaking his head.

Lowrie walked from his cabin in surprise as he heard the sound of several horses approaching the Brigade's camp. Relief, then a smile spread across his rough face as he greeted the men. His eyes focus on the frozen, bloody scalps hanging from the manes of the Crow's horses. Running Dog rode straight and proud. He wanted everyone in camp to see the scalps and to boast of the prowess of the Crow warriors.

"That didn't take long."

"We were lucky. It was a short trail." Pinto dismounted. "You gonna tear into Running Dog for not following your orders?"

"Should I?"

"Not if you want hunters for the winter." Pinto looked over where Running Dog was strutting around like a tom turkey with his chest thrown out, with an ever-present proud walk. "He's proud, Taff. Don't shame him in front of the men. You do, and he'll ride out of here."

"Alright Pinto, but if it happens again, he's going home."

"It'll happen again. You can bet on it." Pinto nodded. "He's wild and he plays by a different set of rules than we do. He can't help it."

"How's the boy?" Lowrie looked over to where Jehu dismounted slowly.

"He carried his load, but he's give out."

"Have him rest a few days."

"Uh huh, you know he'll do just that."

Jehu held their horses and stood watch, while Pinto waded through the cold water of the small lake. He shivered uncontrollably. He knew the water had to be freezing, but Pinto didn't seem to notice. He knew the one drawback to a trapper's life; they were always in knee-deep water. Cold, warm, or hot, it was always wet.

His eyes surveyed the far banks and woods as the sharp crack of the mallet, drove the wooden anchor stake into the muddy bottom of the lake. It had been two weeks since the fight with the Nez Perce. They had already trapped out two larger lakes, and now Pinto was relocating their steel traps. Jehu's strength had returned and his wounds were barely noticeable. Scabs over the wounds were still covering the scars that would always decorate his side and arm, reminding him of the fight with the Cheyenne and Nez Perce.

Snow fell silently over the woods and lake, softly covering the ground like a blanket. Jehu smiled; the scene reminded him of a picture he had seen once in a store, back in St. Louis. The place was quiet, peaceful and serene, just like the picture portrayed. Pinto waved and Jehu led the horses forward, to where the trapper waited.

"Let's build a fire. I'll let you cook us up some coffee, Lad." Pinto mounted his gelding and turned from the water's edge. "I'm pert near froze solid."

"I imagine." Jehu dug around, finding some dry squaw wood, and pulled out his flint and steel. Smoke swirled lightly as the sparks took hold and grew into a blaze. Adding larger, dead wood, he held out his hands to the flames, smiling over at Pinto.

"This overhang will warm up pretty quick. Pull off them wet moccasins and I'll try to find something for the horses to eat on."

"Bring me back some dry leggings and moccasins off the horse, lad, if'n you don't mind." Pinto relaxed back against the warm cave wall.

Snowflakes landed on his face as he tied the horses in the heavy birch timber where they could eat on dead leaves and bark. "It'll have to do boys; best I can do for now." Jehu spoke absently to the geldings.

By the time Pinto thawed out, it was already past midday. The snow blotted out the sun as they made their way silently, around the small lake where they would set their traps next. Slipping quietly, toward the end of the lake, Jehu surveyed everything in his path. Two times now, there had been close, near fatal encounters with hostile warriors. He knew his luck could run out on his next encounter if he was not alert and watchful.

It seemed like years ago, back at Cloud's Trading Post, he heard the Carters, other trappers, and hunters say a man's luck could run out at any time. He listened to their talk and stored it in his memory for future use, and now, here he was. He listened to the tall tales of the hunters, but he never thought he would be out here hunting, trapping, and being hunted himself. Breathing in the cold air deeply, he felt the flakes of snow falling against his face and smiled. Despite the cold and wet, he couldn't help himself; he loved it. The danger and hardships were real enough. Even so, out here he felt exhilarated, full of life, completely free for the first time in his life.

The snow became heavier as he walked back, toward the overhang. He thought of Chauncy and the Carters. He didn't want to admit, he knew she was safe at Miles, but he worried about her. The Carters, he didn't miss at all. They were mean and vicious, but he knew they were experienced hunters, men who should be respected, not for their coldness, but for their knowledge of the frontier.

Their long day ended. Jehu finished unsaddling the horses and turned to where Pinto was sitting beside a fire, inside the cave. "The horses are taken care of for the night, and I brought in your last pair of dry footwear." Jehu handed Pinto the moccasins.

"Well, I'm a thanking you, Lad." Pinto sipped on the hot coffee. "We'll be heading in tomorrow."

Jehu picked up the weathered and burned coffeepot. "How's my coffee?"

"You're getting better at making it Lad, but add a little more beans to the water next time." Pinto rubbed his bare shriveled feet.

Jehu shook his head. "Jethro showed me how to cook the stuff."

"What exactly did he show you?"

"He told me that when it boils to drop a rock in it, and if the rock didn't hit the bottom, it's thick enough."

"A rock?" Pinto shook his head. "Jethro told you to put a rock in my coffee?"

"Sure did."

"Well, did the rock bang against the bottom of the pot?"

"Nope, just sat there on top till I pulled it back out."

Pinto looked down into his tin coffee cup. "Uh huh, one thing's sure; you're becoming a bigger liar than Jethro."

"I am?"

"Yeah laddie, I've gotta get you outta these mountains before you're ruined." Pinto laughed, his voice rumbling, as he put on the dry moccasins.

The snow became heavier, as drifts built up against the walls of the tents and log shelters. The trapping had been the best that Lowrie and Pinto could ever remember. Furs were stacked head high in bundles, ready for the trip east to the rendezvous on the Green River.

"What time of year is it, Pinto?" Jehu sat, bent over, sewing on a new pair of moccasins.

Shrugging, the trapper looked across the wooden shelter. "Couldn't say, but it's still a long pull till spring."

"Feels like February to me."

"It does, huh? Tell me lad, what exactly does February feel like?"

"It feels cold, that's what." Jehu never looked up.

"Well, then it must be February." Pinto puffed on his pipe. "Cause it's sure 'nuff cold out there."

"I reckon we'll be pulling out before long?"

"Won't be long now; soon as it warms up and the trails clear some." Pinto looked over at Jehu. "You ready?"

Jehu nodded. "I would like to see if Chauncy's alright."

Chapter 8

Pinto had been right, as the spring break up closed, the weather turned warm. It was nearing time for the Brigade to head back to the east for the summer rendezvous on the Green River. The winter's trapping had been plentiful. Bundles of plews, wrapped in buffalo hides, completely filled two tents. Never has Lowrie and Pinto had such a run of luck. Now, if their good fortune would only hold long enough for them to get back across the mountains and out of Yellowstone Country.

Riggings, on the packsaddles and riding saddles, were checked and mended as the men waited for the weather to clear. Their timing had to be perfect. Too early and the trails and passes would be covered with ice and snow. Too late and the trails would be muddy and slick, and the rivers swollen with run-off water.

Running Dog and the Crows were excited, ready to be on their way home. The horses and scalps, taken from the Nez Perce, would make them heroes in their villages. The young maidens would sing their praises, and the older men would honor them with gifts. They would be big men in their village and lodges. In Crow society, the scalps were more valuable to them than the furs were to the trappers. They were big medicine, showing everyone the power the young warriors possessed.

"I think it's time for us to move out." Lowrie sat in front of the fire and puffed on his ever-present pipe. "What do you think, Pinto?"

"I'm ready, hoss, whenever you give the word." Pinto nodded slowly. "Running Dog and his men say the trails are clear and will be all the way to the Judith."

"Good enough; we'll pack the mules and pull out first light."

"We've had a good run this season Taff." Pinto looked around the small camp. "Kinda reminds me of our first year with Fitzsimmons."

Lowrie nodded, remembering. "It does and now all we've got to do is get out of these mountains with our hair intact."

"Me and Jehu will take the point with the Crows further out."

"The lad's made a real hoss this year ain't he?" Lowrie looked to where Jehu and Running Dog were throwing a hatchet at a tree. "I'll bet he's gained twenty pounds of solid muscle and grown an inch."

Pinto smiled. "He'll do for sure, but even more important, he's grown in his head. He picked up the Crow language quicker than a blink."

"I agree; Running Dog has taught our young Mister Jehu Wolf a lot." Lowrie smiled. "Watch the way he moves, his actions. Shucks, he's more Crow now than white."

"True enough," Pinto smiled. "It comes to him natural like, and those two have become like brothers."

"If blood makes men brothers, then they are." Lowrie watched the two young men. "You remember young Barnes? Can't recall his first name. Anyway, you remember him and the Indian Blue Bonnet?"

"I remember," Pinto nodded, "our second season with Fitzsimmons. They became fast friends, just like these two."

"Yes, sir. These two remind me of them. I wonder whatever became of Barnes?"

"Couldn't say; they just up and vanished one night and we never heard from them again."

Lowrie looked around at the surrounding mountains. "I feel like, sometimes they're out there, watching us."

"Could be," Pinto agreed, "just could be."

"I believe it; those two loved the mountains."

Pinto shrugged. "No Taff, they went under somewhere up there, or they would have come in by now."

"We'll probably never know for sure."

The Brigade was strung out, following the same game trail on its return trip, as it had taken coming into the Yellowstone Country. Running Dog and his Crows were out in front, with Pinto and Jehu following at a distance. Melting snow dripped from the Cedar and Aspen limbs as they made their way quietly along the wet path. Each trapper led at least two mules strung out in a train a quarter mile long.

The first part of the journey down the mountain trail found the path narrow and slippery. There was no need to put flankers on each side of the column. Lowrie kept all the men on high alert and vigilant. He knew the Brigade was too strong for a small war party to attack, but the Sioux and Cheyenne were powerful allies. Together they could mount a large war party against them if they knew the trappers were in their mountains.

Lowrie knew they had been lucky. The weather had been ugly all winter, with snows heavy enough to block the mountain passes and keep the Indian hunters down lower. The Brigade had not been spotted by hunting parties during the long winter, and for that, Lowrie was thankful. The plews they loaded on the mules would net his share, a small fortune. He contemplated retiring from this dangerous life as his gelding plodded along the muddy trail. Slapping the reins absently against his leg, he shook his head. He knew better, he wouldn't retire this year or even the next. He loved the wildness of the mountains, the freedom of the trapper's life, and the moments just like this. Excitement, danger, and moments of life and death, always rode the mountains with them, kept a man's blood racing, kept him young. Nowhere down in the settlements, could a man experience the mountain man's life or breathe in the pure clean air, or enjoy the company of so many comrades.

Shaking his head, he looked forward, along the trail to where his old friend Pinto rode ahead. He was not alone in his thinking. Something had drawn him and Pinto into these mountains and into a trapper's life. He knew, like himself, Pinto would return again and again to the trap lines and loneliness.

Two weeks passed as the Brigade wound their way slowly toward the Musselshell. Small parties of hunters had been spotted, but so far their luck had held and they had not been discovered. On several occasions, Running Dog had rerouted their course to swing clear of these hunters. Night fires were held to a minimum at each camp. The horses and pack mules were kept hobbled and guarded closely. Lowrie was a natural leader, able to get his men to follow him with little sleep, and less to eat.

They all knew once clear of the Yellowstone Country and the warlike tribes of the Sioux, Cheyenne, and Arapaho, they would be safe. They also knew, when their plews sold, they would be riding high, wide, and wild on their profits. Then, they could live the good life, warm, full of good cooking, and plenty of whiskey. At least until they ran out of money, then it would all start again.

The Brigade had only been on the trail two hours when Lowrie heard the roar of a rifle, then another, followed by yells and war whoops far down the trail. Kicking his gelding into a run, he raced madly toward the sound of battle. Warriors raced back and forth, screaming and yelling their war cries as they charged toward the Crows and the two whites, Pinto and Jehu. Kicking his gelding hard, he raced into the melee as the hostile warriors raced away, yelling their defiance.

"Sioux," Pinto rose from where he had been kneeling. "Dang the luck; we ran smack-dab into them without warning."

"Anybody hurt?" Lowrie looked around.

"Tall Grass got himself a nick in the arm is all." Lowrie looked across the clearing to where Jehu was leaning over a downed warrior. "What's the boy doing?"

"Can't say." Pinto started toward Jehu as Running Dog and the other two Crow warriors raced up and dismounted.

Jehu was standing with outstretched arms, preventing the Crows from finishing off the Sioux warrior that was lying unconscious on the ground. Blood flowed from a deep gash on the Sioux's forehead. Running Dog was demanding that his arrow was the one that hit the enemy and the scalp was his to claim. Owl Man claimed second coup on the Sioux, touching him with his bow.

Lowrie dismounted and stepped closer to the downed warrior. "What's going on?"

"This warrior is still alive," Jehu motioned at the man.

Lowrie looked down at the body then surveyed the clearing as the rest of the Brigade rode up and dismounted. "So?"

"Running Dog wants to kill him." Jehu held his arm out as the Crow furiously tried to duck around him.

Pinto stepped forward. "Stay out of it, lad. The Crow and Sioux are hereditary enemies. They've been fighting for years."

"He's just a kid, Pinto."

"Him Sioux," Running Dog yelled.

The young warrior moved groggily and looked around him. Seeing the hostile Crow, then the white trappers, he tried unsuccessfully to stand.

"He's my prisoner," Jehu argued.

"Me shoot this enemy, me claim coup."

"Running Dog is my friend, and you did shoot this one," Jehu conceded. "I will trade you something for him."

"Why you want this Sioux dog?" The young Crow was in a rage. Before him, was a Sioux, the sworn enemy of the Crow nation.

"Running Dog can see he is just a boy. What do I have that you will trade for him?"

The warrior lowered his war bow and relaxed. Looking at Jehu, he finally nodded. "You give me spotted horse for him."

Jehu looked over where Pinto stood watching. "Yellow Horn gave you the Appaloosa, but I'll pay you for him."

"Is the Sioux that important, lad?" Pinto looked to where Jehu had helped the injured Sioux to his feet.

"Look at him Pinto, he's just a kid." Jehu looked at the boy. "Yes, it is important that he live. We may need him."

Pinto nodded. "Then the horse is yours."

"Thank you." Jehu handed the reins of the Appaloosa to Running Dog who smiled and nodded.

"Him may be boy, as you say my friend." Running Dog tapped the Sioux with his bow. "Soon, him be man; maybe kill you someday."

Jehu quickly bound the head wound then mounted the Sioux on a gelding and handed the reins to Jethro. "Take care of the boy, Jethro."

Jehu hardly cleared the Brigade's eyesight when Jethro dismounted and tied the Sioux's legs together under the gelding. "Doubt you can run off on us now, young'un."

Pinto rode back to the Brigade late in the afternoon, almost at sundown. "Trouble, Pinto?"

"No, just figuring we better find a good fortified campsite for tonight is all."

"You think we're in for trouble tomorrow?"

Pinto nodded and took the plug of tobacco Lowrie offered. "We thank you kindly. Yep, we've killed three of theirs and got one prisoner, which I'm sure they've spotted by now. Yep, come morning we could be hip deep in redskins."

Lowrie swore, as they were almost out of these mountains now. "You're such a bearer of good news."

"Well, you asked, old hoss."

"Reckon I did at that." Lowrie took the tobacco plug back and slipped it in his pocket. "Okay, pick us a good spot where we can pen the animals. We'll be along directly."

Lowrie sat his horse, watching as the big trapper loped his horse to the front, rejoining Jehu and the Crow. He studied the vacant trail then shook his head. Maybe he would get out of this business after all.

Jehu glared at Jethro then cut through the rawhide that bound the warrior's feet. Reaching to help the young Sioux from the horse, Jehu nodded as his hands were slapped away. Backing away, he waited as the boy slipped unsteadily to the ground. Pointing to a nearby dead log, he followed as the Sioux made his way over to it and sat down.

Reaching for the bandage, he jerked his hand back quickly as the youth slapped at him again. "I'm just gonna take a look at your head."

Running Dog walked up and stared down at the boy. "Tell him, I'm just trying to help."

"That one?" The Crow laughed. "Him no want help."

"Tell him anyway."

As Running Dog was speaking, Jehu reached again for the bandage. As quick as a blink, he grabbed the youngster's wrist as the Sioux tried slapping him again. Feeling the power in the white's hand, the Sioux relaxed. He knew this one was very powerful, too strong to try to fight.

"You talk sign language with this one my brother; him understand good." Running Dog tapped the Sioux again then sauntered arrogantly away.

Jehu nodded at the Crow's departing back. "Much obliged Running Dog." Jehu replaced the bandage with bear grease and a fresh bandage. He noticed the hate Running Dog's laughter sparked in the Sioux's eyes as he walked away. The boy spit onto the ground and kicked dirt toward the Crow, who only laughed louder. Jehu smiled, the youth had no fear, but he did have plenty of hate. "You hungry?" Jehu signed.

Only the cold, hard eyes of the captive gave a silent answer as they stared at the tall trapper.

"What is your name?"

Again, the silence came.

Jehu stood up and started to walk away.

"I speak some of the Crow dog's words. Do you white man?"

Jehu stopped and turned. "My name is Jehu."

"I am called Little Elk." The young warrior spoke with mixed Crow and Sioux then used hand signs. "Why do you ride with these warriors?"

"I ride with them because the Crow are my brothers," Jehu nodded. "I am glad to know Little Elk. You are welcome here."

The youth spit. "The Crow are my enemies. You should kill me now."

Jehu walked away, leaving Little Elk sitting alone, unguarded. Looking about, the Sioux started to break for the heavy cedars surrounding the camp. "I wouldn't were I you. The Crow are just waiting for you to run."

Little Elk hadn't noticed that Jehu stopped and was watching him from where Jethro was stirring a large, steaming pot. Turning at the sound of the voice, he kicked at the damp ground and relaxed.

Two more days passed as the Brigade slowly dropped from the high mountains and started across a huge valley. Only foothills were ahead of them. Pinto knew this would be the perfect place for an ambush. Unless he missed his guess, the Sioux would be waiting for them here. Lowrie rearranged the defensive position of the Brigade. One man led several mules while the other trappers rode alongside the flanks of the caravan, ready and waiting for the coming attack.

Lowrie, Pinto, and Jehu rode at the head of the column with the Crow scouts riding point to smell out the Sioux. Jehu turned in his saddle and focused on Little Elk who was riding alongside Jethro's gelding. The boy had finally resigned to the fact he was a prisoner. He relaxed and was waiting out his fate. Actually, he liked the tall white that fed him and put medicine on his head. Nevertheless, the white said the Crow were his brothers and that made him the enemy of all Sioux.

The valley's deep grass had been eaten down short by the herds of buffalo that evaporated away in front of the Brigade as they neared. Almost the entire valley was visible to the Crow. Nothing on the level, grassy plain could escape their sharp eyes. Lowrie knew they would have several minutes of warning if the Sioux appear.

Running Dog held up his war bow and circled the spotted Appaloosa in a tight circle. Pinto and Lowrie both looked in the direction he pointed. Ahead, emerging from the far timber slowly, a line of mounted warriors walked their horses forward. Eagle feather war bonnets fluttered all along the line, showing many older warriors were present, and would be joining in the fight.

"Looks like we have a sure 'nuff battle on our hands, Pinto."

"How many you reckon there is of them heathens?"

"Enough to go around, I figure," Lowrie swore. "Circle the mules and use the furs to make some kind of barricade against them."

Nodding, Pinto whipped his gelding back to where the Brigade had halted. Waving his hat overhead, he watched as the outriders quickly circled the mules and horses then started hobbling them. The packs of furs were not much protection, but they would have to do. There was no other protection out here on the valley floor except the horses. Pinto knew, if it came down to it, Lowrie would order them killed for breastworks against the Sioux. He was also aware, if they killed the horses, they would lose the furs, as there was no way the men could pack the heavy bundles all the way back to the Judith.

Racing his gelding back to where Lowrie, Jehu, and the Crows waited, he saw the Sioux were still advancing slowly toward them. "We're as ready as we're gonna get, outside killing the horses."

"Then I reckon we better get our tails back to the boys." Lowrie started to turn when Running Dog kicked his horse and galloped toward the Sioux.

"What's that fool doing, Pinto?"

"Beats me; trying to commit suicide, I reckon." Pinto watched as the Crow slid his horse to a stop and screamed his defiance, less than a bow's shot from the line of painted warriors.

Several warriors started to ride forward, only to be stopped by the older warriors. Yelling his challenge once more, Running Dog turned the Appaloosa and raced back, toward the Brigade. Halfway there, he dropped his bow and whipped the big gelding across the line of Sioux in a dead run. Jehu had never witnessed such superb horsemanship as the Crow displayed, ducking under the running gelding then appearing on the other side before standing upright on the horse at a dead run.

Even the Sioux were impressed as they waved their war bows and shields and hollered their praise for the rider. Several rode their lunging ponies forward, yelling their war cries and paying tribute to Running Dog. Flipping from side to side then off the back of the horse, the Crow finally pulled the blowing horse to a stop and retrieved his weapons. Retreating to the Brigade, as the Sioux continued forward, Running Dog grinned over at Jehu.

"That was good riding my brother," Jehu smiled.

"I give our people time to get ready for big fight."

Jehu looked at the nearing Sioux line. "We're kinda outnumbered. We're gonna lose some men if we fight."

"We lose many men if we don't," Running Dog laughed. "Sioux people my enemy, but they are great warriors."

Jehu shook his head slowly at the remark, then rode over to where Jethro sat waiting with Little Elk. Reaching for the lead rope, he led the youth's gelding forward, away from the Brigade, before Pinto or anyone else could stop him.

Racing forward, Pinto grabbed for Jehu's reins. "Whoa up there, laddie. Where you headed?"

"Gonna try to get us out of this fix."

Pinto swore, "You're gonna get yourself killed is what."

"It's my hair, Pinto." Jehu looked to where the Sioux had stopped, less than a hundred yards from the Brigade.

Nodding, Pinto released the gelding and watched as the tall youth rode slowly across the grassy floor, toward the waiting Sioux. Stopping thirty feet from the feathered warriors, he turned Little Elk's gelding loose and motioned him forward. Stopping the gelding, Little Elk looked over at the Sioux warriors then back at Jehu. After looking up and down the line of warriors, he offered his hand to Jehu.

Releasing Jehu's hand, Little Elk turned to the Sioux. "This white man saved my life. He is my friend."

A warrior in a long trailing, eagle headdress walked his horse forward and stopped before Jehu. Studying the white face, then Little Elks, he nodded his head slowly. "For my son's life you are free to ride away from this place white man."

"And the others?"

The warrior looked across to where the Brigade waited. "We have dead warriors. The Crow have shamed us. If you give us the Crow dogs, the other whites can leave this place in peace, if they give their word they will not come back."

"The Crow are our brothers. We will not give them over for you to kill."

The warrior kicked his horse forward. "Then you must leave this place alone now, before I change my mind."

"Tell me great Chief; how can this shame be erased, horses, rifles?"

"Blood is called for."

"Only blood will settle this?"

"We have dead; they must be avenged."

"If it is blood you want, I will fight your best warrior. If I die, we will give you the Crow. If I live, we will all leave this place in peace." Jehu looked back at the Brigade. "We have many rifles, many bullets. Many of your men will die if you attack."

"You are a white man. Why would you do this thing?"

"I already told you; the Crow are my friends." Jehu looked into the chief's eyes. "I have given you the life of your son. Their lives, I ask in return."

The warrior turned his horse and rode back to the Sioux line, talking with the other older leaders. After a lot of head and arm shaking from several of the other young men, the chief started back.

"My father is a great and wise war leader."

"What is your father's name Little Elk?" Jehu watched the proud warrior approach.

"He is Wandering Bear, the chief of my people, the Brule Sioux." Little Elk threw out his chest proudly. "He has counted many coups on his enemies."

"Will he fight with me?"

"No, you are beneath the dignity of a chief. Another will face you if they decide to let you fight."

Wandering Bear rode up and looked hard at his son, then turned his eyes on Jehu. "We have agreed; you saved my son. We do not want you to die. Let one of the Crow fight this fight."

"No!" Jehu shook his head. "I am chief of the whites. I will fight."

"The Crow are our enemies."

"If there is to be a fight, it will be me."

Wandering Bear shrugged his shoulders. "There must be bloodshed to save face for the Sioux people. It is the only way."

"So be it," Jehu nodded.

Pinto waited with Lowrie and the Crow, wondering what Jehu and the Sioux were discussing. They looked on curiously, as he turned his gelding and rode slowly toward them at a slow trot.

"What's going on, lad?"

Jehu dismounted and started removing his hunting shirt and possible bag. Pinto looked on curiously, wondering what was happening. "The Sioux demand blood, I have talked them into a fight with just one man from each side instead of getting many killed."

"You what?" Pinto stepped from his horse. "I've never heard of the Sioux doing anything like this."

"You want to lose several men, our friends, and maybe our furs." Jehu looked at the old trapper. "I don't, not when one life will suffice."

"Boy, they got some warriors over there that can fight a grizzly, bare-handed," Pinto spit, "and win."

Jehu shrugged, "I ain't a grizzly bear."

Running Dog listened closely then chimed in when he figured out what they were talking about. "I will fight the Sioux dog; it is my right."

"They will only fight me," Jehu lied.

"If I go out to them, they will have to fight Running Dog."

"You will only shame me, my brother. They will think I am afraid." Jehu looked up at the mounted warrior. "Do you wish to do this?"

Running Dog backed his horse a few steps and dismounted "If you are to do this thing, I give you back your spotted horse. He will bring you luck."

"Thank you, my friend." Jehu took the reins of the Appaloosa. "If I lose, then you can try your luck, because the only way you'll get out of here alive, without fighting, is if I win."

Lowrie looked over at the waiting Sioux. "I think we can whip them in a fight, Jehu. There's no need for you to risk your life."

"And how many of these men and animals will you lose Taff?" Jehu saddled the Appaloosa with his saddle and stepped up on the horse. "This way you will just lose one."

Lowrie studied the lad for a few seconds then nodded. "Good luck."

Pinto shook hands with the young trapper. "Good luck, laddie."

"And I thought he was too green to trap with us." Lowrie shook his head as Jehu rode toward the Sioux.

The Sioux were amazed at the muscles that rippled across the arms and chest of the tall white youth as he slowly approached them. They also noticed the scars covering his body, evidence that he had been in fights many times. Then the loud cheers came, as their Sioux hero rode out in front of the warriors. The warrior was almost as tall as Jehu, and very heavily muscled as well. Dressed only in a breechcloth, he sat his warhorse proudly, his shoulders ramrod straight, as his dark eyes stared quietly at the white man.

Jehu stared across at the warrior, as he knew the man would be a brave, formidable foe. An old man dressed in eagle feathers and a horned buffalo skull, stalked slowly between the two combatants. The medicine man sang a short prayer and tossed some kind of powder to the four winds. Walking to each man, he handed each a war axe and a sharp skinning knife.

Jehu's horse cocked his ears backward, causing Jehu to glance behind him to find Pinto sitting his horse only yards away. Nodding lightly, Jehu returned his attention to the warrior before him.

"Good luck, laddie."

Jehu nodded as he studied his opponent. "Looks like I might need it."

The medicine man pointed to each warrior then toward the two warriors sitting their horses fifty feet apart. Each of the combatants rode their horses to a warrior and turned to face his opponent. The old man raised his hand then dropped it. The pounding horse hooves could be heard across the valley as the two combatants raced toward each other.

Jehu swung his war axe mightily and watched in amazement as the

Sioux warrior disappeared under his hard running gelding. Circling, the two men charged at each other once again. Jehu waited until almost the last minute then reined the Appaloosa horse hard into the oncoming Sioux horse. The collision was hard, causing both men to lose their seat as the horses went down in a pile, both men and horses all mixed up. Jehu scrambled to his feet, looking around for his dropped war axe. Snatching it up quickly, he whirled and swung just as the Sioux sprung forward. Both war axes clashed mightily together as the men slashed, wildly at each other. The two combatants parried, each trying to land a crippling blow. Jehu realized he was up against a dangerous opponent, a superior fighter. The warrior seemed to vaporize in thin air every time Jehu thought he was going to land a lethal blow.

A roar from the Sioux went up every time Jehu missed a blow and the warrior closed in for the kill. Several small cuts showed on Jehu's arms and chest as the sharp knife of the warrior found its mark, time after time. The Sioux warrior was unmarked as he charged forward toward the bleeding white man. The war axes clashed together, causing the Sioux warrior's axe to snap at the head. Jehu smiled slightly and tossed his axe over to where Pinto sat his horse.

Blood dripped from Jehu's chest, running down into his belt as he circled warily around the warrior. Both men clenched mightily as they came together, their knives turned upward, ready to gut their opponent. Muscles corded as they tried to force the other backward, trying to make each other give ground. As quick as a cat, the warrior rolled backward, tossing Jehu over his head. Rolling quickly, the warrior straddled Jehu, trying to force his knife downward. Again, muscles strained as Jehu watched the warrior's knife descend slowly toward his face.

With an amazing show of strength, Jehu tossed the warrior bodily from him. Again, the warrior gained his feet and rushed at Jehu, who was just rising. The two men clashed together, momentarily hanging on to each other. Slowly the warrior slipped from Jehu's grasp as the tall youth stepped back, wearily watching the warrior collapse slowly at his feet. Watching, the Sioux warriors let out with a sigh. They had seen their hero rush foolishly, straight into the white man's knife. They knew the warrior had underestimated the power and courage of this white. He paid for it with his life.

The Sioux line surged forward with cries of rage, only to be held back by their war chief. Jehu straightened wearily and looked across the flat ground as Wandering Bear rode slowly toward him. Studying him closely, the chief stopped his horse in front of the bleeding youth. "You are a brave warrior, white one. How are you called?"

"Jehu Wolf."

"A good name for one such as you," wandering Bear nodded. "My braves are mad. Their blood is up, but you have shown your bravery. You have won this day. Go as we have agreed."

"And the others?"

"You have won; they are free to leave this place."

Jehu walked wearily to where the Appaloosa stood. Mounting slowly, he looked toward the Sioux line and nodded wearily at Little Elk. Looking one last time, as the dead warrior was placed across a horse's back, then he and Pinto turned toward the Brigade.

CHAPTER 9

Pinto followed Jehu back to where the Brigade was waiting quietly. Lowrie stopped the men when they started to cheer, fearing any sign of celebration over the dead Sioux Warrior could start the battle over again.

Pinto reined his gelding in front of the trappers as Jehu dismounted. "The lad saved our bacon, boys. We're free to go. You should thank Jehu Wolf."

As Jethro cleaned the many small cuts, the Sioux had inflicted on Jehu, the others passed by slowly, respectfully touching him on the shoulder. These men respected bravery in a man. The tall youth had not only showed how brave he was, but he saved the Brigade, all the profits, and probably many lives.

Lowrie stepped close to Jehu, and smiled. "Well me lad, you've put your mark on these mountains this day. Your name will be famous, as well known as old Gabe Bridger when word of this gets out."

Shaking his head, Jehu looked up at Lowrie. "I don't want to be famous, Mister Lowrie, not one bit."

"Well, you are," Pinto smiled. "Like it or not, you just killed one of the deadliest fighters in the Sioux Nation, hand to hand."

Running Dog stepped forward and grasped Jehu's hand. The Crow smiled wide, placing the reins of the Appaloosa in his hands. "This is my present to the great warrior Jehu Wolf, for killing the Crow Killer, Wild Horse."

"Was that his name?" Jehu looked where the long line of Sioux were slowly retreating, disappearing back into the low foothills.

"Wild Horse his name; kill many Crow warriors." Running Dog nodded and followed Jehu's gaze. "Many of my people are dead by his hand."

"I gave the Appaloosa to you my friend." Jehu tried to hand the reins back.

"A great warrior needs a great horse. He is yours, brother."

"See, lad," Lowrie slapped Jehu on the back. "Like I said, you will probably never have to buy a drink again, I'll betcha."

"I'll drink to that," Pinto roared with pride.

The Brigade wound their way out of the mountains, then into the foothills that bordered the vast grassy plains. Buffalo were thicker than fleas on a hound. The trappers had fresh buffalo tongue, ribs, or liver every night when they camped. Small bands and villages seemed to materialize out of the ground at every campsite.

At first, Lowrie worried, but with the furs these people brought in to trade, his concern became less and less. The Brigade was nowhere near the rendezvous on the Green and Lowrie had greatly depleted most of his trade goods, trading for small furs and buffalo robes the villagers brought in. He shook his head in amazement. All his mules were already overloaded with many of the men walking and using their saddle horses to provide more transport for the heavy bales of furs. Many were also pulling travois to help carry the furs.

Lowrie shook his head as he sat with Pinto. "I've never seen the like, old hoss. They just keep coming in with plews."

"You know why, don't you?"

"I know why," Lowrie nodded. "Most of them want to see the lad."

"He's big medicine now, very big medicine."

"I didn't believe it, but when you were out hunting, a couple days back, I seen Little Robe, Chief of the Shoshone, offer him his daughter free." Lowrie shook his head. "Never seen the like, before this, the Shoshone had soon cut our throats as not."

"I heard about it. Running Dog said she was pretty and Jehu was crazy for not accepting," Pinto nodded. "You know, if the old chief could get the lad married into the Shoshone Tribe, it would give the tribe much prestige out here."

"Your nephew, Running Dog, thinks every woman is pretty."

Lowrie looked over where Jehu was leaning against a bundle of furs, trying to keep away from the prying eyes of the villagers that sought him out. Several young women stood at a distance, smiling shyly at the young white. Children reached out to touch him as they ran by, playing.

"Well, we're pert near out of trade goods, so we might as well push on to rendezvous, come daylight."

Pinto looked around at the open valleys, empty as far as the eye could see. "By gad Taff, we've sure lived the life, ain't we?"

Lowrie agreed. "Yes, we have Pinto. We've lived high off the hog for sure, but we ain't through by a long shot yet."

"I hope not, but we ain't getting any younger."

"We ain't getting old, Taff. Now Jethro is, but not us," Lowrie threw out his chest. "Me and you can throw down and whip any three men in these mountains."

"We could once, but not anymore, I'm afraid."

Lowrie laughed out loud. "You're right about that old friend. We are getting old, but I still don't figure on going under anytime soon. No, sir, I ain't done yet by a long sight."

The Brigade sat in a line on the mountain slope and looked down across the broad valley. Smoke drifted lazily over the cook fires dotting the rendezvous site, then faded into the great blue skies overhead. Green Mountain Valley was spread out on the plain below them. Tents flapped in the wind and tepees lined the valley, representing every tribe. A simple set of rules kept every warrior at the rendezvous on their best behavior. No fighting was allowed for any reason.

The fur traders that ran the large tents with their rot gut whiskey, fooforah, and trade goods had one rule. Anybody who ignored the rule, was banished from the valley and the rendezvous forever. With all the drinking, carousing, and rough play, the traders couldn't afford trouble. Many of the tribes coming to rendezvous to trade their furs were mortal enemies and some were allies. If a fight erupted, it could turn bloody. The traders wouldn't stand for it, and the trappers and warriors all knew the rules before they rode in. Profit was on their minds and there was no profit in trouble.

Taff Lowrie looked up and down the line of the Brigade, then dropped his hand. Thirty rifles fired, sending a signal into the valley that would wake the dead. Several mules started to pitch and bawl, trying to lose their heavy loads.

Letting go with his wild wolf call, Lowrie kicked his horse forward in a hard run with the whole Brigade following him, screaming their heads off. Over sagebrush, cedars, and small gulleys, the running horses and yelling trappers plunged into their race toward the camp. Everyone at the rendezvous stopped what they were doing to watch and yell their encouragement, waiting for the men racing toward them. Many friends and strangers would unite tonight over campfires and whiskey jugs to renew old friendships, and make new ones.

Jehu had never seen the likes of the place. The trappers and hunters were half wild men that haven't seen civilization in years. Pinto pointed out several bearded, buckskin clad men as they walked by. These trappers were legends here in the mountains; Fitzsimmons, Bridger, Johnson, and many others that left their mark on the Rockies and made their names household words back east. Jehu had heard these names spoken back at Carters. Whenever trappers brought in their plews, they would brag tall yarns, and they seemed to come together.

The Yellowstone Brigade set up their own camp near the large tents, just far enough for Lowrie to keep his men separated from the main camp. First, they must sell their furs, then Lowrie would settle up with each man. Only then would his responsibility to them and their loyalty to the Brigade be finished. Lowrie already put out the word, he would be going back to the Yellowstone next season, and anyone wanting to follow him should sign up before rendezvous broke up.

Jehu had completely healed from the wounds he had received in his battle with the Sioux Warrior, Wild Horse. None of the wounds were deep or dangerous, only shallow ones that would leave more scars across his broad torso. Running Dog strutted along beside him as they walked through the many lodges blanketing the valley. Proud and arrogant, the

Crow laughed and smiled as they mingled with tribes that, outside the valley, were mortal enemies of the Crow.

Talking with Running Dog, from the first days of the Brigade's hunting camp, Jehu had mastered the Crow language and the hand signs the plains tribes used for communication. Conversing in Crow, the two men strolled casually through the large village while the women admired their proud stature and handsome features from lowered eyes. Few men in the camps could match either man in height or physical bearing. Not as tall as Jehu, Running Dog was just as handsome with his straight shoulders and long braids hanging across his well-muscled chest.

"You should have taken the Shoshone woman, my brother." Running Dog still couldn't believe Jehu turned the woman down.

"Does Running Dog have a woman back in his village?"

"They are all mine," the Crow laughed loudly, causing many eyes to glance over at him.

Jehu smiled; Running Dog was impossible to dislike. Even his enemies here at rendezvous seemed drawn to his wild, boisterous spirit. "Then why does my friend wish me to settle down with one woman?"

"It is the way of your people," Running Dog laughed again. "To have only one wife, is it not?"

Exasperated, Jehu looked around the village. "I don't want even one woman."

"My uncle says the Flathead woman, Alamette, looks to you. He says maybe you look to her." Running Dog laughed when Jehu glanced sharply at him. "Maybe Pinto was right."

Jehu swore, "I'll ring his neck."

"Or maybe the white woman, back at the big river."

"I swear; is there anything you two haven't talked about?"

Running Dog laughed again. "It seems the fiery liquid last night loosened the tongue of my uncle."

"I reckon it did at that," Jehu shook his head slowly. If Running Dog wasn't thinking about the war trail, he was thinking about women.

Lowrie sold the furs and settled up with each trapper, cook, and camp skinner. Each man now had money, money that was burning a hole in his pocket. Lowrie wished it was different, but with all the whiskey, women, and gambling in the camp, he knew many of the men would be dead broke before rendezvous broke up. He had done his best to warn them, but he knew it was useless. Year after year, was always the same. The trappers and their money were soon separated. Trappers just love to drink and gamble on anything from a good horse race, wrestling match, drinking contest or footrace. Gambling was in their blood. They can't help themselves. For the ones that signed their mark to join him in the fall, he secretly saved back enough of their money for them to outfit themselves completely.

Ben Scott and several of the brigade sat about the encampment, sipping on the free-flowing whiskey jugs being passed around. Other trappers and warriors walked by and occasionally looked over at the boisterous hunters then shake their heads, wave, and move on.

Scott grinned drunkenly and stood to his feet, swaying in the light breeze that blew across the valley. "What are you boys a looking at? I'm half mountain lion, half grizzly bear, half lobo wolf, and a full-blooded wolverine."

"What you saying Scotty?" A huge trapper squared off at the smaller man. "What are you blowing about?"

"I'm a saying me and my partner can throw down and whip any three men in your camp."

"He's drunk Dugger; pay him no mind," one of the trappers with Scott laughed.

Scott threw out his chest and roared. "Drunk I am, but I've got gold coin here says two of us can out wrestle any three you got."

The big trapper towered at least six inches over Scott and outweighed him by fifty pounds. Looking down at the smaller man, Dugger grinned a snaggle-toothed grin, and poked his finger in Scott's chest. "Why not just you and me go at it, right now?"

"Nope," Scott slapped the big trapper's hand away. "Ain't no fun in that, but you get some help and the two of us will take you for a hundred dollars, American."

"A hundred!" Dugger's eyes grew wide. "You said three of us, against the two of you."

Scott smiled drunkenly. "By gads, he can understand English."

"When?" Dugger questioned. "You're too drunk to stand, much less wrestle."

"Don't let that worry you none at all." Scott patted his leather coin pouch. "I bite like a rattler, kick like a Missouri mule, and I'm slippery as an eel out of water."

"Yeah, and you blow like a prairie twister." One of the watching trappers yelled out, then roared with laughter.

"Little man, you're on." Dugger stuck out his hand. "We'll give you two hours to get sober, then we'll be back."

"You do that," Scott hollered at the big trapper's parting back then did a back flip, landing on his feet. "We got him, boys. We got him hook, line, and sinker."

"You do for a fact, Benjamin Scott." Another trapper spoke up. "But what are you fixing to do with that overgrown bull now that you have him?"

"Why, boys, me and my partner are gonna whip him and take his money." Scott lost his drunken slur and stood to his full height, cold sober. "You fellers get your bets down."

"Not me," a trapper spoke up. "My toes are still frozen from getting them pelts. No, sir, not me. I ain't about to gamble my money on the likes of you."

"Your big chance and you're blowing it?"

"What partner? Who you talking about?" The trapper appeared curious.

Scott grinned. "The Sioux Killer, who else but Jehu Wolf."

"He's kinda funny, Scott. You know what he thinks about stuff like this." A trapper spoke up. "What if he won't wrestle for you?"

"For us, lads, for us."

"He still may not wrestle, then we'll forfeit our gold." Scott scratched at his beard and looked about the camp. "Come to think of it boys, I never thought about that."

"If'n I were you, I'd get to thinking," another spoke up.

"Yeah, well, I've got two hours."

"You best hurry, cause there ain't no one else here in their right mind that would wrestle that gorilla for you, no siree, Bob."

Lowrie walked into the circle of men as Scott hurried off to find Jehu. Listening as his men told him of the upcoming wrestling match, the Brigade leader shook his head in disbelief.

"Don't Scotty remember those two half breed Canadians that ran with Dugger?"

Jethro looked up in shock as his jaw dropped open. "We done forgot about them two French Canadians."

Lowrie shook his head, "I'll betcha Dugger ain't forgotten about them."

"Oh boy, there goes our money," Jethro groaned.

"You mean to tell me, you are all involved in this." Lowrie looked over at the old trapper. "Even you, Jethro?"

Nodding his head up and down, "I'm guilty."

Scott walked quickly through the encampment, asking everyone he went by, if they knew where Jehu was. Finally, he spied Jehu and Running Dog strolling casually in his direction. Wringing his hands nervously, Scott approached the two young men and smiled.

"Ah Jehu, could I have a word with you?"

Jehu looked over at Running Dog skeptically. Never had Scott been so soft spoken and friendly. "Sure, Mister Scott, what's on your mind?"

"Money."

"Yours or mine?" Jehu instantly grew suspicious.

"Money we can win."

"No."

"Now Jehu, you ain't heard me out yet." Scott looked worriedly over at Running Dog. "Tell him to at least hear me out."

"Alright, alright, I'm listening."

"It's just a small wrestling match, and you can make a good deal of money for yourself."

"And if I don't win, how much will I lose."

"No, sir, me and the boys will pay up if we don't win." Scott held up his hand.

"No."

"I've done give my word, Jehu. We'll lose face if'n you don't help me, not to count our self-respect."

"You mean, you'll lose face," Jehu was annoyed. "I ain't said nothing about wrestling anybody."

"Lowrie and our Brigade will lose face if'n we back out, lad," Scott repeated, almost pleading. "You got to do it."

Running Dog looked around the camp. "The Indian people have much respect for you, Jehu Wolf. If you don't fight, they think maybe you scared."

"I don't care about that." Jehu shook his head and glared at Scott. "How do you get us into these fixes, Mister Scott?"

For once, Running Dog was serious when he spoke. Jehu heard the tone in his voice. "If you are going to live here in these mountains my friend, the people must have respect for you, or they will not trade with you."

Breathing easily, the smaller trapper grinned; he had Jehu hooked. "It won't be nothing, lad. We'll take them easy."

"What do you mean them?"

"Well, to tell you the truth, it's the two of us against three of them."

"Great," Jehu threw up his arms. "Now that's brilliant, really brilliant. What else?"

"It'll be a cinch, easy, and we'll be rich."

Jehu looked about the camp and shook his head. "I'm already rich."

Running Dog laughed and slapped Jehu on the back. "You be Great Warrior in village if you win; young women love you."

Jehu looked over at the Crow, "And if I don't win?"

"The boys, your friends, will lose their money." Scott shuddered at the thought of losing, as this had been mostly his idea. He knew his friends in the Brigade could turn nasty if they lost all their hard earned money.

"I didn't tell them to bet their season's earnings."

Scott replied. "No you didn't, but they'll lose everything if you don't wrestle."

"Alright, Mister Scott, but after this, no more, nothing. Do you understand?"

Scott smiled and winked at Running Dog. "Yes, sir."

Jehu raised his hand and stopped. "Yesterday, my Crow friend, you were challenged to a footrace by that Arapaho girl's brother."

"He was but a boy," Running Dog shrugged.

"He was a warrior," Jehu replied. "There is no fighting allowed here or he would have challenged you to fight right then."

"I merely talked to the girl," Running Dog protested.

Jehu shrugged. "Whatever, but if I am to wrestle, then I want your word that you'll race the Arapaho."

"A Crow warrior does not run around on foot. There is no honor in defeating a mere Arapaho." Running Dog looked over at Scott. "Maybe a horse race."

"Your word, some kind of race."

Running Dog shrugged and smiled brightly. "You will let me use the Appaloosa?"

"No, you'll ride one of our pack mules." Jehu thought Running Dog was gonna bust a blood vessel in his face right then.

"I won't; this one will not dishonor the Crow People."

"The people have nothing to do with it. Either you do as I ask, or I won't wrestle." Jehu thrusted out his chin.

Scott took Running Dog by the arm and led him off a few paces, then whispered into the warrior's ear. Nodding several times, Running Dog smiled and turned on the suspicious Jehu. "Alright my friend, I'll do it."

Looking at the two men grinning like a possum up a gum tree, Jehu had his doubts. "I have your word?"

"You've got his word, now let's go." Scott propelled both men toward the Brigade's camp.

Jehu and Scott stood in the middle of the gathered trappers, stripped naked to their waists. Ten feet across from them stood their three adversaries, waiting patiently. Jehu shook his head skeptically as he eyed the French Canadians. Almost twins, the two men were heavily muscled in their chests, with abnormally long arms. Bandy-legged, Jehu knew these two were powerful, worthy opponents, not to mention a giant of a man named Dugger who stood grinning beside the Canadians. Jehu could see the Frenchies were not strangers to fighting as their bodies were covered in scars.

"You sober, Scotty?" Dugger grinned and looked over at the Canadians. "Maybe it would be better if you weren't."

Pinto whispered from behind Jehu. "How did you get yourself into this mess, lad?"

"Weren't my idea," Jehu shook his head. "You can take my place if you want to."

"No thank you," Pinto laughed. "I'll sit this one out."

"Thanks."

"I've heard them Frenchies are pretty rough."

Jehu eyed the pair again. "They look it. You got any advice?"

"Yeah, just faint right now and let them win."

"Can't, if I wrestle them, Running Dog will have to race the Arapaho, and I wouldn't miss that for anything."

"If they break your neck, you might miss it all."

Jehu replied. "Well, I reckon we'll see quick enough."

"If you're gonna wrestle the gorilla, take out his left knee." Pinto looked at the big man. "A mule kicked him once and it's been kinda gimpy since then."

Lowrie raised his hand and silence settled on the surrounding trappers. "There will be only one rule and that is, only four men will wrestle at one time. If a man goes down, another can take his place."

Dugger grinned and motioned at the two Canadians. "Agreed."

"We won't be needing but one man to take the two of them."

"Hurry Jehu, and get your man. I figure I may need help." Scott looked across at the advancing Canadians.

Jehu felt the power in the shorter Canadian as they came together with powerful arms wrapping around each other. Rolling backward, Jehu flipped his man over his head, then broad kicked the one on top of Scott hard, upside his head. As his man rushed in, Jehu whirled, catching him with a hard elbow in the mouth, causing a rush of blood to cover the ground. Again, he slugged at the man wrestling with Scott, then clubbed the man unconscious with a hard right to his temple.

Hearing the murmuring of the crowd and seeing the Canadian collapse, Dugger rushed forward with a roar and grabbed Jehu from behind in a crushing bear hug. Lifting the young trapper bodily from the ground, Dugger was about to crush Jehu's ribs, when Scott hit him hard in the back. Roaring in pain, Dugger released Jehu, and then whirled on the retreating Scott as Jehu was tackled by the other Canadian. Slamming the Canadian's head several times against the hard packed ground, Jehu rolled to his feet. With a mighty leap, he dropped kick the shorter Canadian full in the chest, temporarily knocking the wind from his body.

Rushing to where Dugger was trying to squeeze the breath from Scott, Jehu ripped at the man's strong grasp on the smaller man's throat. Finally, prying Dugger loose, he grappled with the huge trapper as Scott slumped gasping, to the ground. Forearms rippled with muscle as the two giants applied all their strength against each other. Jerking his aching arms downward, Jehu slipped quickly behind Dugger and wrapped his arms around the trapper's throat. Pulling his arms hard around the giant's neck, he wrapped his feet around the man's middle, then slowly squeezed the air from Dugger. Staggering around the watching trappers, his fingers prying feebly at Jehu's arms, Dugger finally collapsed in a heap with Jehu still clinging to his back.

Scott slugged one of the confused Canadians unconscious as he tried to rise and rejoin the fight. Prying Jehu loose from Dugger, before he strangled the man, Scott grinned and slapped the youngster on the back.

"We whipped them boy. We whipped them fair."

Jehu shook his head slowly as the madness of the fight slowly slipped from him. Looking around at the downed Canadians and over to where Dugger was coughing, trying to breathe, Jehu shook his head. "Yeah Mister Scott, reckon we did at that."

Jehu felt the heavy weight of his possible bag that held the gold coins that were his share of the furs and his winnings from the fight. Earlier, Pinto stood back and studied the coins as Lowrie paid off Jehu, then prodded the Brigade leader in his side.

"Peers to me old hoss, you've shorted the lad some."

Lowrie looked over at Pinto and shrugged. "I paid him the same as the others, his fair share for a season's work. A fair price on the plews you two trapped."

"Taff Lowrie, the lad made you a small fortune in furs, not to count saving all of us back on the Yellowstone."

Lowrie finally had to admit Pinto was right and handed over several more heavy gold pieces. The coins, along with the money Scott gave him for the fight weighed down Jehu's leather money pouch, making him feel rich. Smiling, he patted the beautiful bay stallion he had won earlier on Running Dog's mule race.

With all the whispering and sneaking around earlier, before the race, Jehu knew Scott and Running Dog were up to something. Pinto and Lowrie had acted as go-betweens for the two parties, setting up the horse race with the Arapaho, Yells Eagle. Betting is something Jehu knew little about, but one of the Arapaho warriors insisted Jehu bet a good trade rifle against the warrior's bay stallion.

The mare mule Scott led out was the tallest of any of the mules. She was long eared, long legged, long backed, and Jehu had to admit, long headed. Jehu knew she was long on everything except brains and probably speed, but he was resigned to the bet. He knew if the Arapaho weren't appeased in some way, there would probably be trouble when rendezvous broke up.

The Arapaho laughed when Running Dog took his place at the starting line astride the grey molly mule. Jehu smiled and nodded; he knew Running Dog was embarrassed in front of the gathered villagers and especially the young maidens, not happy at all with the situation. Scott insisted on the race being short, only one lap of the camp would be made. The Arapaho Warrior, Yells Eagle, shrugged at the distance. The long legged buffalo runner, he rode, would run the mule down easily at any distance.

Jehu was ready to turn over the rifle when the two hard running animals came into sight from behind the lodges and the mule was several feet in the front. Jehu couldn't believe his eyes as the mule seemed to fly over the ground. Scott was laughing hysterically and doing back flips. It took Running Dog another lap of the village to slow the mule down and get her pulled to a stop.

"I didn't think you could run so fast, my friend." Jehu smiled over at Running Dog. "You look good on a mule."

"When you are as irresistible to the women as I am Jehu Wolf, you have to learn to run very quickly, on anything," Running Dog laughed.

"Uh huh," Jehu grinned. "I was talking about the mule."

The Arapaho were sullen at their loss, but they handed over the reins of the two horses they had bet. Jehu held up his hand as they started to turn away. "These are for my friends, the Arapaho."

Both warriors were presented with trade rifles, powder and shot, which made the two young men, smile broadly, and thank Jehu.

"The white trader, Jehu, is a great warrior. He is always welcome in the Arapaho Villages." Yells Eagle placed an Arapaho amulet around Jehu's neck. Looking over at Running Dog with a frown, the two warriors walked away proudly.

"He didn't say I was welcome," Running Dog laughed.

"I doubt you are."

"His sister chased me. I did nothing." Running Dog pleaded innocence. "I tried to ignore her."

"Uh huh."

Several trappers sat cross-legged in front of Lowrie's tent. Rendezvous was over. The Brigade leader looked to where Pinto sat smoking his old, worn pipe. "Are you two joining me this fall for the season?"

Pinto looked over at Jehu. "Well, lad, are we?"

"Sounds good, if'n you want to," Jehu agreed. "But first, I'm heading down to Miles' Trading Post to check in on Chauncy."

Pinto reached over and shook hands with Lowrie. "See you in the fall, old hoss."

"When are you two pulling out?"

"We're gone, soon as we pick up Running Dog and the Crows."

"Well, luck to you. Meet me on the Musselshell before the first snowfall hits."

"We'll be there."

Pinto loaded all three of the mules heavily with trade goods and gifts for the villagers they would meet on their return trip to the Missouri. He expected and hoped to pick up a few more furs before he reached Miles' Trading Post.

Jehu was itching to reach the trader's post. Something had been eating at him since their departure last summer. He deeply distrusted the Carters. He had heard and seen too much about them when he worked for the older Carter at his inn. On the frontier, might made right, and the Carters definitely had the might.

Two weeks later, the Crow Village of Chief Red Hawk came into sight through the morning mist. Running Dog, Tall Grass, and Owl

Man bathed and put on their finest change of deerskin clothes, brand-new bead decorated moccasins and war paint. Proud and arrogant, the three warriors led the procession toward the lodges. Before riding into the village, Jehu presented Running Dog with a beautiful bear claw necklace, adorned with eagle claws and feathers. Running Dog looked at the necklace in awe before placing it around his neck. The other two Crow warriors, Tall Grass and Owl Man, he presented with the two horses he had won on the great mule race.

"Thank you, my brother." Running Dog fingered the necklace. "It is a thing of beauty. It gives me great pride to wear it."

Jehu bought the necklace from an Arapaho Squaw, knowing someday this young warrior would be a leader of the Crow Nation. The necklace would give his friend great prestige among the Crow people.

Jehu smiled as Running Dog led them into the midst of the village. The bay horse he rode pranced and arched his neck proudly, his nostrils flaring. Red Hawk watched as his nephew led the procession toward his lodge. Before him on the bay horse, covered in war paint, sat the pride of the Crow Nation. Red Hawk smiled; yes, his nephew was proud, arrogant and even conceited, but it did not matter. He was a Crow Warrior, a lance bearer. He had earned the respect of his people.

Pinto dismounted and shook hands with the chief. "It is good to see Red Hawk, the great Chief of the Crow People."

"It has been a long winter, Pawnee Killer," Red Hawk smiled. "Did you have good hunting?"

"Running Dog has made our hunting very prosperous."

"This is good. We have heard of the great fight the young white had with the Sioux dog, Wild Horse."

Pinto was surprised. "You have already heard of this?"

"Tonight we will celebrate his great victory and present this great warrior with gifts." Red Hawk looked in awe to where Jehu stood beside the Appaloosa, almost as if he feared the young hunter. The Sioux warrior known as Wild Horse had been a great warrior. The Crow thought he had supernatural strength and medicine. For many years, Wild Horse had defeated the best of the Crow Warriors sent against him. Here before them stood the young white warrior who had easily defeated their greatest enemy.

Pinto sensed the fear in the chief as he stared at Jehu. The big trapper smiled; maybe it isn't fear, but the Crow believed strongly in a warrior's medicine, and Red Hawk was in awe of Jehu's strong medicine.

"We'll be there." Pinto looked over at Jehu. "Thank you, my friend."

Walking away, toward where they previously camped, Jehu shook his head. "I ain't interested in celebrating. I want to get on to Miles' Post."

Pinto shook his head in disbelief. "Boy, you listen to me. These Crow want to honor you, and you're gonna let them do it."

Jehu unsaddled the saddle horses and mules while Pinto built a small fire and put on water to heat. Rolling out buffalo robes for their beds, Jehu made pillows out of the packs. Several times, on their way back to the Crow Village, they had traded for furs. Miles or Cloud would pay a good deal for these prime plews.

The whole village gathered around the huge bonfire that lit up the village. Rawhide drums beat steadily as several singers chanted the shrill songs of the Crow Nation. Jehu sat at Red Hawk's right side in the highest place of honor. Pinto sat on his left with his children piled up in his lap. Young maidens of the tribe shuffled slowly, in cadence to the drums, smiling invitingly toward the great warrior of the whites. Jehu blushed red at all the attention that was being heaped upon him.

Red Hawk smiled and placed his hand on the young white's arm. "They dance for you, my son."

"Thank you, Uncle. It is a great honor for them to do this."

Running Dog laughingly jabbed Jehu in the side. "They smile at you, my friend. Tonight you are the great killer of the Sioux. Tonight they dance for you. Tonight my friend, they are yours."

Jehu frowned, "I am just a white trapper, nothing more."

Running Dog laughed aloud, his pure white teeth shining in the light of the fire. "Look at their faces. I tell you, they are yours, my friend. All you have to do is ask."

Jehu only shook his head. "I give them to you, Running Dog."

Again, Running Dog laughed, then lunged into the air, landing on his feet and joining the young dancers. "Come Jehu Wolf; we will dance around the fire all night."

Jehu protested loudly, as the warrior pulled him bodily to his feet and shoved him in among the young women. The drums beat wildly into the night as Jehu, despite his protests, danced around and around the great fire. Running Dog showed off his prowess, leaping and jumping wildly around the fire. Jehu's ears rung with the heavy sound of the drums, the warriors screaming out their great victories and coups they took in battle, and the squaws and young maidens shuffling to the drums. All night the village drums beat out a steady rhythm until Jehu finally collapsed, exhausted on a nearby buffalo robe. Pinto and Red Hawk had managed to get themselves drunk with some of the jugs of whiskey Pinto brought from the rendezvous.

Sitting and staring dumbly at the dancers, Red Hawk looked over at Pinto. "My friend, tonight I was to give the young white his new Crow name."

Pinto stared at the pipe he was trying to light. "Alright, let's do it."

Red Hawk shook his head. "I can't."

"Why not?" Pinto could not get his pipe lit. His fingers holding the burning twig could not make contact with the pipe bowl.

"Me no remember name." Red Hawk slowly tilted sideways, passing out cold.

Pinto smiled drunkenly at the chief, then slowly lay sideways and fell off into a sound sleep as the whiskey took its affect. An old squaw looked down on the two and shook her head. Covering both of them with buffalo robes, she led Pinto's children back to their grandmother's lodge. As several young women started over to the young white, she shook her head and motioned them away.

"Ah Grandmother, you would spoil his fun?"

"This one is a good man, Running Dog. I wish I could say the same about another I know." She frowned, then turned away, leaving the young warrior laughing.

Chapter 10

The sun was up and shining brightly, as Pinto stumbled toward the small stream, and then ducked his head under the cold water. Jehu walked up beside his friend, and washed his hands and face.

"You got a headache Pinto?" Jehu laughed, causing the trapper to hold his head. "Perhaps a little too much whiskey?"

"Ssh." Pinto raised his hand. "You can't have a headache without a head."

"You've got your head; I see it."

"Feels like two."

Jehu grinned. "What about the chief? Ain't seen him out and about. Did you kill him last night?"

"Blame me; I've got wide shoulders," Pinto sputtered as the water ran down his face. "You ever thought maybe it was the other way around? He got me drunk, that's what happened."

"Uh huh." Jehu stood up. "It sure looks like that's what happened alright."

"Alright smart aleck, how are you feeling?"

"Fine, just fine."

Pinto had noted how slow Jehu straightened up. "You peer a bit sore to me. Reckon too much jumping around like a grasshopper, huh?"

"Let's eat breakfast." Jehu pointed toward their camp, "I'm hungry."

Both men were shocked as they neared their small fire, which was ablaze with a pot of coffee boiling and thick deer steaks frying. The old squaw, from the night before, beamed brightly up at them as she poured each man a steaming cup of coffee.

Jehu was shocked as he took the coffee and sipped on it. "Dang Pinto, this is better than Jethro's coffee. I didn't know Indians knew how to boil coffee."

Pinto smiled and took his coffee from the squaw. "Normally they don't Jehu, but this here is Little Plum. She used to be the woman of old Slim Mahert before he went under."

"Him plenty good man; you remember that Pawnee Killer," the old squaw looked up at Pinto and dared him to say more about her man. "Him brave; good to squaw."

"Yes, he was, Little Plum."

"She speaks English too?"

Pinto smiled and thanked her for the venison. "Twenty years ago, she was a sight to look at. Old Slim was in love, at first sight of her. He up and gave her pappy many horses, a gun, powder and shot, and blankets."

"He must have wanted her bad."

"I seen old Slim kill a man once at Rendezvous because of her." Pinto chewed on his steak. "Slim gutted that fella like a downed deer."

"What happened? Did he insult her or attack her?"

Pinto shook his head. "Nothing like that, he merely said good morning to her."

"And this Slim killed the man over that?"

"Well, maybe it was a little more. Seems Little Plum was taking a bath at the time," Pinto laughed. "Yes, sir, he picked the wrong lady, at the wrong time and place."

"Him much bad man; look at me, no clothes." The old squaw, who stood listening, spoke up from behind them. "Slim, him very jealous."

"Sounds like he was," Jehu sipped on his second cup of coffee and stared into the small fire. "But I've seen whole villages bathing together out here."

"Funny thing about it was," Pinto looked over at the squaw, "at the time, she didn't think anything of it. You're right; these people bathe together all the time with no clothes on."

The sun was high in the sky when Chief Red Hawk sent Running Dog to bring the two white trappers to his lodge. Pinto and Jehu were saddling their horses as the warrior walked up and told them they were wanted.

Jehu could tell the Crow Chief was still a little wobbly as they stopped in front of the big lodge. Shaking hands, Red Hawk motioned for the two men to sit.

"I am sorry my son." The Chief looked down at Jehu. "I should have given you the honor you have earned, last night."

Pinto nodded guiltily. "It was my fault old friend."

"No matter; I have presents for the great Sioux Killer." Two squaws brought forth a beautiful set of tanned, white deerskin, shirt and britches with matching moccasins.

Another laid a beautiful war axe and deer handled skinning knife at his feet.

Jehu stared hard at the presents. "These are for me?"

"They are for you." Several villagers walked up and were standing in a semi-circle in front of the lodge. The drums from the night before sounded again. "From this day forth, you will be known by the Crow people as White Wolf; I have spoken."

Pinto nudged Jehu. "Stand up and say something. They just honored you, big time."

Jehu stood to his full height and looked about the village. "I thank my friends the Crow people for these beautiful gifts and my new name. I am honored, and will always be at your side if I am needed."

Running Dog leaped straight into the air and yelled, causing several squaws to rush the astounded Jehu, and lift him bodily off his feet. Carrying the struggling youth toward the small creek, they deposited him into the water and start stripping his clothes while Running Dog and the villagers screamed their delight.

Jehu looked like a fresh scrubbed baby as he and Pinto rode from the village. Pinto didn't know if the lad's face was still red from the scrubbing or the embarrassment of the bath in front of the whole village. It was all he could do to keep from breaking out into fits of laughter.

"It's their custom, laddie. The new clothes and the bath give you a new body for your new name, White Wolf. It is the greatest honor they can bestow on you."

"It was embarrassing." Jehu looked behind him at the waving villagers, "being washed like a baby, butt naked, and by women."

"It's sure better than being washed by the warriors," Pinto laughed. "Wave at them White Wolf; wave at your people."

Jehu raised his arm and waved back at the village as the people separated to let a lone rider race after them.

"Looks like Running Dog forgot something." Pinto recognized the racing bay horse of the warrior. The warriors of the Crow nation were the most skilled horsemen Pinto had ever seen on the back of a horse. Bareback, with only a braided piece of rawhide in their lower jaw, the half-wild horses of the Crow were the best-trained buffalo runners and war ponies on the plains. Every tribe did their very best to steal or trade for the valuable animals.

The bay slid to a stop alongside the two trappers and their mules. Pinto noticed the buffalo sleeping robe and that Running Dog had his weapons of war with him. The warrior wasn't just coming out to say good-bye or wish them well.

"My uncle has given me his blessing to go east with my white brother and uncle," Running Dog smiled. "I have never seen the great river."

"You are welcome, my brother," Jehu clasped the warrior's hand. "Where are Tall Grass and Owl Man?" Jehu spoke of the other two Crows who rode with Running Dog to the Yellowstone River.

Running Dog smiled. "Last night the warriors passed the white feather to go on a raid against the Sioux. My friends were invited to go. It is a great honor."

"Why didn't you go?" Pinto spoke up.

"I go with my brother; there will always be days ahead to fight with the Sioux people or the Cheyenne."

Alamette stood smiling shyly as Pinto, Jehu, and Running Dog stood before Yellow Horn and the Flathead Villagers. Their days on the trail had passed quickly without any difficulties or reason to slow their pace, so their journey to the Flathead country had been uninterrupted, except for occasional villagers wanting to trade.

Running Dog eyed the maiden and elbowed Jehu. "She is beautiful, my friend, much more so than the Shoshone woman."

Jehu looked over at the young maiden and nodded. "She is attractive."

"Attractive? What kind of word is that? She is beautiful, as I said." Running Dog looked straight into the maiden's face and smiled.

"Careful nephew; these Flathead are peaceable enough, but they set a great store by their women, especially the young ones like her," Pinto spoke softly.

Running Dog grunted then looked disdainfully around at the surrounding villagers. "They can't outfight a Crow boy."

"Maybe not, but how do you think they hold onto these beautiful and fine hunting grounds they live on?"

Jehu raised his huge arm at the two men arguing. "The Chief wants us to follow him."

Yellow Horn sat before the men that surrounded him in a semi-circle. Several of his sub chiefs and medicine men sat to his right. Older squaws brought forth fresh meat, wild onions, and greens. Pinto's stomach growled in anticipation, as they hadn't eaten all day.

"Eat, my brothers, then we will talk." Yellow Horn looked across at Running Dog and smiled. "When your hunger is satisfied, perhaps we will talk of the many horses you will give for my daughter, Alamette."

Running Dog almost choked on a mouthful of deer meat when he heard the Chief's words. Pinto looked sideways at his nephew and smiled. He knew Yellow Horn only played with Running Dog. The Chief had heard the Crow's remarks about Alamette's beauty and now he was having his fun with the young warrior.

"I fear she only has eyes for the Sioux Killer, White Wolf." Running Dog almost choked as he tried to regain his composure. He loved women, but sure didn't want one for his very own, one he had to marry and live with. "I am but a poor young warrior of the Crow my Chief, not worthy as a husband for one such as she."

Yellow Horn nodded sadly. "Then perhaps my young Crow friend and ally, we will not discuss this anymore."

"Amen to that," Jehu let out his breath.

The Flathead Chief nodded and an older woman standing near the entrance way drew the hide covering back, summoning someone from outside. A tall warrior crouched and pushed through the opening, then stood proudly to his full height. The warrior was not dressed as a Flathead. His scalp lock was tied, as the Paiute would wear.

"This warrior, from our friends the Paiute, brings bad words for your ears, my brothers." Yellow Horn nodded at the tall warrior. "Speak your words to my white brothers, Black Hoof."

The warrior nodded and looked over at Pinto. "I know of you, Pawnee Killer, and the young one. You were at Trading Post on the Missouri before you come this place to trap the flat tail. You are friend with Trader Miles."

"We were there last summer alright, and yes, he is my friend."

"This place is no more; two whites, many Indians, burn trader post; kill trader Miles."

At the warrior's words, Pinto sat upright and stared hard at Black Hoof. "You have seen this yourself?"

"I have seen this thing for myself." The warrior struck his chest, "Miles dead; two white women taken prisoner; all others dead."

Jehu lunged to his feet. "Who done this?"

"Careful, lad; we're still in Yellow Horn's lodge." Pinto pulled Jehu back down beside him.

"Ask him who done this thing?"

"White men," Black Hoof looked down at Jehu. "Men like this one, paleskins, and they had the half breed Delaware Murdockkinn, and his Pawnee dogs with them."

"Murdockkinn!" Jehu spit out the words. "How many days ago?"

"Him with many warriors, but one white man kill Trader Miles and take his hair." Black Hoof shrugged. "Maybe five sleeps ago, they do this bad thing."

Pinto swore under his breath. "Who were these whites?"

"Two men come from big trader man, farther east."

"You mean Cloud's Trading Post?"

"Trader Cloud no there with these men, but me see these same two white men at post last time me go trade furs."

Jehu again, rose to his feet. "He's talking about the Carters, probably Martin and Tate."

"What else Black Hoof?"

"Small trading post, all gone. Murdockkinn burn everything he no steal. Kill any who try stop him."

"And the white girl, Chauncy?"

Black Hoof looked over at the enraged white youth. "Me leave this place before warriors find and kill me. Me not know Chauncy, but two white women go with the whites. Maybe she go with Murdockkinn. Me not know who take her."

"Martin Carter, he took her," Jehu swore. "He always said she was his property, that she belonged to him."

"Maybe he take white girl, maybe not." Black Hoof looked at Pinto and shrugged his shoulders. "No matter, bad Indians have her now."

"Why do you say this?" Pinto felt the warrior knew more.

"White man and Murdockkinn warriors argue over who get woman. Black Hoof leave, come here. Don't know who she go with."

"Did they go back toward Cloud's Trading Post?"

"Me come here; no stay that place. Get this one killed maybe, too many warriors to fight."

"Where you headed, Jehu?" Pinto grabbed the youth's arm as he started for their horses.

"I'm gonna hunt me some men."

Pinto turned and handed Black Hoof a sharp skinning knife and thanked him for coming to tell them of Miles. "Thank you, my friend."

The warrior nodded. "Murdockkinn have many warriors with him; very bad Indian."

"I don't think he'll have enough." Pinto looked over at Jehu retreating. "Not near enough."

Running Dog stood beside Black Hoof. "You come, go with us my friend. Many scalps, much glory."

The warrior shook his head vigorously. "No, this one go alone; see you by and by."

Alamette stood nearby as Jehu finished gathering his weapons. Running Dog walked away to help Pinto with the horses so the two young people could be alone. He patted Jehu on the back and nodded at the young maiden as he walked away.

"You will go away from this place?" Alamette stepped closer to Jehu. Jehu turned and nodded at the girl. "I must go quickly."

"This white woman, she is your squaw?"

"No, she is just a friend in trouble."

She stepped closer and looked up at him. "You will come back when you find her?"

"Yes, I will trap with Lowrie again this year. I have given my word to join him in the fall."

"Alamette will be here when you return to us, White Wolf." She placed a beaded quill pouch in his hand. "You come back to Alamette on a fast horse."

Running Dog passed the girl as she walked away, a slight smile on her face. Looking down at the pouch, Jehu held, he chuckled. "She is indeed a beautiful woman. Now she's all yours, my brother. You belong to her."

Jehu looked to where the young woman stood with her father. "What are you talking about?"

"The pouch; she has put her mark on you, White Wolf."

Absently, Jehu fingered the pouch. In his rage over Chauncy being taken captive, he really hadn't focused on what Alamette had said to him. "What do you mean; she put her mark on me?"

"The pouch," Running Dog pointed at the leather pouch Jehu was holding. "It is a promise pouch, a promise of marriage. It says to all others, you belong to her."

Pinto walked up as Running Dog finished laughing. "What pouch?" The big trapper was curious.

"Nothing, Running Dog's just having his usual fun is all." Jehu jerked hard on his cinch strap.

Grinning, the warrior pointed to the pouch laying across Jehu's saddle. "Our young brother has now been spoken for."

"Oh no I ain't." Jehu grabbed the pouch and started to stuff it in his saddlebag.

Pinto held out his hand for the pouch. "You took this from Yellow Horn's daughter?"

"She gave it to me. I thought it was just a going away present," Jehu shrugged. "And that's what it is."

"It's a going away present alright, and a coming home present." Pinto shook his head. "You see that special beading and soft skin?"

"I see it Pinto, I sure ain't blind."

"Lad, when you accepted this pouch, you promised to return to the girl and marry her."

"Oh no, I didn't. I ain't marrying anybody."

Pinto frowned at the grinning Running Dog. "Providing you survive going after the Carters and Murdockkinn, you will marry the girl."

"I ain't."

"You listen to me good, Jehu. She's the daughter of a big Chief out here." Pinto handed Jehu the pouch. "When you accepted the pouch, you gave your word. You break it and we could be finished out here, maybe even dead if we try to trap or hunt these mountains."

"I didn't know," Jehu stammered. "I sure ain't getting myself married."

"It's their custom, laddie. She caught you dead center," Pinto laughed. "Sides, she is a pretty little thing."

Jehu stepped up on his horse and looked over to where Yellow Horn, Alamette, and several villagers stood watching. The girl smiled, her snow-white teeth reflected in her dark complexioned face.

Jehu nodded, then kicked his horse away from the village. "Let's go; we've got a long cold trail ahead to cover."

Chapter 11

Only the burned walls and caved in cabins remained to greet the small party as Pinto led the way into what was left of Miles' Trading Post. The dead trader's half-starved dogs slinked away from the mounted men as they studied the wreckage of the post. Pinto cursed under his breath as he surveyed evidence of the deadly attack. Stiff human remains lay strewn about the post's yard. Some of the bodies had been partially eaten. Sharp scratches were visible on the exposed bones where animals, probably the starving dogs, had been gnawing on them.

Pinto dismounted stiffly and studied the wet ground. Heavy rains had set in on them halfway from the Flathead Village. By the time they reached the burned post, the rain already wiped out any tracks or signs of the renegade attackers.

"Wolves." Running Dog pointed to several sets of deep tracks in the mud.

"They scatter the bones like this?" Jehu shook his head in disgust.

"They probably helped. So did these dogs and every other varmint passing through here," Pinto swore under his breath. "Wolves are the worst; born killers they are."

"Where have all the villagers gone that were camped nearby?"

"Them go; no come back this place; bad medicine." Running Dog looked around the ruined post, refusing to dismount. "Bad spirit belong here now."

"What's he talking about Pinto?" Jehu looked over at the Crow curiously. "He acts spooked."

"The dead bodies, scattered bones, and the quiet stillness of the place have him that way." Pinto nodded his head. "The Crow people believe if a dead person is not put up on a scaffold when they die, their evil spirit will walk the ground they died on, forever."

"That's ridiculous," Jehu shook his head.

"Maybe, maybe not, but that's their belief." Pinto studied the ground. "If'n you're gonna live out here among these people, you sure better start believing the way they do. It might just keep you alive."

Running Dog was relieved to be sent to look for the trail of the raiders, letting him escape the eerie feeling of the stockade. Pinto knew he would find nothing. With all the rain, any remaining tracks would have been washed away several days before. Gathering up the bodies and what bones they could find, Pinto and Jehu dug a small grave and buried the remains.

Pinto sat on an empty box and studied the fresh grave thoughtfully. "David Miles was a good man. They done him bad."

"What about the women?" Jehu poured himself a cup of coffee. "What about Chauncy?"

"We'll ride on to Clouds and see what we can find out there."

"Running Dog is still out looking." Jehu looked toward the river. "Reckon he'll find anything?"

"Doubt it; trails too cold." Pinto stood to his feet. "Saddle up; he'll catch up to us on the trail. He sure doesn't want to come back here."

"Can't say I blame him for that." Jehu took one last look around the ruined post, then followed Pinto east. For some reason, the burned logs and scattered debris caused a chill to run up his spine as they passed through the ruined gates.

Coming up the river, they used the light canoes. Going back, they had to traverse the rough trails and pathways of the deep forest. Traveling at a steady pace, the horses covered the miles without a mishap. Less than a day from Cloud's Trading Post, Pinto raised his hand and halted the small party for the night.

Four good-sized rabbits lay roasting across a small fire, dripping hot grease, caused it to flare. Running Dog, who had caught up earlier, whistled a sharp warning from the small creek where he was watering his horse. Tying his gelding, he ran quickly back to the fire and pointed to the north. He hardly arrived at the fire when he heard walking horses coming slowly down the forest path. All three men disappeared into the dense forest, their eyes focused sharply on the dark trail. Pinto looked over at the smoking fire and shook his head. There was nothing they could have done to conceal the blaze. The warning came too late.

Two horses appeared through the rough brush, as their riders came into sight. All three watchers breathed a sigh of relief as they recognized the Paiute Black Hoof and another warrior. Rising from their places of concealment, they raised their hands and stepped forward.

"It is good to see Black Hoof again." Pinto shook hands with the warrior. "Come and share our meal."

"How did you find us?" Jehu was curious. The warrior had ridden right into their camp, unconcerned.

Black Hoof pointed over at Running Dog and laughed. "Me follow smell of his horse; horse smell bad."

"The Paiute could never smell very good." Running Dog shook his head, pretending hurt feelings.

"It is good to see my friends again. I have brought a captive." Black Hoof jerked the rope. "Me follow you, almost to Trader's Post, then circle to the west and find this one alone."

All eyes riveted on the bound warrior sitting sullenly on a pinto gelding. "Who is he?"

"Him half breed Injun. He with Murdockkinn when trader post burned and women taken." Black Hoof spit at the captive.

"Half breed?" Jehu looked the captive up and down. "Looks like a full-blood to me."

"Him half Delaware, half Pottawatomie Injun." Black Hoof jerked the rawhide rope tied around the man's neck, pulling him bodily from the horse, landing him in a heap on the ground. "Me watch this one kill many at post; him bad Injun."

"How did you capture this warrior?" Running Dog looked down on the captive.

"Him leave Murdockkinn. Him and woman camp on river. Me find camp in dark time. This one and squaw asleep."

"He was alone, just him and a woman?" Pinto was curious.

Black Hoof nodded. "Him take squaw captive when Murdockkinn and white men raid and burn Trader's Post, and kill Trader Miles."

Pinto's eyes fastened hard on the man's black eyes. "Is he the one that killed and scalped David Miles?"

"I see white man kill trader. This one kill only Indians." Black Hoof nodded at the captive."

"Him steal Indian woman that work for trader."

"Where is the woman?"

"Dead; him kill when I find them."

Pinto jerked the captive to his feet and dragged him over to a small birch tree. Tying the man's hands to a high branch, he walked over to the fire. Looking over at Running Dog and Black Hoof, Pinto picked up a hot ember. "Ask him where the white women were taken." Pinto blew on the red-hot stake. "Make sure he understands."

"Him know what you say."

Pinto nodded and walked back to where the prisoner was tied. "Good." Touching the man's shoulder with the red-hot ember, he stared hard into the warrior's face.

"Him bad man," Black Hoof repeated when the warrior did not move or let out a sign of pain. "Him no talk."

"I want to know where the white women were taken." Pinto pushed the hot stake into the man's stomach. "You can die easy Injun, or you'll regret the day you were born."

Jehu had to admit, the warrior had grit. Pulling his skinning knife, Pinto slowly cut away the man's scalp then touched the warrior's eyelids. Not a groan or word was uttered as the hair was torn from the bleeding head.

"You should tell him breed, or he will cut you to pieces." Running Dog sat calmly watching the man. "Maybe squaw, they no like you anymore."

"Crow dog," the warrior spit.

The heavy report of the Hawken's Rifle resounded across the forest as Jehu placed a well-aimed lead ball through the man's head. Pinto whirled, thinking they were being attacked. Seeing the smoke coming from the rifle, he looked at the youth calmly.

"We're not heathens Pinto, maybe he was, but I ain't." Jehu reloaded his rifle. "We'll find Chauncy and Mrs. Miles without his help."

Pinto shrugged, looking back at the sagging body. "Doesn't matter, lad. He wouldn't have told us anything. I just wanted some justice for David Miles."

"I reckon you got justice," Jehu reloaded the rifle. "I aim to get more, a lot more."

Black Hoof looked over to where Running Dog sat silently. "Is this the great White Wolf of the Crows? He has dishonored the Crow."

"You tell him that Paiute, and he may dishonor you." Running Dog stood and walked over to the fire. "Come, we will eat."

Cloud's Trading Post loomed in the morning light as the four horsemen rode through the palisade gates. Reining in, they studied the flat ground of the post, and then rode in at a slow, deliberate walk to Cloud's Store. Early risers, already working, studied the strange group as they dismounted in front of the store.

Two huge black men stood on the porch as Pinto dismounted. "Get Cloud."

"Yassem, Boss."

Jehu looked about the huge Trading Post, raindrops dripped from the eaves of the roofs, making mud puddles that dotted the wide dirt enclosure. Smoke drifted upward from the rock chimneys above the cabins as breakfast was being prepared. The loud banging of the blacksmith's hammer sounded loudly in the early morning. The post was awake and alive, even at this early hour.

Cloud stepped slowly through the wide door. Recognizing Pinto, he dropped his hand from his pistol and walked calmly out, onto the porch.

"Pinto Stade, good to see you."

"Is it Charlie?"

Cloud's eyes focused on the three heavy-laden mules. "See you've brought me more plews."

"They were for Miles, downriver," Pinto looked coldly into the trader's dark eyes. "I reckon they're yours now."

"That's true; I don't reckon he'll have much use for them now," Cloud smiled easily. "I'll buy them, top dollar."

"Who killed Miles and burned his post, Charlie?"

"Now Pinto, I can't rightly say who was responsible for his demise." Cloud shrugged. "Indians say it was some renegade whites, with a handful of Indians."

Pinto dismounted and stepped up on the porch looking down at the shorter man. "Tell me Charlie, what you heard, exactly."

Again, Cloud shrugged. "Like I said, just heard it was some whites passing through the territory."

"And you didn't bother to try to find the killers, or give those people a decent burial."

"Passing Indians told me about the killings and burned post, but I couldn't take the chance of leaving this place unguarded." Cloud shrugged. "They might have come here and burned me out too."

"Passing Indians, huh?" Pinto turned to where the two warriors flanked Jehu. "Unload the furs Jehu and see that we're paid a fair price, same as before."

"Where you headed, Pinto?"

"Reckon I'll have me a talk with the Carters. You stay here with our furs." Pinto remounted and turned toward Carter's Inn. "Charlie, if Luke Carter doesn't tell me anything, your memory better be clearer when I get back."

"Kinda late in the season for furs to bring top dollar, Pinto. You know the price has dropped back east by now." Cloud knelt beside the furs, answering the veiled threat calmly.

"Reckon that'll be your problem Charlie, same as before, no less."

Cloud smiles, "Alright, alright, but you're wasting your time riding over to Carters."

"Why is that?" Pinto pulled up on the gelding.

"Martin and Tate have been gone since the killing of Miles," Cloud shrugged. "Except Luke, he's over there waiting on his customers."

"Where to?" Pinto turned. "Where'd they go, Charlie?"

"We all know Martin Carter claimed the girl, Chauncy. He was sweet on her. He heard the girl was at Miles' Post. Soon as word came of the raid, him and his brother Tate tore out of here. They've been gone looking for her ever since."

Pinto studied Jehu as he unloaded the packs. He knew the young man was listening to every word spoken by Cloud. "What you think Jehu?"

"He was sweet on her alright." Jehu stopped what he was doing and turned on Cloud. "Mister Cloud, if you're lying to me, I'll come back here and peel your hide."

"Benje might have something to say about that," Cloud nodded at a huge black man covered in muscle.

"If he's speaking the truth, then Martin Carter is still here. He couldn't have taken part in the raid." Pinto rubbed his chin. "Tell me Charlie, this Paiute said that two whites involved in the raid were seen here several times in the past. Who were they?"

Cloud shrugged his shoulders, watching the red face of Jehu nervously. "That, I wouldn't know."

Jehu was in a frustrated rage. He wanted to fight something or somebody. Whirling on the huge black man, fire spit from his eyes. "Turn your dogs loose now, Cloud. When I'm through with him, you're next."

Cloud looked over at the black, thinking better of it, he smiled and shrugged. Something had changed about the young trapper. He was not the same lad that worked for the Carters. "It'll wait for now."

"Point which direction they went," Jehu picked up a bundle of furs and flung them at the blacks, a feat of strength Cloud could not believe. "Mister Cloud, you better point right."

Pinto couldn't believe the distance Jehu had thrown the heavy bundle of furs. Most men couldn't lift a bundle of plews by themselves, without straining every muscle. Here the youth tossed the bundle as easily as if it were a bundle of sticks. Cloud was impressed to say the least.

Pinto doubted the trader would turn the black loose on Jehu, or cross the tall youth, not now anyway. Pinto didn't speak with Luke Carter, as there was no need. Cloud pointed them due west, away from the river and into wild untamed land. All but one pack mule was left behind as the small group would be traveling fast, trying to catch up with the Carters. Before leaving Clouds, they had outfitted with everything they would need for a long trail.

Black Hoof knew the country so he led the way while Jehu pushed them from behind, driving them relentlessly. Twenty miles from the river, Pinto halted the party and ordered a fire built.

"We've got another hour of daylight left, Pinto." Jehu fussed and fumed at the delay.

"We got an hour lad, but the horses don't. They need rest and there's plenty of good graze here."

The group was silent as they sat around the small fire. Even Running Dog kept quiet as he watched Jehu pace around the fire.

"We'll need to set a guard." Pinto puffed on his pipe.

Jehu picked up his rifle, "I'll take it."

"I'll relieve you at midnight."

"No need," Jehu walked away.

Running Dog's eyes followed Jehu as he disappeared into the dark. "White Wolf must care much for the white woman."

"I reckon he does." Pinto blew smoke into the night air.

"What will he do with the Flathead Maiden?" Running Dog looked over at Pinto.

"Maybe him give squaw to Running Dog." Black Hoof laughed at his own words, causing the Crow to laugh as well. Both warriors were young, unmarried men. They couldn't understand why Jehu was so upset over one woman, or any woman.

Black Hoof looked through the surrounding trees and out across a small village. Motioning Running Dog forward, he dismounted and waited for the Crow to move up beside him.

"Small village, maybe Murdockkinn is here."

Running Dog studied the village closely. "These Arapaho people."

"Tell White Wolf and Pinto to leave horses and come up."

Hurrying forward, Pinto and Jehu knelt beside the two warriors and studied the small camp. Counting twenty lodges in the clearing, Pinto figured the village was just a small band of Arapaho moving toward the great council they held every year. He was curious; the small pony herd had eaten down most of the tall grass and yet the village remained where it was. Pinto was aware villages moved often as the grass disappeared and the game became scarce.

"I don't see anything out of place. Let's ride on in, but be ready." Pinto walked back to his gelding and mounted.

The villagers hung back fearfully as the few warriors of the village faced the two whites and the two unknown warriors. Black Hoof spoke to the village leader while the others watched the warriors of the village as they stood around their horses.

Nodding, Black Hoof looked up at Pinto. "Him say Murdockkinn, two white men, and two white women come this place with many warriors."

"How long did they stay?"

"Many days; they eat much; no let Arapaho leave this place." Black Hoof looked up at Jehu. "Chief say Murdockkinn lazy Indian."

"What is it, Black Hoof?" Pinto noticed the look the warrior had given Jehu.

"Chief say Murdockkinn use one white woman very bad."

Jehu's hands clenched the mane of his horse tightly at the words. "Ask the Chief where they were headed."

Black Hoof held up his hands. "There is more."

"What else?" Pinto asked.

"After Murdockkinn and whites leave this place, two more white men come here; ask same thing we ask."

"Two more whites?" Pinto looked over at the Chief.

"Him say, they from Trading Post on big river."

"Tate and Martin Carter," Jehu muttered. "Then who are the whites that rode with Murdockkinn and helped kill Miles?"

"How long they been gone, and what direction?" Pinto listened quietly as Black Hoof questioned the Arapaho Chief who pointed to the west.

"Him say two sleeps."

Pinto swung up on his gelding. "Let's go, we're getting close."

Jehu swore as they left the village. "I reckon Cloud was speaking the truth."

Late afternoon found the hunters following a small game trail. Black Hoof suddenly stopped and summoned Running Dog to the front.

Pointing at the ground, the two warriors dismounted and traced the tracks with their fingers. Picking up horse droppings, the two warriors broke them up and examined them. Leading their horses, the two warriors followed the dim tracks along the trail, studying every scratch on the hard ground.

Two miles further along, Black Hoof stopped again and knelt to study the tracks once more. Excitement sounded in his voice as Black Hoof gestured at the tracks and then northwest. Running Dog walked to where Pinto and Jehu was waiting.

"Black Hoof still can see track on trail." The Crow pointed downward. "Here, no wind, no rain."

"How old are the tracks?"

"Them come this place, one sun."

"Who made the track?"

Running Dog shrugged. "This one doesn't know. The Paiute says it's the whites from the trader's post."

Jehu looked down at the dim tracks. "Why does he believe this?"

"Him say the warhorse of Murdockkinn make track there." Running Dog placed his finger on a larger, half-obscured track.

Pinto and Jehu both instinctively looked down again at the tracks. "Is he sure?"

Again, Running Dog shrugged. "Track fresh; this horse heavy; make deep imprint in ground. He say him plenty sure."

Pinto looked at the tall trees covering the trail, shading it in the heat of the day. The rain had not been as hard along this part of the trail so the tracks were still visible in some places. Occasionally, the huge hoof print of the horse that Black Hoof said was Murdockkinns, would stand out plainly.

"Tell him to follow the track as long as he can." Pinto looked back at Jehu. "Seems the Carters are on Murdockkinn's trail, same as we are."

Nodding, Running Dog turned his horse. After speaking quietly with Black Hoof, the party continued west. In places, the tracks were still visible in the hardpan and where the trail was covered with debris. Black Hoof followed the trail blindly, but relentlessly.

"Why does the Paiute help us?" Jehu was curious.

Pinto shrugged. "Can't say, lad; in time, I expect he'll tell us."

"The way he hangs on to the trail, I'm sure glad he's on our side."

"Me too." Pinto watched the warrior, who reminded him of a hunting dog on a hot trail. "He's sure enough a bloodhound on a track."

The tracks trailed off to the northwest during the afternoon and still, Black Hoof held to the track like a tick on a deer. Mile by mile passed, but now they were becoming excited, as the trail became fresh, and easily followed. The day was long gone. Pinto knew the horses were getting tired so he halted the group and made camp for the night. Earlier in the day, Running Dog had gotten lucky and brought down a small deer with his bow. Deer steaks filled the air with aroma as they sizzled over the small campfire.

The hunters sat around in the dark, hungrily gulping down large chunks of the deer. The small fire sputtered flames as wood was added or when the hot deer grease splattered into the flames. Pinto studied the men's faces and not one seemed tired or discouraged. He knew each one was eager and ready to continue the chase as the trail heated up. They reminded him of a hound on a coon track, becoming more excited and energetic as the trail became hotter.

Black Hoof ripped into a piece of venison with his strong teeth and looked over at Pinto. "Two white man horse, maybe three are with warriors ahead."

Pinto's head jerked up at the announcement. "How do you know this?"

"Two horse's feet small, well-taken care of; others of warriors, bigger, rough edge." Black Hoof reached for another piece of meat. "Maybe this one wrong, don't think so."

"Any sign of the girl, or Mrs. Miles?"

"Maybe one horse carries two women, but Black Hoof thinks only one woman still with these warriors."

Pinto looked over at Running Dog. "What do you think nephew?"

"Paiute, him good tracker; bring us here this place." Running Dog looked over at Jehu. "This one think him right, only one woman with these warriors. Maybe other whites rescue woman."

"You think the Carters caught up with the raiders?" Jehu questioned Black Hoof.

The warrior nodded solemnly. "Maybe, me think only one woman with these warriors."

Jehu bit into his meat and stared into the fire's flames. Black Hoof had already proven his ability to follow and read a trail. Jehu trusted his judgment. He had no reason to doubt only one woman was with the riders ahead, but which one, Chauncy or the Miles woman? Looking up at the half moon that had just risen, Jehu cussed the dark. Tossing his unfinished venison into the fire, he stalked off, into the shadows.

"White Wolf wants to be on trail." Black Hoof chewed his venison as he relaxed on his buffalo robe. "The white squaw, why she so important to him?"

Running Dog shook his head. "I don't know, but he think of white woman all the time."

"We catch up by and by, you see."

Pinto pulled out his old pipe and tamped tobacco in it. "How far ahead are they?"

The Paiute shrugged and looked over at Running Dog. "Maybe we catch when sun come up, what you think?"

"One day, maybe two, no more." Running Dog studied the smoking pipe as Pinto lit up. "They have no fear. Murdockkinn have many warriors. They waste much time on trail. I don't think they know we follow."

Jehu had been listening to the conversation from the dark. Walking back to the fire, he squatted down and looked at the three men. "What happens when we catch up?"

"They'll kill the women before they let us have them back." Pinto shrugged. "That's what'll happen if'n we ain't careful."

"Then Pinto Stade, we'll be extra careful approaching them." Jehu stared hard at the older trapper.

Another day passed as Jehu fretted and fumed with the pace Black Hoof set. Both Running Dog and Black Hoof scouted ahead on the trail, far enough so they wouldn't stumble into the enemy they pursued. Both warriors knew they were closing in on the raiders. Running Dog had been right. With the pace they were traveling, and the plain tracks they were leaving, the warriors ahead did not realize they were being followed.

Pinto had been afoot, walking, leading his horse for several miles with Jehu following close behind him when Running Dog appeared ahead on the trail. Motioning for the trappers to follow, he led them down a small trail to where Black Hoof waited.

"Murdockkinn and his warriors near this place." Black Hoof tied his gelding to a tree. "You maybe wait here until dark come. Black Hoof go; look see."

Pinto, Jehu, and Running Dog relaxed quietly in a stand of box elder trees. Pinto looked to the priming of his rifle and puffed easily on his pipe. The day had been long, but now they were close to the warriors they pursued. Black Hoof would not let them light a fire, so all they had to eat was cold deer meat and creek water.

Hearing the soft walking of a horse coming on the trail, the three men sat up warily until they recognized the form of Black Hoof as he slipped softly to the ground.

"How far ahead are they?" Jehu couldn't contain himself. He had to know.

"They make camp by and by; maybe two hours. Black Hoof shrugged as he tied off his gelding. "They think no one follows; no set guard to watch."

Pinto sat back down beside a tree. "How many?"

"Maybe this many." The warrior held up his fingers.

"And the women?" Jehu asked.

"Black Hoof see only one squaw, she white woman." The warrior looked away. "White trapper keep her close to him. Maybe she his woman now."

"What color hair did she have?" Jehu looked across at Black Hoof.

Black Hoof shrugged. "Woman hair all full dirt. No can tell this thing you want to know."

Pinto lay back on the ground, his old hat covering his face from the gnats and flies that inhabited the timber. "Get some sleep, lads. We're a fixing to get busy come dark."

Jehu looked about the open spaces then up and down the trail before closing his eyes to try to rest. Too excited to sleep, he knew the oncoming cover of dark would bring him closer to Chauncy. His only worry was, could they sneak in on the warriors ahead and rescue the woman before they were discovered. Pinto and Running Dog both had said the men holding the woman would kill her before letting her get away. Black Hoof had described Murdockkinn as a dangerous, cruel, and ruthless war leader among the tribes.

Pinto rolled to his feet in the early dark of the coming night. Seeing the others already sitting about, wide-awake, he checked his rifle, and stood up.

Firelight flickered out of the night, as Black Hoof led the three others quietly forward. Slipping silently, making no sound, the men seemed almost ghostly as they made their way within a few feet of the sleeping camp. One guard stood watch at the edge of the camp. Jehu strained his eyes in the dark, trying to find Chauncy.

Spreading out at intervals, Pinto and Jehu took one side, while Running Dog and Black Hoof waited on the other side. Running Dog silently notched an arrow and took aim on the lone guard. Only the twang and vibration of the bow's string sounded, as the arrow silently took flight and sunk to the feathered shaft into the warrior.

Yelling in unison, the four men fired their rifles and bows, and then charged the sleeping camp, causing the warriors left alive, to leap to their feet and face the demons that were attacking them. Jehu fired once, killing a large warrior, then raced forward, slashing and cutting his way through what was left of the warriors that hadn't tried to flee.

Only moans of pain were heard and then complete silence, before Pinto called from his side of the camp. "Do you see either of the women, or them white trappers?"

Jehu raced to where Pinto knelt beside a dead warrior. "I don't think they're here, Pinto."

"No lad, it appears they be gone." Pinto looked down at the dead warrior. "They must have split off from this bunch and pulled out before we got here."

Searching the camp frantically, Jehu looked about for Chauncy or any sign of her, but to no avail. Running Dog and Black Hoof slipped silently back into the camp. Both warriors had wet scalps hanging from their war belts.

"How many got away?" Pinto looked across the fire at the two warriors.

Running Dog shrugged. "Four or five, maybe more."

"What about the other white woman?" Jehu questioned the warriors. "Was she here?"

Black Hoof shook his head. "She no here, white men no here, Murdockkinn no here. That is why these warriors were so easily killed."

"We'll get some food down and rest a few hours then we'll move out." Pinto looked around the dead warriors' camp. "We can't track them until daylight comes."

For two days, they retraced their back-trail, trying to find where Murdockkinn and the white men split off from the main bunch of warriors. Finally, Running Dog found a hidden path that led away from the bigger trail. The path was well concealed, covered by several cedar trees before opening to a small path that led due south and east.

Black Hoof shook his head as he discovered the large track of the horse Murdockkinn rode only yards down the trail. Pointing at the track, he kicked his gelding hard and rode ahead of the others. The Paiute knew his oversight had lost him the enemy he hated most. Also, it could have gotten them all killed if the dead warriors had been more alert. Running Dog looked at the dark face of Black Hoof. He wanted to say something to calm the warrior, but remained silent. He alone, knew the reason Black Hoof rode with them in their quest to find the Delaware breed.

Pinto sat silently beside the fire, looking at Running Dog. "Where's the Paiute?"

"Him scout ahead, try see which way the whites travel."

"You mind telling me why this Murdockkinn is so important that he risks his life to help us." Pinto knew Indians; the Paiute was not tracking the Delaware just because he liked to fight. No, there was more to it.

"Him tell you, uncle, by and by, maybe." The warrior shrugged. "Running Dog no tell; not for this one to speak of this thing.

Pinto knew further questioning would do no good. If an Indian was a friend, he was loyal to the end. However, if he didn't want to speak of something, even tearing out his tongue, he wouldn't say a thing.

"Have you seen any sign of the white woman with this bunch?" Jehu looked sharply at Running Dog.

Running Dog shook his head negatively. "Me no see."

Jehu only nodded quietly then leaned back against his saddle. He knew they had only been on this trail one day; maybe tomorrow. Her track would be hard to discover unless she dismounted and walked where the ground was soft.

Black Hoof flung himself from his gelding and walked over to the fire. Pinto couldn't see how these warriors could ride many miles and never show fatigue. He knew, from an early age, Indians lived on a horse's back. They were more at home on a horse than on the ground. The Paiute took the food he was offered with a nod, and sat down across from Jehu.

Biting into the meat, he looked into the hard eyes of White Wolf. "Murdockkinn is ahead with the white trappers from the trading post on the big river."

"Who else rides with them?"

Black Hoof knew what the white youth was asking. "There is a white woman with them, a light haired woman."

"Maybe it is Chauncy." Jehu let out a sigh of relief. "Is she well?"

"She is well. The white from post watches her every move."

"Who else?" Pinto spoke from across the fire. "Who else rides with them?"

"Murdockkinn has maybe ten warriors with him."

"We'll ride at daylight. How far ahead are they?" Pinto asked.

"When I turn back, they near. Now, maybe one day ride ahead." Black Hoof shrugged. "We catch tomorrow."

Chapter 12

Black Hoof led the small party in a hard trot to the southeast. All day they rode, stopping only to let the horses drink out of the many small streams that coursed through the flatlands and hills. The trail led through timbered mountains, then dropped off into the small valleys dotting the countryside. Flowers and tall grass stood belly deep on the horses as they passed. The fragrant smell the forest emitted was fresh and invigorating to the trappers as they rode along.

Small bands of elk, deer, and buffalo, drifted quickly away from the fast moving horses. The recent rains made the tracking easy for the sharp-eyed Paiute as they went along the trail. New grass had been laid over, as the horses trampled it down in their passing, making the tracking easier. Crossing a boxed in valley, the trail led straight up a slippery, shale-laden hill, then fell straight down, making the horses slide hard on their haunches to keep their feet. At the bottom, Black Hoof pulled in hard on his blowing gelding.

"What is it?" Pinto reined in beside the Paiute.

Black Hoof pointed to where the trail parted. "Many warriors come down trail and meet Murdockkinn and the whites."

"How many?"

The Paiute ignored the question, slipping from his horse to study the trail. "Maybe five more come this place."

"Who were they?"

"Same ones we fight before."

Pinto swore. "You mean they circled in here ahead of us? Now this Murdockkinn knows we're here and following him."

"Him know we here. Now they come for us maybe."

Jehu looked across at Pinto. "What happens now?"

"Well, if we were smart, we'd high tail it out of here, quick." Pinto scratched his head and looked at Jehu and Black Hoof. "They've got us outnumbered. They're bound to be waiting for us somewhere up ahead."

"I'm not leaving her here."

"Figured as much," Pinto nodded. "What about you, Black Hoof?"

"Me come this place to kill Murdockkinn, not run away like coward."

"That's good, real good. They only outnumber us, maybe fifteen against our four."

"You go if you want to Pinto, I'm staying." Jehu set his jaw firmly.

"Didn't say I was going anywhere, just telling you the facts is all." Pinto looked over at the Paiute. "Tell me Black Hoof, why are you so set on killing this Murdockkinn?"

Black Hoof looked solemnly at the tracks at his feet then raised his arm and showed them a scar. "I have sworn my blood to kill this one or lose my own life."

"But why?"

"Three years ago, I come home from long hunt, find village burned, many dead, my woman, two small ones and mother all dead."

"Murdockkinn?"

Black Hoof nodded. "Him lead war party of Pawnee warriors to our village."

"And now you're sworn to kill him?"

"I must kill him, this one already dead." Black Hoof drew his long skinning knife and pulled it across his chest, causing a small trickle of blood to run down his stomach.

Pinto grabbed the warrior's knife hand before he could commit any more damage. "You better save your strength. We've got to catch him first."

Again, the Paiute took the lead, far ahead of the others. Running Dog followed at a trot behind Jehu. Outnumbered the way they were, Pinto didn't figure on an ambush. To attack a weak enemy, without warning, was considered cowardly to the Pawnee. No, when the warriors were ready to fight, they would turn and be waiting somewhere ahead in plain sight.

Jehu slowed down and let Running Dog catch up. "My friend, tell me, what did Black Hoof mean when he said he was a dead man?"

"Him dead man, him not return from this war trail."

"You believe that?" Running Dog nodded. "Black Hoof say his medicine tell him he die on this raid. I believe him. You see."

Ahead, the Paiute sat his horse and waited for the others to catch up. A few feet further along, the trail forked, leading off to the east and west. Black Hoof slapped the braided riding crop across his leg and studied the track as he waited.

"You lose them?" Pinto pulled up and looked at the warrior.

"No, Murdockkinn take one trail. I think white men and woman take another." Black Hoof pointed to where the trail branched.

"You sure?"

Running Dog rode around Pinto and studied the tracks. "Him speak truth, Murdockkinn ride west with warriors, white men go east."

Jehu looked over at Black Hoof. "How many white men and have they got warriors with them?"

Black Hoof nodded slowly. "Five maybe six horses go east."

"Why would they split up?" Jehu was curious. "Especially if they know we're following."

"Maybe they argue," Pinto spoke up. "Maybe they just want us to split up so they can attack somewhere along the trail."

"I've got to follow the trail to the east. I'm going after her." Jehu kicked his horse, just to have Pinto reach out and grab his reins.

"You wait up just a minute, and let's talk this over a bit."

"This is my business, Pinto."

"I asked the Paiute why he wanted to kill the Delaware, now I'm asking you the same question."

Jehu looked over at all three men. "Chauncy Lee is my sister, Chauncy Lee Wolf."

Pinto's mouth fell open. "Your sister!"

"I thought it would be safer for her if we didn't let on we were related."

"Why?"

"I figured if no one knew, they would talk in front of me. That way I would know when it was time for us to move on." Jehu shrugged. "Dumb thinking I guess, but we done it."

"Well, you sure had me fooled on that one," Pinto nodded.

"Yeah, we had Martin Carter fooled too."

"Alright Jehu, what do you figure we should do?" Pinto looked over at Black Hoof. "We're too few; I don't think we should split up."

"I told you, I'll take care of my sister. You go with Black Hoof and Running Dog."

"No." Black Hoof raised his arm. "We will all go to the east. I will return and follow the trail of Murdockkinn when my brother, White Wolf, has his sister back."

Running Dog nodded his head in agreement. "The trail will lead to a white village somewhere."

Pinto looked over at the warrior. "Why do you think that?"

"Whoever this white man is, he will try to hide in village with other whites. Him know White Wolf follow his trail." Running Dog shrugged. "Him think in white village, he be safe."

"Let's ride." Jehu motioned for Black Hoof to lead out. "I'm thanking all of you."

Pinto studied the tracks several seconds and released the reins of Jehu's horse, looking over at the youngster. "We'll get her back, lad."

Jehu nodded, "thank you, Pinto."

"We ride now, waste much time talking." Black Hoof looked off to the west. "We will all go after woman and whites, and then I will find Murdockkinn."

Black Hoof pushed the horses hard, but still the white men stayed ahead of them. Knowing they were being followed, the ones ahead used every strip of hardpan ground or water to slow the followers down. Black Hoof clung to the trail with the tenacity of a bulldog. The horses were tiring, but the horses ahead were just as tired, and it was only a matter of miles before they caught up with the men.

Riding into a small creek, with an abundance of grass, Black Hoof held up his hand and stopped the men following him. "We rest horses here."

Pinto nodded and dismounted tiredly. "How far ahead are they?"

"Maybe we catch tomorrow."

"You sure?" Jehu questioned. "Really sure this time?"

"Black Hoof sure."

Pinto lit his pipe and relaxed against a small birch tree. The ground felt good. It had been a long trail. His body was aching from the hard pace the Paiute set.

He watched as Jehu staked out the horses on the lush grass. Running Dog and Black Hoof wanted fresh meat so they went to hunt. Nodding, he looked approvingly at the tall youth. The lad had come a long way since their first meeting. Pinto figured he had put on twenty or more pounds of muscle and had grown another inch, but it was his presence and proud carriage that was so noticeable.

One season in the mountains had made the youngster into a man and had given him the legendary name of White Wolf. One day, the old trapper knew, the youth's name would be remembered and spoken of the same way as Bridger and Fitzsimmons.

Daylight found Black Hoof following the trail of the whites to the east. Fresh horse droppings and tracks littering the trail led the Paiute forward at a hard trot. Pulling in his gelding, the warrior motioned the others forward to him.

"We are close; they just ahead."

From where they sat, atop a ridge, Pinto looked across the valley, through the trees. Sitting forward, he pointed a finger. "There."

Six riders were crossing the open valley holding their horses to a walk. The white woman rode in the middle of the line of riders. Pinto studied the far side of the valley. A small game trail could be seen leading out of the valley and into the timber. They watched as the last rider in the line turned his horse and studied their back trail.

Black Hoof nodded. "Pawnee know they're followed."

"How are we going to get across the valley without being seen?" Jehu studied the small figure of the woman in the distance.

"We go around the valley or wait until dark," Pinto spoke up, before Jehu could say anything. "No choice, they see us coming in on 'em, and they're liable to kill her."

Jehu dismounted and walked forward on the trail where he could see the valley better. He had her almost in his grasp. He couldn't stand to see her ride out of his sight again. Remounting, he whipped the Appaloosa into a hard run down the narrow trail before any of the others could stop him.

"What the?" Pinto could only swear as he watched Jehu hit the bottom of the trail and raced his horse across the valley. "He's gone loco."

Almost in a trance, the three watched as the last two Pawnee warriors in line heard the running horse and turned their horses, waiting across the trail for the oncoming Appaloosa. The two whites, with the woman, kicked their horses into a dead run to the east. The last of the Pawnees, watched in awe, as the crazy, white man raced his horse forward, charging and screaming like a banshee, right at the other Pawnees. The warrior hesitated, scared of what he thought was a crazy demon racing at him.

Running Dog, with Pinto and Black Hoof, came out of their trance and whipped their horses downhill toward the valley. Ahead, over the hoof beats of their racing horses, they heard the loud report of Jehu's rifle going off. Clearing the timbered ridge, they were shocked to find two Pawnee already dead and Jehu racing the Appaloosa across the valley, ignoring the third warrior, who was running his horse away from the madman.

Pinto turned his horse and raced after the fleeing Pawnee, while Running Dog whipped his horse, trying to catch up with the flying Appaloosa. Black Hoof dismounted and scalped the two dead Pawnee. One had been shot and Jehu's rifle butt had knocked the other in the head. Black Hoof held up the two scalps and watched as the White Wolf disappeared into the far mountains.

"You are truly a White Wolf, my brother."

Pinto raced his tired gelding almost to the end of the valley then dismounted the horse in a sliding stop. Leveling the Hawken, he sighted in on the hard running Pawnee. Holding steady, he gently pulled the trigger, feeling the recoil of the rifle against his shoulder. He watched as the warrior slipped slowly from his blowing horse. Riding carefully up to the dead warrior, he pulled his skinning knife and approached the dead man.

Throwing the scalp from him, Pinto looked at the blood covering his hands. "One more for you, Lintamine." Remounting, he slapped the gelding in the flanks and caught up with Black Hoof who was leading the loose horses of the Pawnee. "The White Wolf, I heard his rifle shoot again, up the mountain."

"I heard it." Pinto spit and kicked his horse into a lope. "Let's go take a look."

The two whites, with the woman, pulled their horses to a stop and dismounted. With the woman slowing them down and the speed of the Appaloosa, they knew they would be overtaken quickly. Both men were dressed in buckskins and carried heavy fifty caliber Hawken rifles. "If'n we can kill the crazy coot that's coming on that App horse, the others may back off."

The redheaded man looked over at the woman, then over at his partner nervously. "Yeah, if we don't end up like them Pawnee did."

The other trapper looked over at the redhead. "Keep your nerve, you hear?"

"I hear." The redhead looked over at the woman. "She ain't worth dying over, let's just leave her and ride."

"She's mine; I ain't leaving her or running. Sides, I ain't sure leaving her behind would stop that lunatic."

"We could try."

"I'll kill her first."

The Appaloosa could be heard running hard on the rocky trail, his hooves echoing loudly on the hard ground. Jehu had reloaded his rifle while in a dead run after he took his last snap shot at the two whites. Rounding a small clump of trees, he sighted riders standing together, a hundred yards away. Kicking the App hard, he felt the horse surge forward as one of the men fired at him.

"You missed him clean." The bigger man cussed at the redhead.

Jehu watched one of the men raise his rifle and saw the belch of smoke at almost the same time he felt a sharp blow and burning sensation in his side. Clinging hard to the saddle, he managed to pull himself straight once again. Looking down the trail for the two whites, he found the men trying to reload their rifles. Raising his rifle, Jehu took aim on the man on the right and pulled the trigger. Watching, as the man was thrown backward, Jehu ducked off to the horse's side as the other man fired again.

Jehu kicked the Appaloosa hard, watching in horror as the man pulled his skinning knife and raced to where the woman had collapsed on the ground. Veering the Appaloosa, Jehu shoulders the big gelding into the running man, knocking him sideways, away from the woman. Lunging from the horse, Jehu landed on top of the man. The war axe did its job as Jehu split the man's skull.

Standing unsteadily, he staggered over to the woman. Rolling her over on her back, he wiped his eyes, trying to clear his vision. "Mrs. Miles, I thought you were Chauncy."

The woman could only cling to him and sob uncontrollably. Jehu held her tight and looked over his shoulder as Running Dog raced into the clearing.

"Is your sister alright?" The warrior knelt beside Jehu and the woman.

"She is alright, just exhausted and scared out of her wits," Jehu tried to stand, "but this is not my sister."

Running Dog grabbed the wobbly youngster, helping him down against a large boulder. "You're bleeding, my brother."

"Yeah," Jehu tried to look down at his bloody side. "They got a piece of lead in me, I reckon."

"He saved my life." The woman crawled over beside Jehu. "Tully was going to kill me, as he did David."

"Tully?" Jehu now focused on the fact the two dead trappers were not the Carters. "Where are the Carters?"

Pinto and Black Hoof raced into the clearing and quickly dismounted. Pinto looked around at the dead bodies and knelt beside Jehu. "How bad you hurt, lad?"

"Feels like the bullet went clean through."

"Let me take a look."

"Wait, first ask Mrs. Miles about Chauncy."

"No, first I'm gonna stop the bleeding, before you bleed out on me." Pinto pulled bandages from his saddlebags. "Dang fool, why didn't you wait?" Pinto felt Jehu go limp against the rock and looked sharply at him. Quickly cutting his bloody shirt away, Pinto examined the wound of the unconscious man. The wound had gone completely through Jehu's side, but he was losing a dangerous amount of blood.

Running Dog looked over Pinto's shoulder at the wound. "Him need medicine man. Lose too much blood."

Pinto nodded. "You're right; I wish Jethro was here. Rig a travois; we'll take him back to Yellow Horn's village."

Mrs. Miles looked to where Pinto was cleaning the wound. "Will the young man live?"

Pinto looked up at the woman. "Maybe, he's strong, but he's lost a lot of blood."

"He saved my life."

"I know," Pinto nodded. "Tell me, what happened to the other white woman, and who are these men?"

The woman looked over at the two dead men. "That one's name was Tully, and the other they called Red. They came with the Pawnee to our trading post. Tully killed David, and then the Indians killed more people, burned the trading post, and destroyed everything they didn't want."

"And Chauncy?"

"Martin Carter and his brother Tate caught up with us on the trail. Martin bought the girl back from the Pawnee."

"The Carters weren't involved in the killing and burnings?"

"They came later. They heard there was to be a raid on our post. Martin Carter came after the girl later."

"How did he know Chauncy was with you at the post?" Pinto was curious.

"I figure that heathen Murdockkinn told him." Mrs. Miles rubbed her face almost in a trance. "Martin had come twice before; earlier in the fall, trying to get her to go back to Cloud's with him."

"And she refused?"

"She did," said Mrs. Miles. "He was infatuated with her, but he didn't try to force her to go with him."

"The Carters weren't involved in any way with the killing of your husband?" Pinto asked again. "Are you sure?"

Looking over at Tully's body, she shivered uncontrollably. "He's the one that killed my husband, and did horrible things to his body."

"Why didn't they buy you back?"

"Martin Carter tried; I don't think he really cared, but the girl made him."

"Murdockkinn wouldn't sell you?"

"Tully claimed me as his prisoner. He wouldn't sell me to them." The woman dropped her head. "That animal threatened to kill both of us if Murdockkinn interfered. Finally, they left with Chauncy."

"Where did Martin and the girl go?"

"I don't know, maybe back to Clouds."

"We'll find her when the boy gets back on his feet," Pinto nodded slowly. "First, we've gotta get him back to the Flathead Village."

Mrs. Miles looked down at Jehu. "He may be disappointed."

"Why do you say that Mrs. Miles?" She shrugged almost as if she was in a trance speaking over her shoulder. "It doesn't matter."

Running Dog and Black Hoof brought the travois and tied it behind one of the gentler horses. Easing the unconscious Jehu onto the buffalo robes, Pinto examined the wound and tightened the bandage.

"We'll return to the Flathead Village. Their medicine man will be able to tend to the lad better than we can." Pinto looked over at Mrs. Miles. "You up to riding, mam?"

"I can ride."

Black Hoof kicked his horse as Pinto pointed south. "Take the lead, my friend. We must hurry and get him back."

Black Hoof looked down at the ashen Jehu. "White Wolf will live. He is as strong as the buffalo bull."

"Yes, he is strong, but the lead doesn't know that." Pinto mounted his horse and looked down at Jehu concerned. "It's the poison I fear."

Black Hoof and Running Dog leaped to their feet as the two Crow Warriors, Tall Grass and Owl Man came riding slowly into the Flathead Village, their right hands extended in a sign of peace. Walking to where his friends sat their horses, Running Dog escorted them back to the fire.

Tall Grass stood before Yellow Horn and motioned sideways with his hand. "Peace to you, Great Chief. We wish permission to enter your village and speak with our brother Running Dog."

Pinto knew, while the Crow and Flathead People were not mortal enemies, they have, at times in the past, stolen horses and fought each other. Not only personal safety, but also good manners were behind Tall Grass asking permission to enter the village.

"Sit my sons, you are welcome." Yellow Horn motioned for the warriors to be seated. Turning, he spoke to an old squaw. "Bring them food."

Good etiquette always necessitated that guests must eat before speaking about whatever brought them to the village. Pinto knew there had to be something mighty important to bring them alone into the village.

Tall Grass set down his bowl, thanking Yellow Horn for the food and turned to Running Dog. "We have heard of the white man's fort being burned, my friend. We have come looking for you, to offer you our protection."

Running Dog laughed. "I thank my friends, Tall Grass and Owl Man."

Tall Grass looked about the camp and over at Pinto. "Where is the White Wolf?"

Pinto motioned at the lodge. "He has been wounded. He lies inside the lodge."

"He will live?"

"The old one doesn't know for sure." Running Dog nodded at the medicine man. "The Great Spirit will not let one such as him die."

"This is bad news. We have need of him." Tall Grass shook his head.

Running Dog looked sharply at the warrior. "Why do you say this, my friend?"

"Two Paiute Warriors came to our village. They look for Black Hoof." Tall Grass looked over at the Paiute. "They only know Black Hoof was with Running Dog and two white trappers, one known as White Wolf."

"What did they want?"

"They have news of Murdockkinn."

"What news?" Black Hoof sat forward.

"The Pawnee dog and many warriors attacked a Sac and Fox Village many days to the west." Tall Grass looked across at Black Hoof.

"Murdockkinn is far away from his village and safety. Now, if you hurry, you can kill him."

"This Murdockkinn must have attacked the village after we turned south to bring Jehu here." Pinto rubbed his chin.

"Where are the Paiute Warriors who look for me?" Black Hoof asked.

"We not know where you travel. We come here; others look for you to the west." Tall Grass pointed west. "They say if we find you, say you come to Dead Horse Canyon fast."

"Dead Horse Canyon?" Pinto murmured the word.

"This place is between Crow Village and Pawnee hunting grounds." The warrior nodded knowingly. "They say maybe we can trap the Delaware dog there if we hurry."

"Who goes with me?" Black Hoof looked around the group.

"We will go." Running Dog looks over at Tall Grass and Owl Man.

"How far is this place? How many days ride?" Pinto looked over at Black Hoof.

Black Hoof shrugged. "Maybe five, six suns, if we hurry."

"I'll ride with you." Pinto looked over at the lodge.

Black Hoof held up his hand. "No, the Pawnee Killer should stay here with White Wolf."

"You came here and helped me save the lad, now I will help you," Pinto argued. "The girl and the old one will take good care of him until I return."

"It is a good thing you do," Black Hoof nodded. "We will leave now."

Dead Horse Canyon was amply named. Years before, the Sioux and the Blackfoot fought a running battle on the flat sandy land. Bleached horse bones from the battle still littered the rocky floor of the canyon. That long ago battle was still sung in the Blackfoot Villages. The mighty warriors of the Blackfoot had won a hard fought battle against the raiders from the Sioux Nation. It was a great victory.

Traveling hard, Black Hoof and his small party arrived at the valley six days later, after a long, tiring journey over the rough mountain passes. Pinto slid slowly to the ground as Black Hoof and Running Dog rode forward across the valley, looking for any sign Murdockkinn had passed through the canyon before their arrival. He was tired. He hadn't participated in such a forced, non-stop ride, in many a year. Stretching his sore back, he knew Lowrie had been right. They were getting old. The two warriors rode back from the canyon floor and dismounted.

"Murdockkinn no come this place. No horse come through canyon in many days." Black Hoof looked across the canyon floor. "We should put out a guard to watch the north entrance."

Pinto looked along the walls of the canyon, looking for a likely place for a sentry. "We sure don't want any surprises."

"We will do this thing," Running Dog nodded.

"Can Murdockkinn and his warriors go another way back to their villages?" Pinto asked.

Black Hoof shrugged. "They can go many ways, but they come this way; quicker to get back to their village."

"Always before, Pawnee enemy come this way fast after raid to the east." Running Dog kicked a few sticks of wood together for a fire. "Them want to go to village to show off their new scalps and captives, to their squaws."

"Yeah," Pinto looked over at Running Dog, "I've noticed somebody else around here likes to strut and show off."

Running Dog laughed at the words. "A brave and mighty warrior should always brag about his victories over his enemies."

Pinto unsaddled his horse and turned around. "Where are the warriors that were to meet you?"

"They come here soon, maybe."

"I hope so," Pinto spit. "I'm curious, Running Dog. You say this Murdockkinn is a Delaware. Why do Pawnee Warriors follow him?"

"Him Delaware, but he is a great warrior, many coups, and many scalps." The Crow looked to the west. "Him come here many suns ago. He live with Pawnee."

Jehu had lain around the lodge several days after Pinto and the others departed. The feverish delirium and fever had finally broken. His appetite was back, and he slowly swallowed the stew that Alamette fed him. He was in a sour mood after finding out Pinto left him behind when he rode out to help Black Hoof fight Murdockkinn. Only the weakness in his body kept him from saddling the Appaloosa and following Pinto and the warriors. Several times, he had tried to rise from his bed, but he had lost too much blood. He was too weak.

"Mrs. Miles, Alamette said you know where Chauncy was taken?" Jehu looked up at the white woman as she entered the lodge.

"You're awake," she was surprised. "How are you feeling?"

"Weak as a baby."

"Yes, I know where they took the girl." Mrs. Miles knelt beside Alamette. "Why don't you rest my dear? You haven't left his side in days."

Jehu was surprised when Mrs. Miles signed to the girl. He never thought the white woman would know sign language. Alamette only shook her head, and refused to leave.

"You're a lucky young man, Jehu. She hasn't left your side once since Pinto brought you in last week."

"Tell me about Chauncy."

"It was Martin Carter that followed the Pawnee and took her back east like I told Pinto."

Jehu looked hard at the woman. "Was she hurt?"

"No, she had not been harmed, nothing permanent anyway." Mrs. Miles shivered and looked away from Jehu's probing eyes. "Carter found us a few days after they killed my husband. He ransomed her from Murdockkinn then departed immediately."

"He took Chauncy and rode out and left you there?"

"He had no choice. He tried, but I was the prisoner of the man you killed, not of the Indians."

Jehu nodded. "Did Murdockkinn let Tully have you?"

Mrs. Miles touched his forehead. "Out here Jehu, when a warrior captures a prisoner in a raid, the captive belongs to that warrior and no one can take them away from him, not even a chief."

"What will you do now?" Jehu looked up at her.

She shrugged. "Pinto says he will take me back to St. Louis when he returns."

"When I'm on my feet, I will take you east."

"I figured you'd go after Pinto."

"I need to find Chauncy. I don't know where Running Dog and Pinto might be, and it's large land out there."

She smiled. "You don't know where Chauncy is either, and what about Alamette?"

"What about her?" Jehu looked over at the girl. "She's fine."

"She adores you. She is dedicated to you." Mrs. Miles looked at the girl. "She says you are her husband. She nursed you day and night, never leaving your side."

Jehu focused on the tall lodge poles overhead. "I know she did."

Three days after Pinto and the warriors staked out Dead Horse Canyon, six Paiute warriors rode cautiously into the canyon. Recognizing the men as some of his tribesmen, Black Hoof let out with a shrill whistle and hurried down the rocky slope to meet them.

"What has happened, my brothers?" Black Hoof blurted out as he noticed fresh blood on some of the warriors.

"Murdockkinn; we rode into his trap on our way here." An older warrior looked at Pinto and the warriors behind Black Hoof. "This is all the warriors you brought?"

"How many did you lose?" Running Dog helped a wounded warrior from his horse.

"Three are dead."

Black Hoof was beside himself. "Where is Murdockkinn?"

"He follows us; him come this place soon."

"How did you get away from him?" Pinto asked curiously.

"Him come from long raid. His horse very tired; our horse fresh. We outrun Pawnee." The warrior shrugged. "We lose Delaware; him have to track us; take more time."

"How far behind is he?" Pinto tapped out his pipe. "How many warriors does he have?"

"Him be here soon. Him have maybe ten warriors."

Murdockkinn and his raiders spread out in a long line as they entered the mouth of the canyon. They knew Black Hoof and his warriors were waiting inside the canyon. Pinto tried his best to stop Black Hoof, Running Dog, and the other warriors from riding out into plain sight to confront the raiders, but to no avail. Black Hoof had already seen Murdockkinn, the killer of his family and a blood rage was on him. Running Dog and the others were young and in their fighting prime. Their pride would not let Black Hoof ride out alone to face the enemy warriors. As the two lines of warriors faced off across the canyon floor, Pinto shrugged and kicked his horse forward.

"You're a dang fool, Pinto Stade." The big trapper swore, as he counted the warriors Murdockkinn has, almost twice as many rode with them. "Only a dang fool lets his temper and foolish pride, get him killed."

Seeing the warrior once again, Pinto now remembered the Delaware Murdockkinn as he sat his horse calmly in front of his warriors. He was the same warrior Jehu pointed out at Miles' Trading Post.

Black Hoof kicked his gelding forward and rode out a few feet, facing Murdockkinn. Turning, he looked over at Pinto. "Do not use the rifle on this one. He is mine." Black Hoof pointed at Murdockkinn.

"If I kill him, maybe the others will run," Pinto argued.

"No, it is a personal thing. He is mine."

Pinto shrugged. "He's yours then."

Black Hoof yelled out his battle cry and the two lines surged forward. Pinto held his gelding in check and killed one of the Pawnee before charging after the line of warriors.

Jehu's strength, along with his appetite had returned with the vitality of youth and a strong body. His side was still stiff and sore. It was painful when he made a sudden move, and riding a horse was still days away. With Alamette at his side, he stalked the village like a caged animal.

"I thank you, Alamette, for taking care of me all this time." Jehu sat on a downed log along the river and looked over at her.

The dark eyes looked across the slow moving stream, the small brown hands rested lightly in her lap. "You will be my husband when you are well. It is my duty as a wife to you."

Jehu looked over at the beautiful oval face and nodded. "Alamette."

"Yes, White Wolf."

Shaking his head, he changed the subject. He owed her much and he could not bring himself to hurt her. "Nothing."

Jehu studied the young maiden and felt guilty about his thoughts. He told Running Dog that he didn't want a wife and he still didn't, but how could he explain his feelings to her. He was young and ignorant of women. He didn't have the words. The beaded pouch Running Dog called a marriage vow, had been a mistake, a mistake of his ignorance to the customs of the Flathead People. Now, he had to tell her he didn't want to marry her, but how. He could always do as Pinto suggested and just ride away, but that was the coward's way out, and he was no coward.

Rising slowly, he started toward the village with Alamette following. His side was still very sore to the touch, but the wound was no longer bleeding. It had closed and scabbed over. He would be able to ride in a few days and he would follow the tracks of Martin Carter and Chauncy wherever they led. He hadn't spoken of it to Pinto, but he swore to his dying mother, he would always see after his sister.

Coming up the slight slope to the village, Jehu noticed a commotion among the lodges. Several of the villagers circled a lone warrior sitting astride a hard ridden, spraddle-legged, gelding. Recognizing the Crow warrior, Tall Grass, Jehu hurried his pace toward the gathered people.

Pushing through the crowd, Jehu found Limping Deer already bending over the wounded warrior. Rising from the warrior, the old medicine man motioned at the two warriors standing nearby. "Take him inside my lodge."

"I would talk with him, Father." Jehu used the term of respect for the older man.

"There will be time to talk with him after I see to his wounds." Limping Deer noticed the look in Jehu's eyes. "He is not hurt bad. The wounds are minor. He is more tired than hurt."

Jehu, with Alamette by his side, watched as the medicine man poured some kind of powder onto the warriors' wounds then smeared it with a salve. The medicine smelled terrible, but Jehu knew it worked. These same herbs healed the bullet wound in his side quickly. Tall Grass leaned against a backrest as Limping Deer finished with his wounds.

Standing erect, the old man nodded, down at the warrior. "You will be sore. Your wounds are slight."

"This one thanks you, Uncle."

Nodding at Jehu, the old man left the lodge.

"What has happened?" Jehu slipped beside Tall Grass.

"We go Dead Horse Canyon. Soon Murdockkinn come this place.

Black Hoof, him crazy with hate. Him see his enemy, he no wait. Alone, he charge the Delaware and his warriors."

Tall Grass took a deep breath and shook his head. "Too many enemy warriors against our few."

Jehu knew it was the Indian custom to wait stoically for a guest to finish talking at their own pace, but he couldn't hold still. "Then what happened?"

"Black Hoof charge right at the Pawnee dogs. The rest of us followed." Tall Grass shrugged. "We have no choice; we must go help Black Hoof."

"And Pinto, the white trapper?"

"He kill two Pawnee warriors with his long gun, then charge into the fight with us." Tall Grass took a sip of water from the bowl at his side. "Pawnee have many more warriors. The fight turned into a bad thing. Everyone was fighting with knives and war axes."

Tall Grass took his time telling about the fight, causing Jehu to sit forward expectantly. "What happened to the white trapper, my friend?"

The warrior seemed to study on his next words, then nodded his head slowly. "Black Hoof push his horse hard into middle of fight, straight at Murdockkinn. The Delaware ride big, powerful horse. He charge Black Hoof and knock him and horse into dirt. Then everything hard to see, with all the dust and sand drifting on wind. Too much dust make enemy hard to see. Me fight with one Pawnee Warrior when another stab me in back with knife. When I fall, white trapper stand over me and fight two Pawnee from me. Someone shoot Murdockkinn horse with arrow; big horse fall. The Delaware fall in front of Black Hoof. They fight with knives in the middle of enemy. I see Black Hoof bleed much, so did Murdockkinn."

"Go on." Jehu was beside himself with apprehension.

"Pawnee lose many warriors. White trapper and Running Dog kill many. Murdockkinn see many of his warriors on ground. He back away from Black Hoof and grab loose horse. Pawnee run away from canyon, but Black Hoof, him still crazy. He grab horse and chase Murdockkinn. Running Dog see me bleeding, think I hurt bad. He tell Pawnee Killer to bring me here, then he take off after Black Hoof with few warriors that can catch horse."

"That's the last you seen of them?"

"Many Pawnee no have horse, try run away on foot." Tall Grass raised his hand as he was pointing. "Black Hoof, he only want Delaware. He race by running Pawnee Warriors and chase Murdockkinn. Running Dog, Owl Man and Paiute Warriors kill many Pawnee Warriors as they catch up with them."

Jehu wiped his face. "Go on, my friend."

"Pawnee Killer help me up on horse. When he try to get on horse, a Pawnee, we thought dead, shoot him in leg with arrow. He shoot Indian, then we leave from canyon."

"Where is Pinto?"

"Him bleed much; grow weak, and fall from horse. Me hide him in cave, then come here get help."

"You left him wounded and alone?"

Tall Grass shrugged. "Me must leave him, leg bleed too much. Him big man; me very weak and tired. No can get white man on horse. Him tell this one go quick, get help. If trapper try ride horse, I think him bleed more, maybe die."

"And you haven't seen Running Dog or any of the rest since?"

"Me think they all dead. Blood make Black Hoof crazy; he want die." Tall Grass looked up as Limping Deer walked back inside the lodge and shook his head. "Black Hoof much crazy; want to kill Murdockkinn."

"Maybe they're not all dead." Jehu walked from the lodge with Alamette following closely behind him. "They could be alive."

At the edge of the village, he stared out across the large horse herd, finally spotting the Appaloosa grazing quietly on the deep bottom grass along the river. Feeling of his side, he leaned over and touched the ground.

Alamette walked up quietly behind him. "Are you going after your sister or your friend?"

Turning, he looked down at the small woman. "How did you find out she is my sister?"

"Running Dog told me before he rode away with Black Hoof."

"Running Dog shouldn't have told you." Nodding thoughtfully, he turned back, toward the herd. "She is my blood, my responsibility."

"Is she not my sister now, husband?"

Jehu looked down at the small woman and smiled. "I guess she is."

"Is not the white trapper your friend too?"

"He is my friend," Jehu nodded. "He is a grown man, she is but a girl."

"Do you wish for your friend to die alone?"

The small twig he grasped tightly in his hands, snapped as he looked out across the large herd of horses. The decision was his, and it was difficult. He could remember Chauncy's face as he last saw her when they departed Miles' Trading Post. A mere girl, and she was in the hands of Martin Carter. Pinto was indeed his friend, and he was alone out there, wounded. Sister or friend, which would he try to save?

"Alamette," Jehu looked down at her.

"Yes, my husband."

Jehu shook his head as he looked at the love and adoration emitting from her beautiful face. "What would you do?"

The girl shook her head. "This is for you to decide, but whatever you do, I will understand."

"I can't ride two ways at one time."

"No, you must decide who you will help."

"Will you catch my horse?"

Nodding, she looked up at him. "Are you strong enough to make a long ride?"

"If I am to help either, I must ride, now." Jehu watched as the young woman walked across the open grassland toward the Appaloosa. She was indeed a thing of beauty, graceful in her movements, pleasant to be around. He also knew he should consider himself a lucky man, but was he ready to be tied down by a wife, someone he would have to be responsible for?

CHAPTER 13

Jehu waited patiently in front of the gathered villagers and mounted warriors. Yellow Horn stood before his people and looked to where Jehu sat the spotted horse, waiting for the chief to speak. Nodding, as Yellow Horn finished talking to his warriors, Jehu gave the hand signal of friendship to the chief, and then looked down at Alamette who stood beside the Appaloosa. Touching her black hair, he nodded slightly and looked over at Tall Grass.

"Are you sure you can ride my friend?" Jehu knew the warrior had rested only one night.

"I must lead you back; I will ride."

Jehu looked to the east, then back at Alamette. "Maybe I will ride to the east and follow the trail of my sister."

Sitting his horse quietly, beside them, Tall Grass shook his head. "You are the White Wolf of the Crows. You are the blood brother of Running Dog. You, my friend, are as a son of the one called Pinto. I do not think you will ride away from this place to the east and leave them to die."

Jehu knew Tall Grass spoke the truth. Nodding, he turned the spotted horse back to the west. Looking down at Alamette, he touched her cheek lightly. "I will be back."

She followed him a short way from the village, and then waved as the warriors, led by Tall Grass, disappeared into the trees along the small river. At Alamette's insistence, and after much pleading, Yellow Horn gave in and sent several warriors to ride with Jehu and Tall Grass back to Dead Horse Canyon. She was his favorite daughter. Nothing was denied her if it was in his power to give it.

The day had been long and the horses were tired. Deer meat sizzled over the open fire as Jehu leaned against his saddle and looked into the small campfire. He was sore, but at least his wounds did not reopen.

The Crow warrior, Tall Grass, sat across from him, also staring into the red embers of the fire. "How are you, my friend?"

Jehu looked over at the warrior. "How are your wounds?"

"We are both weak." Tall Grass looked across the fire at Jehu. "A Crow Squaw could defeat us in battle, but still we must hurry."

"We will rest tonight. Tomorrow, with the new sun, we will ride faster." Jehu poked at the fire. "How far is the place where Pinto waits?"

"If we ride hard, maybe three sleeps."

Jehu nodded. "We will ride hard."

Tall Grass was right, as Dead Horse Canyon lay before them three days later. Their tired horses pushed hard without rest and very little graze. The Flathead Warriors sat in a long line, staring across the flat canyon. Buzzards floated lazily on the air, their sharp eyes focused in on the bloating bodies below. Jehu watched as several wolves tore hungrily at the dead horses strung across the valley. Pulling his rifle, he was about to fire when Tall Grass placed his brown hand on the barrel.

"No my friend; the Pawnee could still be close and hear."

"Where did you leave Pinto?"

"Come." Tall Grass kicked his horse forward. "It is near this place."

An hour later, the Flathead Warriors sat their horses in a semi-circle facing the cave where Tall Grass had led them. Jehu dismounted and followed Tall Grass quickly into the small enclosure and knelt beside the cold fire. In the dim interior of the cave, Jehu could see the deep imprint of Pinto's moccasins. Nothing else remained only the prints and dead ashes from the fire.

Tall Grass studied the ground closely. "Your friend walked away from this place."

"Maybe the Pawnee came back here and attacked him?" Jehu was skeptical, looking around the ground for tracks.

"No, no Pawnee track here. Him leave this place alone." Tall Grass shook his head. "No blood, no body, him gone."

"Why?" Jehu questioned. "If he was bleeding so badly, why would he leave unless he had to?"

Tall Grass shrugged, then turned from the cave. "Me not know this thing, but there his track; him leave."

Motioning to the Flathead Warriors, Tall Grass sent them to scouring the grounds and surrounding woods for any signs of Pinto. Jehu watched as the warriors covered every inch of the sandy trails leading from the cave. Higher up on the ridges, the winds blew harder, erasing tracks from the sandy trails where they now stood. Slowly, the mounted warriors worked their way farther and farther away from the cave and Dead Horse Canyon.

Tall Grass dismounted beside Jehu, and looked over at the tall trapper. "We find no track of the white man."

Jehu looked down at the soft, sandy ground. "He should be easy to track in this ground."

"Him smart like Indian. Him no leave track for enemy to find. He hide track. I no think we find."

"What should we do, Tall Grass?"

"We go find Running Dog. Maybe white man try to help Crow Warriors after I leave."

"I thought he was too weak to travel far?"

"Him say this, I do not know," Tall Grass shrugged. "Maybe him lie. Maybe not hurt so bad."

Jehu nodded. "That would be like Pinto."

The trail of the battle was strung out for several miles leading due west, away from the canyon. Tall Grass led the mounted warriors slowly along the trail, studying the surrounding woods and open grassland carefully, watching for any sign of ambush. Jehu rode with his Hawken resting lightly across his arm, ready for action if needed. With all the dead horses along the trail, he doubted either side would still be in the mood for more fighting, or for an ambush. He was curious, as only blood showed where bodies had been knocked from their horses.

"Pawnee my enemy, but they brave warriors, no leave friends behind for Crow to count coup on." Tall Grass noticed the blood spot that Jehu was looking at.

Jehu studied a large stain of blood on the ground. "You mean they carried their dead away from this place?"

"No take; I think they hide in tall grass." Tall Grass looked about him and rode his horse toward a solid line of woods. Dismounting, he pushed some tall grass back, pointing at the hidden body.

"Why would they take time to try to hide him?" Jehu was curious.

"They know if they leave bodies, Crow Warriors will take scalp, cut bodies of their friends." Tall Grass turned from the dead body. "Pawnee no have horses to carry dead warriors away from this place."

Late afternoon found Jehu and the warriors many miles from the canyon and the start of the running battle. Tall Grass reined in his horse and sat there looking down at a dead horse. Studying the tracks, he could read the signs. The ground was torn and blood splotched. More fighting had taken place around the horse.

"Much fight here in this place." The warrior looked at Jehu and pointed toward a tall ridge line of rock. "I think no more fight now. Crow Warriors there, they wait high on ridge. Pawnee are gone from this place."

Jehu looked toward the rock formation Tall Grass pointed at, curious how the Crow knew his friends were up in the rocks. Somewhere ahead, in a stand of trees, a horse nickered, as he smelled the oncoming riders. Jehu's horse started to answer when a hard yank on the reins silenced him. Riding up, below the rocks, Jehu spotted three horses tied to the trees below the rock wall.

"There." Tall Grass pointed at a head that showed from behind a boulder.

Dismounting, Jehu followed a small rocky trail slowly up, toward the boulder. Feeling Tall Grass touch his shoulder, Jehu stopped and let the warrior pass him.

"Maybe Crow Warrior no recognize the White Wolf." Tall Grass looked up the trail. "I will go first."

Three warriors greeted Tall Grass and the others as they arrived at the top of the trail behind the large shelf of rock that had protected them from the Pawnee. Two others lay propped up on the ground. Jehu recognized the bloody face of Running Dog and rushed to his side.

"Get some water!" Jehu hollered at one of the Flatheads as he knelt beside the warrior and examined his wounds. "How bad are you hurt my friend?"

"It is good you have come," Running Dog tried to smile. "Are the Pawnee dogs gone?"

"They're gone," Jehu nodded. "At least we didn't see them."

"Did you see Black Hoof or Owl Man?"

"No, only the bodies of dead horses were on the trail." Jehu took the water bag from the Flathead Warrior. "We found only one body."

Running Dog took several swallows of water, and then rested his head against the rocks. "Big fight down there; Pawnee too many. They chase us back to this place and they ride to the west. Murdockkinn not let Pawnee come up here. Too many of his warriors would die. Black Hoof crazy, still want to fight. Him hurt bad, but he still want to kill Murdockkinn."

"Did he go after Murdockkinn?" Jehu washed the blood from the warrior's face. "Why would he do this if he was hurt bad?"

"Murdockkinn may be hurt bad too, I don't know, but Black Hoof no care. Him no listen, he only want to kill his enemy."

Tall Grass knelt beside Jehu, and looked down at Running Dog. "My friend Owl Man, does he live?"

"He lives or did. He follow Black Hoof after the Pawnee." Running Dog shrugged. "I tried to stop him, but he no listen either."

"The Flatheads will stay with you and get you back to their village." Tall Grass stood and looked at Jehu. "I go after my friends. Does the White Wolf come with me?"

Jehu looked over at Running Dog. "Have you seen Pinto since you sent him with Tall Grass?"

"No," Running Dog shook his head. "Him no come this place. We not seen him."

Nodding, he looked over to where Tall Grass waited. "I'm coming."

After washing and tying up Running Dog's wounds, as best he

could, Jehu turned to where Tall Grass stood waiting. Thanking the Flatheads, and then guaranteeing each of them several trade goods if they would help the wounded warriors back to their village. The two men started back down the narrow trail to where the horses stood tied. Stopping at the top, Jehu looked back to where Running Dog lay, watching him.

"Am I still pretty? Will the women still want me?" Running Dog spoke weakly, his old spirit still showing through the pain. "The Pawnee almost took my scalp off."

Jehu nodded. "The scars will make you even prettier, my friend. They will prove how brave you are. Take care and I'll see you back at the village."

"I will tell her, you will be back." Running Dog smiled as Jehu waved.

Tall Grass pushed the horses hard to the west, disregarding Jehu's words of caution. Several times, the warrior stopped his gelding and studied the ground carefully before pushing the horse on. Jehu was feeling stronger, but he knew both he and Tall Grass were still weak from their wounds.

There were no signs on the ground of any other fighting, only the tracks of several horses pushing slowly to the west. Tall Grass stopped his horse beside a small stream and slipped to the ground.

"They are too far ahead to catch up in time to help them." Jehu unsaddled and turned his tired gelding loose on the abundant grass along the stream. "They have too much of a lead on us."

"They have wounded. Several times they stop today," Tall Grass argued. "We will catch them soon."

"When?"

"Soon," Tall Grass was agitated. "If we do not catch them before they reach the safety of their village, we can do nothing to help our friends."

Jehu looked over at Tall Grass. "Surely Black Hoof won't follow Murdockkinn into the Pawnee Village."

"I told you, Black Hoof crazy. Him want to kill Murdockkinn. Him no wait. Yes, Black Hoof will follow Delaware into Pawnee Village." The warrior looked off to the west. "Even if it means the life of Owl Man."

Jehu shook his head. "We should have kept some of the Flathead Warriors with us."

"No, this is our people fight, not Flathead people."

Jehu chewed on a piece of jerked meat as he looked into the dark. Suddenly, he tensed and smelled the air. Never would he understand these people, or the way they think. Surely, Murdockkinn would not have made camp early and let them catch up. "Smoke, I smell smoke."

Both men stood quickly to their feet and looked across the stream. A small flare of light showed them where a campfire lit up the night.

"It wouldn't be them, would it?"

"No, the ones we follow are far ahead, unless something has happened to slow them." Tall Grass shook his head. "Come, we go see this camp."

Leaving their horses behind, Jehu and Tall Grass slipped quietly forward to where they could gaze directly into the firelight. Three Pawnee boys sat laughing and joking around the small blaze. The warriors were young, too young to follow the war trail or accompany a war leader like Murdockkinn. Jehu looked over at Tall Grass and wondered if he would charge into the firelight and attack these youngsters.

Tapping Jehu on the arm, the warrior pulled back, away from the camp. "Young Pawnee, no warrior yet," Tall Grass whispered. "They come this place to hunt, have good adventure; no fight."

"You mean you're not gonna kill them?"

The Crow looked curiously at Jehu in the darkness. "This warrior not kill children."

Jehu was shocked. As mad as the Crow were, he figured Tall Grass would kill any Pawnee he came across. "Did you know what they were saying?"

"No, this one not understand Pawnee words."

"I don't think they would be out here so openly if they had crossed paths with Murdockkinn or Black Hoof." Jehu followed Tall Grass back to their camp.

"Me think so too," Tall Grass agreed. "If Black Hoof or Owl Man see these young ones, they would kill them quick, I think."

"Would they be far from their village?"

"This Pawnee hunting grounds. They feel safe here. They not know Crow come this place to fight."

Slipping quickly back to their horses, the two men mounted and circled far around the Pawnee camp. Tall Grass wanted to wait and rest the horses until morning. However, with the nearness of the two camps, any shifting in the wind could bring their smell to the Pawnee horses, causing them to warn the young men. Riding a few miles to the west, Tall Grass dismounted and stood beside his horse.

"We wait here until sun comes up, then we find track of Black Hoof." The warrior found a soft spot and settled down with the horse standing almost on top of him. "I think it close; village of Pawnee close."

Tall Grass pushed the horses hard, following the tracks of the westbound warriors. The trail led straight, due west, not changing direction at all. Only deep gullies or river crossings varied them in any direction, but they always came back on course, making it easy for the warrior to follow the trail. For two days, they rode hard, bringing them closer to their quarry.

Tall Grass sat his horse, looking across the swollen river as it ran sluggishly along its banks. "Must have big rain upriver. Much water come this way."

"We gonna swim it or wait?"

"We no wait; we must hurry." Tall Grass slapped his gelding on the rump with his bow.

Jehu kicked the Appaloosa and splashed into the deep water. Holding his Hawken clear of the muddy water, he slipped from the saddle and held onto the saddle horn of the hard swimming horse. Tall Grass looked back at Jehu and the Appaloosa, grinning as they passed midstream and started into the slower backwater of the river.

Wading onto dry ground, Tall Grass nodded at the horse. "Spotted one great swimmer, maybe brother to flat tail."

"That he is, for sure." Jehu patted the wet neck of the horse.

Water dripped from the bay horse as Tall Grass kicked him up out of the river bottom. Following a buffalo trail due west, a short way, he pulled the gelding to a stop and pointed down at the ground.

"There Black Hoof and Owl Man track. They still follow Pawnee to the west."

All night, Tall Grass rode west, unable to see the trail or tracks, following by sheer instinct alone. Reaching the narrow valley, they dismounted and waited for the coming of dawn. Heavy fog lay like a blanket over the small valley as Jehu and the Crow watched quietly from their hiding place at the edge of the heavily timbered woods. Unknown to them, the trails, and the one they followed, all ran due west, converging into the head of the valley where they now waited.

Campfire smoke drifted on the morning breeze, coming from the north end of the valley as the two stood beside their tired horses holding their muzzles. The Appaloosa's small ears pricked forward as several horsemen rode boldly out across the flat ground. Jehu counted seven riders as they appeared from under the low heavy fog.

"Murdockkinn lead warriors." Tall Grass pointed at the lead rider. "Look, White Wolf, the Pawnee have two prisoners. See, their hands bound behind them."

"Prisoners?"

"They are my people, Crow Warriors." Tall Grass gritted his teeth in anger.

Jehu could also see the ropes that bound the warrior's feet underneath the horse's bellies. "Is that Murdockkinn in front?"

Tall Grass nodded. "That is Delaware dog."

"He doesn't seem hurt too bad, leastways he's still sitting upright on his horse." Jehu strained his eyes trying to see the great warrior he had heard so much about.

"Him bloody, but him great fighter, brave warrior." Tall Grass stared at the two prisoners. "He is very dangerous enemy."

"A compliment for an enemy?" Jehu looked over at Tall Grass.

The warrior nodded at Jehu's question. "Him Crow enemy, me want him dead, but Murdockkinn still great war leader." The warriors disappeared into the far trees at the end of the valley when Tall Grass remounted and rode at a trot to the grass field where Murdockkinn had just passed. Turning his horse to the east, he looked over at Jehu and nodded.

"We wait here. Black Hoof and Owl Man come to this place pretty quick, I think." Tall Grass looked back to the east. "If they still live."

Jehu followed the warrior's gaze. "Tell me, why would Murdockkinn take prisoners?"

"He lost many warriors on this raid, no horses, no nothing." Tall Grass looked over at Jehu. "He lose face; these prisoners will help him regain honor."

"You people, and your honor."

Tall Grass looked over at Jehu, and smiled. "There is nothing more for a warrior."

"How about life, happiness?"

"If Murdockkinn kill Black Hoof, him have scalp on coup stick." Tall Grass changed the subject. "I think they still live. Soon we will know."

Tall Grass had predicted right. Hardly an hour passed when their horses raised their heads and pricked their ears. The ground in the valley was covered with deep grass so the approaching horses made no sound. With the coming of day, the deep fog had closed in once again, making visibility almost nonexistent. Black Hoof rode almost within touching distance, only a few feet from Tall Grass and Jehu when he jerked his gelding to a stop and reached for his war axe.

Kicking his horse forward, Tall Grass approached the startled warrior and stuck out his hand. "It is good to see my friends, Black Hoof and Owl Man, once again."

Owl Man could not believe his eyes. "How did you come to this place before us?"

"We rode hard."

The warrior shook his head. "Black Hoof wounds give him much trouble, but he will not rest to let them heal. We ride slowly and with great caution. We already fell into the Pawnee's trap once."

"We see Pawnee pass. Murdockkinn has taken two warriors captive."

Owl Man nodded. "Pawnee wait in ambush for us. We kill three of them in fight, but Little Bull and White Feather did not have chance to fight before they were captured."

Tall Grass looked at the blood staining Owl Man's leather shirt. "The Delaware has just passed this place. He is not far."

Black Hoof kicked his horse. "Now, he will die."

Reaching out, Jehu grabbed the rawhide rein. "The Pawnee Village is near, my friend. Murdockkinn has already reached its' safety. If you wish to die, that is your right, but what about us, your friends?"

"My friends may ride away from this place." Black Hoof pulled on the rein. "I go to village; kill Delaware."

"You are weak, Black Hoof. If Murdockkinn kills you now, he will live." Tall Grass looked into the face of the warrior. "Then he will escape your justice forever."

"What would you have me do, Tall Grass?"

Tall Grass looked over where Jehu was watching their back trail. "If you will trust the White Wolf, he has a plan."

Black Hoof looked hard at the warrior before him, then down at his scarred body, he was weak. He had wounded the Delaware, but he did not know how serious Murdockkinn's wounds were. Nodding his head, he placed his hand on Tall Grass' shoulder. "You are right; I am too weak to fight. I must rest and trust my friends, Tall Grass and White Wolf, with my life, but the Delaware must die."

"Does it matter who kills him?"

"It does not matter, but I must fight this one first. If I die, then my friends can kill him."

Tall Grass led the small party back east in a hard trot. Jehu brought up the rear, watching and listening closely for any warriors following them. Finding a small stand of cedar, far from the trail, the small party dismounted and hobbled their horses to graze on the knee-deep grass.

"We will rest here. When the night comes, me and Tall Grass will ride further east and put my plan to work."

"What will you do?" Black Hoof sat down weakly against a small tree. "What is to the east?"

Tall Grass smiled. "First, we will eat. You and Owl Man must rest and regain your strength if you are to fight."

"I do not need to eat. Tell me, what is your plan? How will you bring the Delaware here?"

"Eat, Black Hoof, my friend and regain your strength, then we will speak of this." Jehu motioned for Tall Grass to follow him as he walked over to where the horses grazed eagerly on the lush grass.

Black Hoof bit into the dried meat and watched as the two men spoke together briefly and returned to where he waited.

Chapter 14

The moon was full, the music of the small tree frogs, locusts, and owls rang out through the night as Tall Grass and Jehu made their way quietly back to the east. Casting back and forth, looking for the light of a night fire to show itself, Jehu strained both his eyes and ears, trying to see into the dark. Several hours passed as they rode slowly through the flat valleys and into the more forested land that lay along the slopes of the mountains. Tall Grass' sharp eyes missed nothing as he surveyed each valley they passed through.

"Maybe they've taken another trail back to their village." Jehu whispered as they sat quietly along the river that had swelled only a day before.

Tall Grass nodded slightly. "I think they are close by. We will find them on the other side."

This time the river was back to its normal depth. The horses reached deep water and only had to swim a small way, but nothing like their first crossing. Riding from the water, Tall Grass led the way across the open valley taking the same path they took earlier. Jehu looked behind him to the north. He hoped Black Hoof and Owl Man, who they left in the valley to rest, would remain where they were until he and Tall Grass returned.

Five miles further along, Jehu sniffed the unmistakable smell of campfire smoke. Relieved, he breathed deeply, hoping they found their quarry. Both men dropped quietly to the ground and tied their horses. Silent as a stalking cougar, Jehu and Tall Grass approached the blazing fire, surprised to find the same young Pawnee boys sitting before their fire laughing. Lying around the fire, the youngsters had no idea two sets of eyes watched their every move. Motioning for Jehu to stay where he was, Tall Grass made his way silently to where the boys left their horses. A small chunk of wood thrown at one of the horses made the animal jump sideways and stomp the ground. Hearing the commotion, one of the youngsters scowled. He left the campfire, and made his way to where their horses were tied. The boy never knew what hit him as Tall Grass knocked him senseless and bound him securely with rawhide thongs.

Jehu saw the young boy leave the light of the fire, but not reappear. Figuring what had happened; he blinked as another boy left the firelight in his direction and walked right to him. Laying the Hawken aside, Jehu quickly subdued the youngster and bound him hand and foot. Again, Tall Grass caused a commotion, only this time, the lone boy noticed his two friends never returned to the fire. Calling out into the darkness, the young Pawnee backed up to the small fire and waited anxiously, not knowing what to do. Suddenly, from the darkness, both Jehu and Tall Grass hurled themselves right in the middle of the lighted area, bringing the lone youth to the ground.

"Well, my friend, we got 'em. Now what are we gonna do with them?" Tall Grass helped the trapper drag the bound youths together.

"We trade for our Crow friends." Jehu waved his skinning knife at the boys. "Or maybe we take their Pawnee scalp locks."

Black Hoof and Owl Man blink in amazement as the Pawnee youths were led single file into the small clearing where they were waiting. Stepping forward, the two warriors looked into the young faces then over at Tall Grass.

"What will you do with these?" Black Hoof touched his knife.

Tall Grass dismounted and pulled the boys from their horses, pushing them down against two cedar trees. "Have you rested and regained your strength my friend?"

"I am rested," Black Hoof looked down at the dried meat in his hand. "Dried deer meat doesn't have much strength in it."

"You're in luck my friend. These youngsters have brought you some real food." Tall Grass handed Black Hoof a leather pouch filled with buffalo, deer jerky and dried berries. "Eat, my friends, and then we talk."

Passing the bag to Owl Man, the warrior nodded his thanks. "This is your plan, White Wolf, these boys?"

"You want Murdockkinn; Tall Grass wants his people back from the Pawnee." Jehu pointed at the youngsters. "These boys will help us get them."

"And how do you propose this thing?" Black Hoof bit into the meat.

Jehu looked up at the sun. It was almost midday. "We wait until morning, and then we will spring our trap."

"Until morning." Black Hoof nodded and looked down at the dried jerky. "The Pawnee women are good cooks."

Tall Grass laughed. "We are all cut up, hungry, and tired. We have many enemies about us, and what do we talk about, food. I, Tall Grass think we are becoming crazy like Running Dog. Eat and rest my friends. Tomorrow we will need our strength."

Jehu looked around the small camp. Tall Grass was right; they all were wounded in one way or the other. They were tired, dirty, and plain worn out. Now they were fixing to stir up a hornet's nest when the new sun came up. Yep, one thing was certain, they were going to need their strength come morning.

Jehu walked over to where the young Pawnee boys lay bound, hand and foot, then looked down at them. The oldest, he figured to be about fourteen, and the youngest, no more than twelve. Signing to the oldest, he asked if he understood his hand signs. The boy's hands were tied, but he could still nod his head.

Jehu smiled and signed again. "Providing you do not try to escape during the night, you will be released unharmed with the new sun."

The youngster spit, an attempt at bravery.

Jehu had to admit, the youngster had spunk.

The sun peeked from behind the tall trees that shelter and hide Jehu and the warriors. Rolling from his sandy bed, he looked over to where Tall Grass stood beside a large cottonwood tree, his eyes trained on the valley. Motioning to the warrior, he walked with him to where the boys lay bound hand and foot.

Cutting the oldest boy's hands free, Jehu nodded at Tall Grass. "Tell him we turn him loose to return to his village."

Tall Grass motioned silently with his hands and waited as the boy returned the signs. "He wishes to know if the others go with him."

"Tell him we will bring the others unharmed to the valley near their village." Jehu looked down at the lad. "Tell him to have his people bring our two warriors and Murdockkinn to the valley."

"And if they refuse?" The young Pawnee signed with his hands then threw out his chest.

Quicker than the eye could see, Jehu pulled one of the other boys to his feet and placed his skinning knife at the boy's throat. "If they refuse, I will cut their throats and cut out their hearts myself."

"My people have heard of a tall white man, brother to the Crow. They call this one, White Wolf." The youth studied the tall trapper. "Is this you?"

"I am White Wolf," Jehu signed this time.

"They also say you are a mad dog. Now, I believe it."

"Good, I don't like repeating myself." Jehu drew the blade slightly across the youth's throat. "Could be I'm wasting my time sending you."

"Do not kill the young ones. I go to my village to speak your words."

Jehu nodded. "That's more like it, but you better believe me. If our two warriors are hurt or they're not out front with your people come morning, these youngsters will die."

The youth nodded. "I believe the White Wolf; I go."

Tall Grass led a horse forward and watched as the youth kicked the horse into a lope toward his village.

Three hours passed as Jehu paced back and forth underneath the tall oaks, watching to the west toward the Pawnee Village. Only the swaying of the tall grass in the slight wind moved on the flat floor of the valley.

Tall Grass leaned against a small cottonwood tree and relaxed. "It will take time my friend. They will have to hold council with their elders before they come to this place."

"How long?"

"They come to talk soon, or they come to fight." Tall Grass studied the valley. "Maybe when talk over; they will want to fight, then what White Wolf do?"

Jehu smiled. "Reckon there's only one thing to do."

"What's that?"

"Run."

Tall Grass shrugged. "Black Hoof, I no think him run. There is too much pride and anger in this one."

"Then he's on his own. They probably have a hundred full-grown warriors and my pride sure ain't gonna let me commit suicide, no sir." Jehu shook his head, looking around. "We've only got four against the whole Pawnee Nation."

Tall Grass rose slowly to his feet and pointed. "We see soon enough. Pawnee there, they come to this place."

Turning to see what Tall Grass was looking at, Jehu's eyes narrowed as he focused on the long line of Pawnee. Mounted warriors were strung out in a long line across the whole north end of the valley. Long flowing eagle feather war bonnets and headdresses showed there were many older chiefs and war leaders among the ranks of the Pawnee. The warriors appeared miraculously from the nearby woods they front, seemingly from out of the ground.

Jehu could see the two Crow Warriors standing out in front of the line. He could also see the rawhide thongs still wrapped around their neck and arms. Grabbing the Pawnee boys from the ground, he pushed them forward into plain view of the line of warriors. Suddenly, a splendid, mounted warrior raced his warhorse across the short distance separating the two parties. Only a single feather adorned the big warrior's topknot, but Jehu knew this man was a warrior of prominence among the Pawnee. Pulling the horse to a sliding stop on the tall grass, only feet from where the boys stood, he looked over the captives carefully.

Black Hoof stepped forward beside Jehu. "Him Straight Arrow, War Chief of the Pawnee. He is a great warrior. His words can be trusted."

Jehu studied the warrior and waited for the chief to speak. Tall for a Pawnee, the warrior was straight as an arrow, with a broad intelligent face encircled by grey sprinkled hair and wide set dark eyes. The hard eyes of the chief locked on Jehu, and studied the white man closely for several seconds.

"You have come to my people, my land, and taken our sons captive." The tall warrior slashed his hands through the air. "You threaten to kill mere boys. Why does the White Wolf of the Crow People do this thing?"

Jehu was surprised as the chief spoke in the Crow language, then replied. "You have let your warriors follow Murdockkinn to the east where they have killed many whites, my friends."

Straight Arrow twisted on his horse and looked back at the long line of warriors. Straightening, he turned around and looked again at Jehu. "Some things cannot be helped. Some of my warriors follow the one with the black heart."

"You speak of the Delaware, Murdockkinn?"

The chief nodded slowly. "You have not killed our sons. I will not kill this time. Take your warriors and leave this place. Do not return to Pawnee lands."

"No." Black Hoof stepped in front of Jehu. "I have come for Murdockkinn. You will send him out to meet me."

The Pawnee Chief looked down at the bloodied and torn shirt of Black Hoof, then over at Jehu. "This one who speaks is wounded. He speaks brave words. I think he would be killed if he faces the Delaware."

"Why does the great Chief of the Pawnee care if I am killed?" Black Hoof raised his voice, glaring at the chief. "Send him out to fight or I will kill one of these boys. I will not leave this place as long as one of us lives; I cannot."

Straight Arrow shook his head. "You wish to die so badly, Paiute? All can see you are not able to fight. You are weak from many wounds."

"Straight Arrow is right. You are weak. I will fight Murdockkinn for you." Jehu placed his hand on the shoulder of Black Hoof.

"No, it is for me to kill this one." Black Hoof shook his head vigorously. "I have challenged the Delaware dog. It is my blood right."

Straight Arrow looked down at the warrior then over at the boys. "It will be as you ask, Paiute. You have asked for a warrior's death, and you shall have it."

"Do we have your word that your warriors will not interfere in this fight?" Jehu questioned.

"The Delaware is a crazy dog, but some of my warriors follow him. This I cannot do anything about. You have my word that no one from my people will interfere until this fight is over."

Jehu nodded, "and then?"

"Then white eye, you are on your own. I cannot speak for your safety."

Looking over at Tall Grass and Owl Man, Jehu motioned at the bound boys. "Turn them loose."

Black Hoof whirled, hatred spitting from his dark eyes. "Do not trust this Pawnee."

Jehu looked up at the chief. "I trust him to keep his word. Turn them loose. We do not make war on children."

Straight Arrow slipped from his horse and stood in front of Jehu looking long into his blue eyes. Reaching out his hand, he pulled one of the boys to him. "This is my son, Bright Eyes. You have given him and his friends back to his people. For this, I thank you."

Black Hoof turned to Jehu as the Pawnee Chief rode slowly back to the line of warriors with the boys trailing him. "I thank the White Wolf for his offer to fight Murdockkinn, but I, Black Hoof, must kill the Delaware. My people's blood calls out for it to be so."

"And if you fail?" Tall Grass spoke up.

"I cannot fail. He must die." Eyes flashed as the warrior looked across to where the Pawnee and Murdockkinn waited. "I cannot fail."

Jehu had seen the warrior Murdockkinn, several times around the trading posts, but not knowing who he was, he had never paid much attention to the Delaware. Now, as Murdockkinn stood in front of the gathered warriors, stripped of his leather-hunting shirt, Jehu knew why warriors followed the man. Average in height, the warrior was well muscled and stood straight as a lodge pole pine. Long powerful arms and a broad chest with a tapering waist showed this warrior possessed great strength.

Jehu turned his eyes to where Black Hoof removed his hunting shirt. Several fresh scars showed on his body. Any normal man, cut up as Black Hoof was, would be in bed, not fighting a life or death battle, hand to hand with a dangerous opponent like the Delaware. Not heavily muscled as Murdockkinn was, Jehu was aware, unless his friend was very lucky, he stood no chance against the Delaware. If Black Hoof were completely healthy, it would still be a close match between the two. Wounded and weakened as he was, Jehu felt Black Hoof had no chance. He wanted to step forward and challenge the Delaware, but to do so would be worse than death to Black Hoof who would lose face in front of the whole Pawnee Village.

Murdockkinn looked his opponent over. Jehu could see the contempt he held for the wounded Paiute standing before him. Smiling slightly, he stepped forward to meet the challenger with a sharp skinning knife in one hand and a war axe in the other. Tall Grass stepped forward and extended a long skinning knife to Black Hoof. The knife had a curved, razor sharp blade that was much longer bladed than most knives. The other hand of the Paiute held an iron handled, double steel edged hatchet, the kind most trappers carried with them. These were heavier and clumsier to handle, but would not break like the wooden handled axe Murdockkinn carried.

When seeing the longer knife and double-edged hatchet, Murdockkinn protested to Straight Arrow.

"The Paiute is weak from his wounds. Surely the great Murdockkinn does not fear him or his weapons." The Pawnee Chief smirked.

The sharp words from Straight Arrow were like a slap in the Delaware's face. Glaring hatred, he advanced across the grassy space toward Black Hoof.

Tall Grass looked at his friend and smiled. "He is mad. He will make a mistake. Let him come to you then use the iron hatchet."

"I will kill him, I must." Black Hoof adjusted his hold on his weapons, and then started forward. "My dead people will give me strength."

The two warriors circled each other slowly; their weapons held in readiness, ready to lunge forward and deftly cut the life out of their opponent. Neither man had any qualms about killing the other. The only difference between the two men was Murdockkinn wanted to kill, but he also wanted to live. Black Hoof wanted only to kill the Delaware. Living meant nothing to him. His family was dead. His wife, children, and mother all lay dead where Murdockkinn and his warriors killed them. Only his aged father waited for him, back in the Paiute Village. For Black Hoof, life held little meaning.

Jehu watched in anticipation and worried for Black Hoof. This was not a game. It was a gamble of life and death, one he had been involved with himself. He had learned to like and respect the Paiute warrior as both a man and friend. Now, all he could do was to wait and watch as the fight played out. Any interference could get them all killed immediately. Maybe they were all dead anyway. Jehu knew Indians had strange ideas, never understanding what they would do next.

The fight appeared lopsided, as Murdockkinn was only slightly wounded, and was larger and stronger of the two warriors. None of the onlookers could see inside the two men. They couldn't see the hatred driving Black Hoof on, the hatred that gave him the strength he would need to defeat the Delaware.

The sharp blades, of both men, shone brightly in the morning sunlight as they circled and parried each other with lightning strokes. Black Hoof brought first blood as his knife cut a furrow along the extended arm of Murdockkinn. Repeatedly, the Delaware's war axe and the Paiute's hatchet crashed together as they swung with mighty strokes at each other. Both men were fast, fast enough so far to avoid a crippling blow from either weapon.

Black Hoof was retreating slowly as Murdockkinn steadily pressed forward, pushing the weaker man across the grassy field. Jehu watched as the slashing and cutting weapons missed their targets, and so far only caused slight harm to either fighter. Suddenly, quicker than the eye could detect, Murdockkinn slipped under the defense of Black Hoof and caused blood to spurt uncontrollable from a deep slash across the rib cage of the warrior. Only pure hatred showed across the dark face of the Paiute as blood ran down his left side. Jehu wanted to step forward, but the strong arm of Tall Grass held his arm in a death grip.

Again, the sharp knife of the Delaware found its mark as Black Hoof tried desperately to reach Murdockkinn. Grinning evilly, the Delaware advanced arrogantly, raising his war axe high above his head for the final blow. Jehu started forward again, only to have Tall Grass restrain him.

"Black Hoof will lose face if you interfere."

Jehu shrugged loose from the warrior. "He will lose his life if I don't. You know he doesn't stand a chance."

Tall Grass nodded. "This is true, but he will die with his pride. If you help him, he will have nothing."

Murdockkinn grew impatient and careless as he stalked the unsteady Black Hoof who was barely able to retain his footing. He laughed as blood ran down the Paiute's body and legs, dripping onto the slippery grass.

"You are a woman Paiute, just like your people." The Delaware laughed wickedly. Suddenly, quick as a cougar, Murdockkinn launched himself forward, swinging his war axe with all his might.

Black Hoof raised the double-edged iron axe to ward off the blow and bowed down from the tremendous power as the two weapons crashed together. The force was too powerful, causing the wooden handle to shatter against the stronger iron handled weapon of Black Hoof. Stepping back, Murdockkinn's eyes grew wide as he stared down at the broken axe. Now, the fight evened up a bit, even though Black Hoof was becoming weaker with the loss of blood.

Flipping his knife from hand to hand, Murdockkinn feigned a rush, trying to weaken Black Hoof to the point he could not defend himself. Slowly, the Paiute retreated before the deft knife handling of the Delaware. Repeatedly, the blade snaked forward, sometimes reaching its target, sometimes missing. The ever-forward movement of Murdockkinn went, as the Delaware wanted. It was sapping Black Hoof's strength.

Reeling from loss of blood, Black Hoof went down on one knee and released the heavy iron axe from his grasp. Seeing the axe fall to the grass, Murdockkinn screamed forth a fierce war cry of victory and lunged forward for the kill. Black Hoof's timing was perfect as he rolled sideways scooping up the iron axe and slashing downward at Murdockkinn's exposed back as he landed where Black Hoof was kneeling. Too weak to extract the buried hatchet from the Delaware's back, Black Hoof pushed himself forward driving the skinning knife's long blade into the Delaware several times before scalping his enemy.

Staggering to his feet, he raised the bloody trophy over his head and screamed defiantly at the Pawnee warriors. Several yelled in anger and started forward, only to have Straight Arrow extend his arm and stop them.

Looking into the faces of his enraged warriors, the Pawnee Chief motioned to Black Hoof. "The Paiute has defeated the Delaware. I have given my word; he will leave our land unmolested if he did so. It will be as I say. They will go unharmed from our hunting grounds."

"He must die." A warrior stepped forward and pointed at Black Hoof.

"Hear me White Bull, return to the village now or your blood will be on the ground with the Delaware's." Straight Arrow touched his own skinning knife. "Go now; leave this place."

Chapter 15

Straight Arrow waited and watched as the followers of Murdockkinn reluctantly turned their horses back to the Pawnee Village. Only a few of Straight Arrow's most loyal and trusted warriors waited behind him, making sure no harm would come to their leader as he spoke with the Paiute.

The Pawnee Chief turned back and looked toward Black Hoof. "You have shown the great heart and bravery of a true warrior today, Paiute. Go safely from this place."

Jehu and Tall Grass led the horses forward and helped Black Hoof mount. Owl Man mounted behind the wounded man and wrapped his arms around him for support.

Jehu stepped in front of the Pawnee Chief and extended his hand. "I would give more to Straight Arrow for our lives, but this is all I have to give."

Straight Arrow nodded and took the offered hand. "You have given me the life of my son that is payment enough."

"We go now; maybe I will return to trade with my friends the Pawnees one day."

"The White Wolf, someday, will be welcome in the village of the Pawnee. For now, I cannot say you will be safe."

"I understand some of your warriors wish our blood."

Straight Arrow glanced to where the warriors were disappearing into the far timber and brush. "Ride hard and fast my friend. I will not be able to protect you after I ride from this place."

"We go."

Recrossing the Republican River, Jehu rode up alongside the horse that carried double. "How is he?"

"He must have rest and his wounds treated, or Black Hoof will die," Owl Man looked over at Jehu, "soon."

"Ahead, where the gorge grows narrow, we will stop and let him rest."

Owl Man nodded. "That is a good place. If the Pawnee come, a few can defend the pass. It is better than getting caught out in the open."

Black Hoof raised his head weakly. "We will not stop; we must go on."

Jehu smiled, "Owl Man, did you hear something?"

"I heard nothing."

"Then my friends, we will stop at the pass as I said." Jehu kicked his horse forward.

"You are a fool, White Wolf. This one is already dead," Black Hoof, slurred his words. "Leave me, go now."

A small spring lay at the base of the gorge where Jehu halted the small party and prepared to make a stand against the enemy he knew would follow. Owl Man and Tall Grass tended the wounds of the protesting Black Hoof while Jehu picketed the horses on deep grass and built a small fire. Walking close to where the wounded man lay on a soft buffalo robe, Jehu watched as the wounds were washed and cleaned, then covered with bear grease.

Motioning for Tall Grass to follow him, Jehu walked close to the fire. "How long do we have before they come?"

Tall Grass shrugged. "When Pawnee Chief go his lodge, they leave village, maybe come this place with new sun."

"You don't trust Straight Arrow, do you?"

"I trusted a bear once."

"And?"

"He killed me," Tall Grass laughed.

Jehu smiled slightly and looked over to where Black Hoof lay. "Will he live?"

"Only the great ones know what's in a man's heart. If he wishes it so, he will live."

"And if he doesn't?"

Tall Grass tossed a small stick in the fire. "Black Hoof wishes to die. I think it will be so."

Jehu nodded. "Either way, he is a great warrior, a man to be honored." Jehu sat beside the wounded man and looked up at the brilliant stars above. Not a cloud in the sky, only millions of bright sparkling stars lit up the dark sky. Not a sound stirred in the surrounding darkness that consumed them. Only quiet, stillness that seemed to make a man's ears go deaf.

Black Hoof stirred slightly and opened his feverish eyes. Seeing Jehu sitting cross-legged before him, he smiled. "The White Wolf waits here for the Pawnee?"

Surprised, Jehu looked over at the warrior. "You said you wanted to kill your enemies my friend, now maybe you can do so."

"White Wolf is crazy, maybe."

"Rest Black Hoof, we will need your strength and strong arm tomorrow."

"I told you to leave me and go from this place."

Jehu nodded. "Yes, you did, now I tell you to rest so you can help tomorrow."

"I think the White Wolf of the Crow people is crazy like the fox." Black Hoof closed his eyes. "I will fight with you tomorrow. Maybe then, I can die in peace."

Jehu smiled and leaned back, against a rock outcropping. "A warrior as ornery as you my friend is not gonna die for many years."

"What is this word, ornery?"

"Tomorrow, I will tell you, tomorrow if you're still alive."

"Yes indeed, you are as the fox, smart and crafty." Black Hoof shifted slightly then relaxed.

Tall Grass shook Jehu slightly, then retreated, waiting alongside the rock wall of the pass until the white trapper joined him from the dark. Earlier, the small fire burned itself out, leaving the small clearing in complete darkness.

Stepping close to the warrior, Jehu could barely see his silhouette. "What is it, Tall Grass?"

"They are here, White Wolf."

"Already?"

"They wait where the trail start upward, toward this place."

"How many?" Jehu could barely make out the shadow of the warrior as they talked.

"From the sounds they make, maybe twenty," Tall Grass shrugged. "Until the new day comes, I cannot be certain."

Jehu looked upward at the tall rocks towering over the pass. "They can get above us, but not without a lot of climbing or riding clear back, around the cliffs."

"They will not turn away. The Pawnee will come straight at us when the new sun lights their way."

"Then we will fight here."

Tall Grass nodded. "It is good, Black Hoof is weak. He cannot ride or he will die."

Almost two hours remained before the coming of light. Jehu, Tall Grass, and Owl Man busied themselves, blocking the small pass with dead trees and heavy brush. It will not hold back the Pawnee long, but they will not be able to charge their horses or use them in the upcoming battle.

The sun flickered slowly in the east as both sides readied for the upcoming conflict. Jehu waited calmly, staring down the narrow trail that led upward, toward the pass. On one side, the walls were too steep to climb. On the other side, the ground sloped straight down where a man could easily fall to his death. If the Pawnee charged up the trail, many would die before they reached the barricade.

"They come," Tall Grass whispered, pointing down the trail as the early morning started to bring forth new light.

Black Hoof tried to sit upward. "Help me to my feet."

Looking over at the wounded and weak warrior, Jehu shook his head. "No, my friend, you are too weak to stand, let alone fight."

From where he stood, Jehu could hear the hooves of the horses as they reverberated up and down the cliff walls. Suddenly, the Pawnee came into sight, stopping their horses in a cluster, slightly out of bow range.

Dismounting, they started forward on foot, up the rocky trail.

Sighting calmly down the sights of his Hawken Fifty, Jehu slowly tightened the trigger on the closest warrior. Blinking his eyes, Jehu recognized White Bull, the big warrior from the day before, who wanted to kill Black Hoof, the one who had argued with Straight Arrow. If he killed this one, the others may not be so ready to die.

The strong brown finger of White Wolf, squeezed slightly on the trigger, then abruptly held fire as the ringing echoed of another rifle sounded above the pass, causing White Bull to collapse in a ball. Jehu fired his rifle and watched as another warrior fell almost on top of White Bull. Again, the rifle from above fired and another warrior clutched at his breast before careening head first over the trail. The rest of the Pawnees, hearing the rifle blasts and seeing many of their warriors fall, quickly retreated down the trail. Jehu stood slowly and looked up at the rock cliffs above him.

"Well, laddie, you've managed to keep yourself alive, I see!" A laughing, familiar voice boomed down at him.

"Pinto?" Jehu couldn't believe his ears. "Pinto Stade is that you?"

"Aye lad, it be me," Pinto laughed again. "Looks like I caught up with you just in the nick of time."

"That's a fact indeed." Jehu strained his eyes trying to see where the voice came from. "Your timing, as usual, is superb old friend, and that was some mighty fine shooting, Pinto."

"I have another surprise for you."

"What else do you have up your sleeve?"

"Wait right there, me boy, I'll join you presently," Pinto laughed. "Just hold your horses and I'll show you."

The words were hardly spoken when a horse passed Jehu running full out, down the narrow trail. Jehu could not believe his eyes as the bay gelding cleared the barricade and raced away with Black Hoof clinging to his back.

Whirling, Jehu noticed Owl Man standing beside the trail, watching as the horse disappeared out of sight. Tall Grass stood off to the side of the barricade, a blank expression on his face.

"He was too weak to mount a horse." Jehu looked over at Owl Man. "How could he have gotten onto that horse?"

"I helped him." The warrior looked calmly at Jehu.

"Why, why would you do such a thing? You know he is too weak to fight." Jehu shook his head. "You sent him to his death."

"No," Owl Man nodded. "Death is what he seeks. It is his right."

"We are too few to fight so many out in the open. We will wait here for Pinto. When he gets here, we will go to try save Black Hoof."

Tall Grass stepped forward. "We will go bury our friend, but it will be too late to save him from the Pawnee."

Two hours passed before Jehu heard the unmistakable sound of horse's hooves coming down the trail from the east. Tall Grass had already gathered their horses, plus three extra the Pawnee left in their fast retreat from the pass, horses belonging to the dead warriors. Mounting his horse, Jehu, with Tall Grass and Owl Man following, rode up the trail to meet Pinto.

The reunion of the two friends was loud, boisterous, and even more so when Jehu discovered his good friend Running Dog was the surprise Pinto had mentioned. Clasping hands, the friends smiled and laughed, standing back to look each other over. Running Dog was covered in dried blood, but Jehu knew most head wounds seemed worse than they actually were, as they bleed a lot.

Jehu could only shake his head as he looked at the gathered men who still wore their bloodied deerskin shirts. "Well, we're the most cut up and wounded bunch of men I've ever seen."

Pinto laughed aloud. "One good thing, at least the fighting is over."

"Is it?" Jehu looked at his friend.

"You mean there's more?"

"Black Hoof took off in pursuit of the Pawnee. Now, with your help, we're fixing to go after him."

Pinto scratched his head. "Why would he do a fool thing like that?"

"He wants to kill more Pawnee, then join his ancestors," Owl Man spoke up. "A warrior such as Black Hoof should do as his medicine tells him."

"Was it his medicine or his hard head?" Jehu looked across at Owl Man.

Owl Man shrugged. "It was his wish. He has nothing left in this life. I will speak no more of it."

Jehu knew the discussion was finished. No good would come of him speaking of it further. Motioning to Pinto and the warriors, he mounted and turned his gelding to the west, following the path Black Hoof had taken.

Only a few miles passed before they discovered the battle site where Black Hoof finally was granted his wish of death. Sitting their horses, they looked down at the body of their dead friend. A dead horse lay beside the still body, along with his weapons.

"The Pawnee have honored Black Hoof in death." Tall Grass knelt beside the dead warrior. "He has not been scalped and his weapons were left with him."

Jehu was confused. "Why would they honor a warrior that only yesterday, they wanted dead?"

"One always honors a brave enemy." Owl Man stood beside Tall Grass. "That is why they have killed a pony for him to ride into the next life."

Pinto dismounted stiffly, limping on his swollen and sore leg. "Black Hoof was a brave man. You have to give him that."

Tall Grass looked about the small clearing they stood in. "This is a good place. We will build his scaffold here in the maple trees for all to honor as they pass by."

The campfire blazed brightly as a small deer roasted over the hot fire. Owl Man examined Pinto's swollen leg and rubbed bear grease onto the wound. Wrapping the leg with a rabbit skin, the warrior nodded at the trapper and moved on to examine the wounds of Running Dog.

"He missed his calling." Jehu watched the warrior examine the wounds of the men. "He should have been a medicine man like the old one of the Crow, Blue Acorn."

Tall Grass looked over to where Owl Man was helping Running Dog. "Soon he will be, when we reach our village again."

"He has learned the art of healing from the medicine man of our village," Running Dog spoke up. "His vision was seen and interpreted by Blue Acorn as a sign that someday he would become a great medicine man of his people."

"Well anyway, he sure made my leg feel better," Pinto smiled, and then bit into a large piece of steaming deer meat.

"The White Wolf of the Crow People has been lucky too," Running Dog laughed.

Jehu looked over at him curiously. "And why is that?"

"The Pawnee horses he has captured, they will be given to the father of Alamette as payment for his new wife."

"What?" Jehu jumped at the words as if he had been pricked with a sharp needle.

Running Dog laughed. "They will be payment for the woman, Alamette."

Jehu shook his head and looked over at his friend. "I told you, I have no need for a wife."

"No, but she has need of a husband, my friend."

Pinto laughed, wondering how long was this argument going to last before Jehu finally gave in and married the lass?

Running Dog was a devout bachelor, but he truly enjoyed seeing Jehu's discomfort at the thought of having a wife.

"I'll take the first watch. The rest of you get some sleep." Jehu's eyes lit on Running Dog who was still enjoying his little joke. "At this hour, children should be asleep."

Tall Grass led the small body of white trappers and warriors at a leisurely pace toward the east and their own hunting grounds, far away from the Pawnee. Several times, Owl Man swung back to their rear and watched for any sign of enemy warriors following their trail. Finally satisfied that none followed, the warriors rode on toward their village leisurely; listening to Running Dog brag about all the honors, they would soon be given. Every man among them was sore from the wounds they had received on their journey to the land of the Pawnee, but not one would have missed the adventure.

Tall Grass pulled in his pony on the banks of the small river that flowed by the Flathead Village and waited for the others to ride up beside him. People from the village were already gathering and pointing at the group of riders, trying to be certain the strangers were not a raiding party after horses. Finally, one of the younger warriors let out a war whoop as he recognized the riders and rushed toward the river. Tall Grass kicked his horse and splashed across the shallow stream.

The Flathead Chief, Yellow Horn, stood before his tall lodge as Jehu and the others dismounted, and approached him. Running Dog grinned widely as the scalps, tied in his horse's mane, brought much exclamation from the gathered crowd. Throwing out his chest, he elbowed Jehu in the side.

"Tonight, my friend, we will be greatly honored." The warrior laughed lightly. "Tonight they will sing our praises."

Jehu shook his head as he noticed his friend looking over the gathered maidens of the Flatheads. "And tonight you just be sure to be on your best behavior. I've had all the trouble I can stand for a while."

"I do not see your woman, Alamette." Running Dog looked around the expectant faces. "Maybe she has taken another for her husband."

Jehu was surprised at the jealousy the remark sparked in his heart. As much as he rejected the idea of marriage, he too looked for the beautiful maiden. Fear gripped his heart, as he knew if she were in the village, she would be here to welcome him back. Had she married another as Running Dog said? Is she sick?

"I told you to marry her before you left for the Pawnee lands." Running Dog grinned. He already spotted Alamette walking toward the gathered crowd with a large basket of berries under her arm. "Now you have lost her forever."

Pinto smiled. "Don't fret yourself, here she comes now."

Glaring over to where Running Dog had broken into a fit of laughter, Jehu shook his head. "One of these days Crow, one of these days."

"If you would marry the woman, then you would have no more fears."

Jehu knew Running Dog spoke the truth. The uncontrollable fear that engulfed him with the thought he had lost her, was almost unbearable. "Pinto, will you speak with Yellow Horn about arranging the marriage?"

Did he hear right? Pinto's jaw dropped open. "Alright Jehu, if you're plumb positive." He was in doubt, as the youngster had always been dead certain against getting married.

"I promised her; I'm dead certain." Jehu nodded as he looked down on the shining face of Alamette as she walked up. "She will be my wife."

"White Wolf only has three Pawnee horses to give for such a beautiful woman." Running Dog looked to where Yellow Horn was talking with Tall Grass. "He will want many more."

"I will bring more from Cloud's Trading Post when we return."

"And what if she won't wait?" Running Dog teased.

"I will wait." Alamette walked up and caught the last of Running Dog's remarks and the deep slash across his forehead. "I see a Crow whose boastful ways almost lost him his head."

Running Dog's deep laughter echoed through the village. "The scar helps with the women. I was too beautiful the way I was."

Alamette could only shake her head and smile. No one could not like this warrior. "I think it is Running Dog that needs a wife."

Still inflamed from the Pawnee arrow that struck him through the calf, Pinto fumed and fussed as he watched Jehu prepare to depart. In addition, the arrowhead buried in his back, the old trapper had plenty to grumble about as Jehu saddled the Appaloosa and gathered his possibles. The old medicine man warned Pinto about infection, saying he shouldn't ride until the wound healed itself. Now he watched as Jehu prepared to ride east in search of his sister, Chauncy, and Martin Carter.

He knew Jehu Wolf had come far and matured since coming with him west from Clouds. Nevertheless, he was still young, too young to take on the whole Carter Clan, not counting Charlie Cloud and his blacks. Looking down at the swollen leg, he cussed his luck and the Pawnee. They were the ones to blame for his predicament.

"You sure you should take the girl with you, lad?"

"I'm sure." Jehu looked to where the girl sat perched on her horse waiting. "Sides, ain't no way she'll let me ride out alone again."

Pinto nodded. "Well, you can always take a stick to her backsides."

Jehu looked over at his new wife and smiled. Only the evening before, Running Dog convinced her father, Yellow Horn, how good a husband Jehu would make. The Chief argued loud and long, but to no avail. His daughter was determined; the young white trapper would be her husband and his new son-in-law. Actually, Yellow Horn was elated with the marriage, as it would give the Flathead People much prestige, and it would give the Chief a good son-in-law. Somehow, Running Dog found the horses Yellow Horn asked for the bride price, and the wedding had taken place. Jehu didn't know where his friend came up with more horses, and Running Dog declined to say.

The victory celebration over the Pawnee and the wedding celebration had been rolled into one, keeping the village wide-awake and dancing to the beating drums almost until the new sun. Despite Running Dog and Tall Grass insistence on him staying up all night, Jehu managed to slip away quietly, leaving his friends to wonder where he and his new bride disappeared. He doubted either would miss him as long as they were the center of attraction to the village and the young maidens.

Jehu looked to where Pinto was fidgeting with his leg. "You gonna be alright, Pinto?"

"Aye lad, I'll lay up here until you return." Pinto squinted his eyes in the morning sun. "Wish I could ride with you and help find the lass."

Jehu nodded. "You rest and let that leg heal. I'll find her and make sure she's okay."

"Keep your eyes on the skyline."

"I will old friend, and you keep off that leg."

"Laddie," Pinto extended his hand to Jehu. "Thank you for coming after us."

"You would have done the same for me."

"Yeah, reckon I would at that."

Stepping into the saddle, Jehu looked down once more on the trapper. "I'll be back before summer's end, then we'll ride to find Lowrie. You rest and be ready."

"I'll be ready." The big trapper squinted through the morning sun. "One thing, lad, if you go back to Cloud's, you be careful. He can be mighty ornery when he's a mind to."

"Yeah, I've seen him and his men in action."

Two weeks after leaving the Flathead Village and Pinto, Jehu sat the Appaloosa alongside the Big Muddy, looking across the open trail that led to Cloud's Trading Post. Alamette sat her horse quietly behind him, her long black hair blowing slightly in the breeze.

"There it is." Jehu looked back at her. "We'll ride in and see what we can find out."

Alamette looked anxiously at the tall walls and wide open gates. She had never been to a trading post or fort. It reminded her of a bear's den. "Will there be trouble, my husband?"

"We won't know that until we go in and see."

"There are many whites in this place?"

Jehu nodded. "Sometimes many come here to trade. You can remain here and wait for me if you wish."

A small frown came to her face. "You know I will not do this thing. Where you go, I go."

Shaking his head, trying to hide a grin, Jehu nudged the Appaloosa and rode slowly toward the post. Looking around as they passed through the gates, Jehu could see nothing had changed. Even the blacks of Clouds were sitting at their usual place alongside the busy trading post, keeping a watchful eye on the wharf for any travelers coming their way. A heavy early summer rain had muddied up the wide flat ground that lay inside the palisades. Their walking horses slogged noisily through the mud as they neared the post.

Jehu noticed one of the blacks as the man retreated quickly inside the post. Letting the horse walk slowly up to the porch, Jehu pulled him up and waited. He knew Cloud would come outside as soon as the black tells him strangers, loaded down with furs, were riding in.

Cloud had not changed a bit. Jehu would have recognized the owlish look of the small man, even in the big city of St. Louis. Cloud smiled grimly, his lips curled back over his teeth, reminding Jehu of a coyote fixing to have a rabbit for dinner. Looking around, the dark eyes center on Alamette.

"I see you're carrying a squaw now, Wolf?"

"She's my wife, Mister Cloud."

"That a fact? Where's Stade?"

Jehu looked behind him toward the gates. "He's around."

"Summer furs don't fetch much." Cloud looked at the loaded down packhorse the young squaw led.

"Don't remember asking you to buy them." Jehu despised the man, and it showed in his voice.

Cloud smiled. "We've heard about the Great White Wolf of the Crows, even way back here in civilization."

"And just what have you heard?"

"They say this White Wolf is a white man, that he's a mighty warrior of the Crow, undefeated in battle. Word is, he's killed many with his bare hands."

"I'm looking for the girl, Chauncy, nothing more." Jehu stared down at Cloud.

Cloud smiled slightly and looked over at the porch where the big black, Benje, was sitting against the post wall, his eyes locked on the Indian girl. Turning his eyes back on Jehu, the trader's face suddenly became blank of expression. The black eyes narrowed and became as flint.

"Perhaps, Mister Wolf, you should leave my post and keep riding." Cloud pulled his long coat back, revealing a small flintlock pistol stuck in the sash that bound the slender waist.

"I will leave when you have answered my question, Cloud." Jehu cocked the hammer of his Hawken. "Where is she?"

"Wouldn't know," Cloud smiled, then looked over at Benje. "Take him."

Jehu couldn't believe a man of such size could move so fast, as the black lifted him bodily from the saddle, throwing him across the tie-rail, landing on the rough porch. Jehu hit hard on his side and felt the heavy body of the dark cyclone land atop him. Rolling quickly and kicking out hard with both feet, he knocked the black bodily, back onto the muddy ground.

Rising swiftly to his feet, he clenched with Benje and felt the power in the big black's grasp. Muscles bunched and strained as the two giants applied all their strength, trying to force each other to their knees. A hammering blow knocked Jehu sideways into the post's wall. Shielding his head from the next blow, Jehu hooked the black's legs with his own, tripping the man onto his back.

Never has Jehu felt the power Benje applied as they wrestled across the rough oak floor of the porch. Rolling on his side, Jehu flipped the black sideways and hammered at the big man with two hard rights. The blows seemed to have no effect on the dark face that grinned wickedly and flung him backward onto the muddy yard. The air was knocked from his lungs as the heavy man landed atop him, landing several hammering blows to his face. A large cut opened down the side of Jehu's cheek, causing blood to run into his eyes, blinding him.

"I will have your woman white man, after I kill you," Benje laughed. "She will be mine."

Feeling for the black face, Jehu ran his fingers in the large nostrils of the man and ripped his head backward. A crushing blow to Benje's throat caused his breath to come in hard rattles. Rolling sideways, Jehu managed to land on the man's back and enveloped his throat with his powerful forearm. Locking his legs together, around the black waist, he tightened his hold slowly on Benje's throat.

He could feel the feeble tugging of Benje's hands as he tried in vain to break the stranglehold the strong arm held him in. The arm cut off his air as he staggered blindly around the yard with Jehu on his back. Several hands pulled at Jehu, forcing him loose from Benje's dark face. Throwing the men backward as he rose to his feet, Jehu focused his eyes on Cloud.

"You've killed Benje." Cloud looked up at Jehu in dismay.

Never in his life had he feared any man, but looking up at the hulking madman standing over the body of the black, Cloud shuttered. Whatever stood before him was not human. Perhaps the stories of the White Wolf were true. Maybe this was an evil spirit or the incarnation of the devil wolf. The face was contorted, insane. The eyes were red as fire and blood seemed to drip from this devil's face.

Cloud shuddered involuntarily again. Across from him, the other blacks backed away in fright. The figure before him seemed to snarl like a wolf ready to pounce. Wiping the sweat from his face, Cloud backed away slowly, his legs trembling.

Slowly, the rage and fury left Jehu's face as he straightened. "I'll not ask you again, Cloud. Where is she?"

A trembling finger pointed to the south. "Down river about forty miles, they've got themselves a farm."

"She with Martin Carter?"

"Yes, last time they were here for supplies, she rode in with him." Cloud touched the grip of the little pistol. "They are married."

Jehu approached the shaking trader and looked down into the dark terrified eyes. "One last question, Mister Cloud."

"What do you want to know?"

"Did you have anything to do with David Miles' Trading Post being burned and him killed?"

"Nothing, I swear, nothing."

"You'll live today Cloud, but when Pinto gets here, I ain't sure what might happen." Jehu walked back to the Appaloosa. Picking up his fallen Hawken, he mounted and looked down at Cloud. "I'm riding over to talk with Luke Carter. You look over them plews and get my money ready."

"And the packhorse, you leaving him here?"

"Fill my packs with supplies, lead, shot, and powder." Jehu reined the Appaloosa around. "My payment for you sicking your man on me."

"Yes, sir, Mister Wolf." Cloud cowered before the trapper, his hands trembling. Never has he feared any man, but Jehu Wolf struck fear in him, fear he couldn't cast off.

The blacks looked over at their terrified owner then looked down at the dead Benje who they thought was unbeatable. Never had they known Charles Cloud to fear any man, but the man riding away was no mere man. They too had seen him change before their eyes. He was a demon, a devil. No mortal man could change as this one had just done. The whites of their eyes still showed fear as they cowered on the porch of the trading post.

Luke Carter had already heard the commotion across the street and watched the approaching rider and Indian girl. From a distance, he could see one of the blacks being carried behind the post. Blood completely covered the face of the man before him as he reined to a stop.

"You remember me, Luke Carter?"

"You've grown some, Wolf."

"Never mind about me, where is she?"

Carter looked across at the trading post. "You kill one of Cloud's blacks?"

"Benje, and this day's young yet." Jehu looked down at the man. "There's time for another killing today."

"I've always treated you fair." Carter wiped his face. Like the others, he couldn't believe Benje could be killed. "I gave you and that girl a job so you wouldn't starve."

"You did that. Now, where is she?"

"She's on a farm down river, near where the fork of the Blue meets the Big Muddy."

Jehu nodded. "If you're lying, I'll be back."

"She's there."

Alamette spread bear grease on the long cut on Jehu's cheek. It would forever leave a nasty scar, giving him the evil look of a dangerous man.

Gazing directly into the blaze of the small fire, he nodded his thanks and patted her on the hand. "Thank you." Jehu felt the bloody scab running down his cheek. "Does it make me ugly to look at?"

The beautiful girl smiled and placed her small brown hand on his cheek. "You are a fine looking man, my husband. The scar makes you even more handsome."

"If you say so, young lady."

"We have camped here for a week. Why do you not speak with her instead of watching the white man's house?"

Jehu looked toward the small farmhouse. "I wait for the swelling to go down in my face."

"It is gone my husband. Only the red scab remains."

Jehu nodded. "Tomorrow we will ride to the farm."

"Do you wish me to go, my husband?"

"You are my wife. Why wouldn't I want you to go?"

"I am Indian; perhaps you are ashamed of me."

Pulling her against his chest, he softly stroked her dark hair. "Never say that again. You are my life."

Smiling, she curled up against his broad, strong chest.

Chapter 16

Chauncy shielded her eyes against the eastern sun as she tried to make out the two riders crossing the cornfield through the new stalks of knee-high corn. Glancing over at the barn where Martin worked on a leather harness, she was about to holler a warning when she hesitated. Something about the shape of the lead rider held her attention, something about the way he sat the big spotted horse. Glancing at the other rider, her eyes focused on the buckskin-clad figure, an Indian woman.

Not a word was spoken as Jehu reined the Appaloosa to a stop ten feet from the astounded woman. Jehu studied her smooth face, blond hair, and eyes the same color as his.

"Is it truly you, Jehu?" She stared at the bobcat skin covering on his head with the fierce face and ears sticking out, and the long red scar that appeared fresh running down his cheek. The bloody buckskin clothing, the hard, cold eyes, all tell a story, a story of hardship and battle. She also noticed the powerful shoulders and chest. He had filled out since she has last seen him. "Is it really you, my brother?"

Jehu looked behind her to a small, dark head sticking up from a cradle. Hearing a door squeak open, he looked over at the barn, then cocked the Hawken as Martin Carter appeared in the doorway.

"He is my husband, Jehu. The child is his." Chauncy stepped between the rifle and the approaching Martin. "Do not harm him brother, this is our home."

Jehu looked to where Carter had stopped in his tracks as he recognized the wild looking, bloodstained man, and noticed the Hawken

Rifle pointing right at him. Kneeing the Appaloosa, Jehu rode closer to the porch and looked down at the dark skinned baby. Turning, he studied the woman's face for several moments, slowly riding from the yard and across the cornfield without speaking a word.

"I'll be danged, Chauncy." Martin Carter walked up. "How could a short year change a man so much? I thought I was a dead man for sure when he looked at me."

Chauncy looked back at the baby. "You almost were Martin. I could see it in his eyes."

"I've heard the stories told in the mountains and around campfires of his fights. I thought they were just that, stories."

"My poor, Jehu." She watched as Jehu and Alamette disappeared along the river bottom. "Oh Martin, you should have seen his face, the scar, the blood."

"They weren't stories. I've seen most of the bad ones around Cloud's Post. I'll tell you this, none put the scare in me like he just done."

Picking up the baby, Chauncy held it to her. "He never even spoke; never said a word."

"What was there to say? He hates me, that's for sure, but when he saw you were happy here as my wife, and the baby, well that was enough."

"Where will he go, Martin?" Chauncy cried. "I can't even help him."

Carter shrugged. "Back into the high mountains I reckon, following his trap lines."

"Who was the woman?"

"Probably just a squaw he picked up. By her hair and do dads, I'd say she was Flathead."

Her eyes teared up more as she walked to the edge of the cornfield with the baby. "Good-bye Jehu, my beloved brother."

Jehu's second and third season riding with Pinto and Lowrie proved to be the worst winters the high Rockies had seen in years. Temperatures plummeted colder and colder, causing the small lakes and streams to freeze solid. Heavy winds blew through the frozen trees, causing them to snap like the roar of a rifle going off. Huge snowflakes blew sideways, causing snowdrifts to build up against the log cabins that had been built.

They had been lucky. Running Dog told of how the old medicine men of his village predicted the terrible winter that was to come. Lowrie, wise leader that he was, had listened to his scout and meat hunter, and had moved into the valley the little cabins occupied. While the trappers were out, running their trap lines, the camp hostlers were busy putting up cabins that would withstand the heavy snows that were predicted.

Running Dog, now fully recovered from his wounds, kept busy bringing in deer and elk meat that would be made into jerky to feed them through the cold times. It was good that they had the large supply of meat stored. Some of the meat hung high in the trees, away from hungry varmints, and some hung safely in the cabins. With the coming of the colder days, the deer and larger animals, like buffalo and elk, had disappeared from the high ridges, moving into the lower valleys far from the cabins.

Earlier in the fall, the trapping was good. Beaver skins, fox, otter, and mink were brought in daily, but not now. With the water frozen over two feet thick, there was no way of setting their traps. The snow was deep, the cold so penetrating, the woodland animals held to their warm burrows and dens underneath the ground. Most of the trappers stayed inside the cozy cabins, sitting around the warm fires, telling tales and yarns of bygone hunters and their adventures. Others, feeling cabin fever coming on from days of idleness, braved the deep snows and cold temperatures to explore the far-reaching valleys and forests for places to set their trap lines the following fall.

Jehu built a small cabin for Alamette and him to be alone. Except for Pinto, Lowrie, and Running Dog, who were occasional visitors for supper, or for the night, no one bothered the young couple. Most of the men were now in awe of the tall trapper the Indians called White Wolf. They either feared him or held him in deep respect. They had heard of his fight with Cloud's black. They had heard how he had changed into a wolf. None really believed the tale, but none tried to carry on idle conversation with Jehu, as they found him distant. Only around Pinto or Running Dog did he seem his old self. The mountains were reclusive and now they had a recluse to share their quiet and loneliness, a strong man, strong as the mountains themselves.

After rendezvous, each year, Jehu and Alamette drifted away to stay alone, until it was time to reunite with Lowrie for another season. Only

Running Dog and Pinto knew where they went. Occasionally, out on a raid, Running Dog stopped by the peaceful, but isolated valley where Jehu and Alamette stayed by themselves. He would stay a few days visiting, bringing Jehu tobacco or maybe a bolt of cloth for Alamette, and then he would ride away.

The call of a huge hawk sounded over the valley, causing Jehu to shield his eyes and look skyward. Something had disturbed the high flying bird from his perch high in a tall sycamore tree. The hunting bird circled slowly, his sharp eyes scanning the flat valley and the small creek that flowed through it. Jehu stood up from where he had been sharpening a skinning knife. His clear blue eyes searched out the trails that led to the cabin, looking for any interloper that might bring danger. He knew no warrior dared enter his valley. They knew this was the lair of the White Wolf and they feared him.

Jehu was no longer the green youngster that came into these same mountains years ago with Pinto Stade. He had matured and grown, and his reputation had grown with him. Most Indians were superstitious. Some believed Jehu could turn himself into the white wolf he was named after. Many, meeting Jehu at rendezvous or at a trading post, were in awe of the trapper, stepping wide around him to avoid meeting him face-to-face. None could look him in the eye.

The blue eyes of Jehu quickly found and focused in on a brown movement of an object far down the mountainside. Reaching for the Hawken, Jehu whistled a warning to Alamette, and then trotted away in long powerful strides. Suddenly, from below, Jehu heard the unmistakable scream of a Crow war cry. He smiled and relaxed, slowing to a walk. Running Dog and Tall Grass rounded a bend in the trail and came face-to-face with the tall trapper.

Dismounting, the warriors hugged Jehu, all the while laughing and pumping his hand. Running Dog hadn't changed one bit. He was still full of laughter and good cheer, and still ready to argue with anyone who would listen about the good virtues of a woman, any woman, as long as she wasn't his wife. The three friends made their way slowly along the trail to the cabin, all the while laughing and telling Jehu why he should join them on their upcoming raid on the Pawnee.

"Straight Arrow is my friend. He treats us fairly." Jehu shook his head vigorously. "I won't ride against him and his people."

Running Dog acted sad and hurt. "We only go to steal horses. We will do no fighting or take any captives."

Tall Grass looked impatiently at his friend. "Do not believe this liar, my friend."

Jehu looked over at Tall Grass, a warrior, he knew to be serious, not like Running Dog who would rather tell a small lie and get you upset, than tell you the truth.

Laughing aloud, in his rich vibrating voice, Running Dog suddenly grew quiet as Alamette appeared in the doorway of the cabin. His dark eyes went immediately to her stomach. With a whoop, he dashed to the porch and lifted her off her feet.

"Careful, put me down, you'll hurt the baby." Alamette was laughing almost as hard as Running Dog was. Even though he was a Crow and she was a Flathead, she had grown fond of him over the years as if he was a brother.

Tall Grass could not believe his eyes. He just stood there, looking at the girl who suddenly became a woman in his eyes. It was as if he had never seen a woman fixing to become a mother.

Running Dog slapped his friend on the back and laughed. Turning to Jehu, he pointed at their horses. "We have brought meat, if you will have our woman cook it, we will feast."

"Our woman?" Alamette stared hard at the warrior. "What do you mean, our woman? I have only one husband."

"Yes, and if I hadn't convinced him to marry one such as you, he would still be free like me."

"Free like you, Running Dog?" The redness started to show in her face.

"And you would not have him if I hadn't given your father the horse price he asked for." Running Dog grinned. Nothing tickled him more than to get her mad.

"The only reason you are still unmarried is no woman will have you. You are not to be trusted, and you brag too much," the black eyes of the girl flashed.

"A great and handsome warrior such as I should brag. It is his right."

"Okay, okay, I'm hungry, let's eat." Tall Grass raised his hand. "You two fight later."

Suddenly both Alamette and Running Dog burst out laughing, causing Tall Grass to shake his head as he pulled the deer meat and grouse from his horse. Turning to Jehu, he congratulated the soon-to-be father.

"Now this one knows why you come to this place, away from all people." The warrior looked over at Running Dog. "Especially this one."

"Amen my friend, but some things you just have to put up with." Jehu started plucking the fat hens. "Are you two alone?"

Running Dog shook his head. "We leave the rest down mountain while we come to talk to White Wolf."

Jehu looked over at his two friends. None had been more loyal and trustworthy as these two men who he would trust with his life. "I would ask you not to go to the lands of the Pawnee."

"Why you ask this thing, White Wolf?" Tall Grass looked curiously at Jehu.

"Let's just say I had a premonition of doom if you go." Jehu shrugged. "I wish you would stay away from the Pawnee."

Running dog laughed lightly. "Our friend, Tall Grass, has asked for a woman to be his wife, but like my friend the White Wolf, he is poor in horses."

"And that's where you two are going," Jehu shook his head, "to get him some horses?"

Again, Running Dog shrugged and laughed good-naturedly. "No horse, no squaw, you know this to be true my friend."

"Yes, I know, but if you get yourself killed, you won't need a woman."

"Bah, the Pawnee warriors are women."

Jehu disagreed. "Both of you know better than that. They are great warriors."

"We will steal their horses without waking them up," Tall Grass argued. "Then we will leave their hunting grounds fast."

"My friends, you both know Straight Arrow is a great war leader. You steal his horses and he will come after you."

"Good, I wish to fight with the Pawnee again." Running Dog smiled. "You should come and go with us to the west."

Jehu shook his head. "How many are going with you?"

"A few wait at the small river by the rocks." Running Dog stood up and walked into the cabin. Handing Alamette a bundle, he looked down at her stomach and smiled. "I will be an uncle soon; maybe when I return."

"It will be soon." Alamette opened the deerskin wrapped bundle. "It will be a boy."

Turning, the warrior stepped from the cabin and shook hands with Jehu. "We go."

"Will you scout and hunt for Lowrie this winter?" Jehu walked with the two warriors toward their horses. "Providing, that is, if you survive this crazy idea?"

"I have to, who else will keep the White Wolf from getting lost," Running Dog laughed. "Good-bye, my friend. When we meet again, you will be a father, and I will be an uncle."

"What about me?" Tall Grass spoke up. "Two of those horses you paid for Alamette were mine."

Running Dog looked over at the warrior. "You are too ugly to be his uncle."

Jehu smiled; he never knew how these two could steal horses when all they did was argue. "You both will be his uncles."

"This is good," Tall Grass laughed.

"Tell me, my brothers." Jehu looked up at the mounted warriors. "Why do you raid the Pawnee? Why not the Cheyenne or Sioux?"

For the first time since Jehu knew him, Running Dog grew serious. "Our friend Black Hoof is dead because of Straight Arrow and his Pawnees."

"Cripes, that was three, four years ago."

"We will only take horses, nothing more, then we will never return to Pawnee land again." Tall Grass whispered, "Black Hoof must be avenged."

Alamette stood beside Jehu as the warriors rode from sight over the mountain trail. A lonely feeling came over the tall trapper as he watched them wave from the ridge.

"Maybe my husband, you should go with them." Alamette looked up into his worried face.

Wrapping his great arm around her small shoulder, he smiled down at her. "No, they are grown men. My place is here with you."

"But you would like to go. I can feel your blood racing." She persisted.

"If my blood races, it is because of your beauty my wife, nothing more." Jehu turned her toward the cabin. "I will not steal ponies from my friend Straight Arrow, or his people."

Two weeks passed and Jehu had not heard a word of Running Dog or Tall Grass. He knew Running Dog would bring word that he was back safely. He was worried. Alamette bragged on the warriors and the many raids they had been on and returned from safely, trying to ease his fears, but she too, was worried. Surely, Running Dog would have sent word if the raid was successful, especially if the raid netted many horses. Alamette knew how he liked to boast and brag.

Suddenly, Jehu made up his mind. "Cook food and prepare your things today."

Alamette looked over at him curiously. "Yes, my husband; may I ask why?"

"It is near your time. We will ride to your people where the old women will be there to help when the little one comes."

"I do not need their help husband, but it is thoughtful of you to think of the little one," Alamette turned toward the cabin with a smile, "and Running Dog."

She was right, but he did not want her here in these valleys if she did need help having the baby. Yes, he was worried about Running Dog and Tall Grass, but her safety came first. Taking down the Hawken from above the cabin door, he checked the primer and looked to where she was cooking.

"I go after the horses." Stopping in the door, he smiled. "We will leave in the morning."

"I will be ready."

The small pasture that held the four horses was down a small trail less than a mile from the cabin. A rail gate kept the horses confined in a box canyon with deep grass and a small stream. Climbing through the rails, Jehu stopped beside the clear water and looked up and down the valley floor. Seeing no horses in sight, Jehu knelt down and cupped his hand for a drink of the cold mountain water before splashing across. His hand froze before touching the water. His hair seemed to stand up on the back of his neck, and then he shivered uncontrollably. In the sandy, wet bank was the huge track of a grizzly, a deep wide track that was still oozing water, showing the bear was close, very close. Slowly, Jehu raised his eyes to look across the small stream. Nothing, only the sandy banks standing empty meet his eyes as far as he could see. Turning his head slightly, Jehu blinked. Before him, less than thirty feet away, a huge grizzly reared on his hind feet and tested the wind.

Frozen motionless in his tracks, Jehu waited. He knew the bear had poor eyesight, but if he moved a hair at this distance, he could charge. Dropping to the ground, the bear raked the ground with his forefoot and charged a few steps forward. Jehu rotated on his knee and cocked the rifle. The silver tip was a big bore grizzly, weighing at least eight hundred pounds, close to nine or ten feet tall on his hind feet.

Trapping with Pinto, the last few years, Jehu had seen many grizzlies. He had even killed two of the beasts when he was forced to. Grizzly meat was too greasy for his taste. However, the trappers valued bear grease for the many different things it could be used for and the skins made good rugs for warmth against the cold.

The bear retreated a few feet then stood up on his hind legs, sniffing the wind. Jehu held his breath and waited. The grizzly was in his prime, rolling fat and healthy, ready for the long hibernation of winter. Would he charge for no reason? If he does, Jehu had heard the old-timers talk of the terrible damage the long claws could do to a man in seconds. He also remembered they said only a brain shot would kill one this size quick enough to stop him cold.

Again, the bear dropped down and ambled slowly toward him, stopping every few feet, smelling the wind. He was close, too close. Jehu could smell the musty smell of the brute. He could see the small, dark nose, trying to sniff out and identify the unseen enemy. Jehu wondered if the bear, living way up here in these remote valleys, had ever seen a human before.

He was coming too close, and Jehu had no choice. Yelling at the top of his lungs, he waved his arms, slowly retreating before the animal. The scream stopped the bear momentarily, causing him to spook backward a few yards before he stopped again and rose to his feet. Checking to make sure his skinning knife was at his side, Jehu raised the Hawken slowly. He would only have time for one shot and if it didn't stop the huge beast, the knife was all he had left. The beady little eyes split the sights of the rifle as Jehu slowly started to squeeze the trigger.

Unsure of what stood before him, the grizzly slowly turned sideways and then started for the near woods. Jehu eased up on the trigger and watched unbelieving as the big bear disappeared from his sight. Relief washed across him as his legs slowly folded and he sat down on the sandy bank. Wiping his face, he felt the cold sweat that had broken out on his forehead. Never had he feared anything, but never had he met a foe as huge and ferocious looking as this grizzly up close. With shaking hands, he washed his face and stood slowly to his feet. Watching behind him, as he crossed the water, he slowly regained his composure and started to laugh. If only Pinto and the boys could see him now.

Jehu smiled, now he would have a tale to talk about around the fires this winter. Would any of the older trappers believe him, he wondered. Shoot, he didn't believe it himself. Hitting a short run, he hurried across the valley to find his horses.

The Flathead Village of Chief Yellow Horn, Alamette's father, lay before them in the misty early morning. Jehu sat, letting his horses drink their fill while he studied the smoky fires of the women. Alamette smiled, they had not arrived any too soon. She was having pains and the baby was on his way. Jehu kneed the Appaloosa and splashed into the belly deep water.

"Maybe my husband, maybe you should hurry." Alamette held her stomach painfully. "Hurry."

Yellow Horn smiled knowingly, as Jehu paced back and forth before the council fire, occasionally looking over to where the squaw lodge sat by itself. He laughed, to himself, the White Wolf, brave in battle, was beside himself, nervous as an unbroken pony.

Walking to where Yellow Horn waited, Jehu sat down beside his father-in-law. "How long does this take?"

"Who knows, sometimes very quick, sometimes days."

"Days?" Jehu shook his head. A scream came from the lodge and Jehu leaped to his feet. "Are they killing her?"

"Much noise when new life come into world, same as when one dies, much noise." Yellow Horn smiled knowingly.

Jehu shook his head slowly. "Shucks, if this keeps up, I'll be ready to do a little screaming myself."

"Screaming good for squaw, no good for White Wolf."

"And why is that?"

"You brave warrior, great fighter, killer of Sioux and Pawnee Warriors. White Wolf no scream like woman." Yellow Horn looked worriedly over to where Jehu sat, causing the white hunter to chuckle. "White Wolf no scream."

Jehu remembered a few days earlier when he had the run in with the grizzly. He wondered what Yellow Horn would have said if he saw the Great White Wolf almost faint after the bear retreated. He had no doubt in his mind, he was scared.

Jehu's thoughts were snapped back as Yellow Horn let out a war whoop. "Your son is born. The great spirits of our ancestors have given you a son, White Wolf."

Looking over at the lodge, Jehu watched an old woman motioning to where they sat. "How does Yellow Horn know it is a boy?"

"I knew before you came back to this place, that my daughter would have a boy child." The Chief looked over at the old medicine man, Limping Badger, and nodded.

"Uh huh, and I knew that bear wasn't about to eat me," Jehu whispered under his breath.

"Go see your son, White Wolf. Give thanks to the great ones for their gift," Yellow Horn smiled.

Pinto rode into the Flathead Village two days later and dismounted before the lodge of Yellow Horn.

"My friend, it is good you have come home to your people. We have not seen you since you stayed with us two summers ago."

"It is good to be back once again." Pinto shook hands with the chief. "Have you seen anything of White Wolf this summer?"

"Him here," Yellow Horn pointed. "There, him have new son."

"A new son? I'll be dogged," Pinto smiled easily. "Alamette, is she okay?"

"Daughter fine; she must stay in squaw lodge a few days."

"I'll bet Jehu loves that," Pinto laughed. He knew a warrior wasn't allowed to visit a woman when she was in the squaw lodge. "Yes sir, has he seen the baby?"

"Him see."

Pulling several twists of tobacco from his saddlebags, Pinto handed them to the chief. "Where is the lad?"

"Him hunt with warriors; be back soon."

Pinto unsaddled and was watering his horses when several voices sounded from the far end of the village. Looking at the small knoll that lay to the west, he focused on many warriors riding down the steep slope toward the village. Raising his hand to shield his eyes from the sinking sun, he picked out the Appaloosa he knew belonged to Jehu. Shaking his head, he smiled. Even from this distance, he can see the rider was a big man, straight as an arrow on the horse and from the way he rode, he was proud.

Slowly the face came closer and Pinto could not believe his eyes, as Jehu had grown and matured. The man underneath the bobcat skin cap wore a light brown beard and the leather-hunting shirt couldn't hide the muscled up torso or the hidden strength. Pinto could only shake his head, as he always knew, one day Jehu would make a real hoss, and he had. The prominent grey scar was so pronounced, before it became half hidden under the beard, gave the young trapper character, and even class.

"Well, old pard, you made it back to the mountains." Jehu picked Pinto bodily from the ground, almost as if he were a feather.

"Yes I did, laddie, for a fact."

"You're looking fit as a fiddle."

"Would you believe it, lad, I went to St. Louie after last year's season. I stayed with my friend Sutton and his wife Arabella for a few days. He took me to see a sawbones, a friend of his, and the doctor removed that old arrowhead from my back that's been giving me fits for so long. He even fixed my leg almost good as new, he sure did."

"That's great. I'll bet you feel a lot better now," Jehu laughed.

"No, I'm ashamed." Pinto dropped his head slightly.

"Ashamed of what, old friend?"

"Well you see, that weren't no Pawnee Arrow at all when he got the blamed thing out. It was Cheyenne, after all."

Jehu was confused. "So?"

"Sutton kept telling me it weren't Pawnee, and I wouldn't believe him." Pinto shook his head. "To think of all the Pawnee I've put under just because of an arrowhead that wasn't even Pawnee."

"Well, we all make mistakes." Jehu nodded solemnly seeing his friend wasn't joking. He was actually taking the news badly. He was curious, was it because of all the dead Pawnee, or because now he wouldn't be able to hate the Pawnee as much. "Let's eat; I know you're famished."

The old squaw set steaming bowls of meat and wild onions in front of the two trappers, then retreated to her fire, out of earshot. Another brought the baby out of the women's lodge for Pinto to see and ogle over. Jehu held the small bundle and let Pinto study the small face before handing the kicking bundle back to the woman who retreated to another lodge with the baby.

"I stayed with Sutton a whole week. He's got himself a prime piece of land along the Big Muddy." Pinto looked over to where Jehu sat. "I gave him most of my fur money to buy me a piece of land lying alongside his place."

"You aiming on quitting the trap line?" Jehu looked curiously at his friend. "Maybe taking up the plow?"

"Someday maybe I will, but not this year," Pinto laughed. "At least I'll have the land and not waste my money on drink and foolishness."

"Good thinking, maybe I should do the same for me and Alamette."

Pinto looked around the village, then at the squaw lodge, then over at the half-wild young hunter, he had befriended what seemed like years ago. "No, me boy, I don't think you'll ever leave these mountains."

Jehu nodded slowly; Pinto was probably right. "Did you pass through any Crow Villages on your way here?"

"Crooked Leg's Village and a smaller village with a subchief named Paints His Face." Pinto looked curiously at Jehu. "Why?"

"I'm worried about Running Dog and Tall Grass."

"I met up with Owl Man at Cloud's Trading post before coming here." Pinto bit into his supper. "He told me they had gone west on a horse raid."

"I know; I tried to warn them not to go."

"You know Running Dog, he's wild, and adventurous," Pinto smiled. "He ain't that wild. He's too smart to get himself done in. He'll turn up."

"Soon as Alamette recovers, I'll be riding out to look for him."

"Why, for Pete's sake, you warned him."

Jehu looked across the small fire. "Because, he would do the same for me."

"How long have they been gone?"

"Almost a month now."

"I'll ride out with you."

"Why was Owl Man at Cloud's Post?"

Pinto laughed again. "Seems his friend Tall Grass, is wanting to marry and his bride's daddy wants new metal pots for part of the squaw price."

"Metal pots, horses," Jehu smiled. "Must be some woman to cost that much."

"Well, Owl Man got his pots, but I don't know about the horses."

Jehu looked over at the woman's lodge. "Limping Badger said Alamette can leave the lodge tomorrow. We'll be pulling out."

Chapter 17

Once again, Jehu sat on the banks of the Republican River looking off to the northwest. He said good-bye to Alamette and his son days before. Now, he and Pinto rode alone toward the Pawnee hunting grounds. No sign of Running Dog or his raiding party had been found. Kicking the Appaloosa into the water, Jehu started across the deep river.

Pinto kicked his bay gelding, grumbling all the while. "I've got me a bad feeling about this laddie."

"Crossing the river?"

"Yes and riding back into Pawnee lands where we've not been invited."

Jehu smiled back at his friend before the Appaloosa reached swimming water. "You could wait here, old friend."

"Uh huh."

The Pawnee Village came into sight two days after crossing the Republican. Jehu and Pinto had carefully avoided the many small hunting parties that come and go down the small trails leading to the village. Sitting their horses quietly, in the midst of a tangle of trees and brush, the two trappers studied the camp.

"It may not even be the village of Straight Arrow. We don't know for sure." Pinto shook his head.

"You got any ideas?"

"Yeah, let's get back where we belong while the getting's good."

"The village looks peaceful enough."

"Yeah, a rattler's den looks peaceful enough until you stir them up." Pinto shook his head. "Then they bite."

"Well, if we're gonna find out about Running Dog, we might as well ride on in." Jehu kicked the horse.

"Whoa up there." Pinto grabbed the Appaloosa's reins. "You ain't gonna ride in there without an invite."

"Figured I would."

Jehu counted the lodges as they rode slowly into the village. Almost a hundred tepees and other shelters sat scattered around the clearing. Horses wandered through the village grazing on the abundant grass. The tall grass had not been beaten down or grazed flat so Jehu figured the village hadn't been encamped there long. Children ran playing through the brightly painted lodges, rolling their hoops and laughing.

Suddenly, the village became aware of the two intruders and transformed from a place of laughter and games into an armed camp. Mounted warriors appeared from behind the lodges, as women and children retreated out of sight. Jehu kept walking the gelding slowly toward a group of warriors who stood up in curiosity as the white men approached their lodge.

Stopping before the tepee, Jehu looked across at the warrior; he recognized as Straight Arrow and raised his hand in greeting. "It has been a long time since we have talked, my Chief."

"You have changed White Wolf, but I recognize the great warrior that saved my son and gave him safely back to me."

Jehu dismounted. "I am glad you remember."

"I also remember Murdockkinn was killed, and many of my warriors at the rock pass beyond the river."

"Murdockkinn was killed in a fair fight between two warriors. The other Pawnee were killed when they attacked me and my warriors against your wishes."

Straight Arrow nodded thoughtfully. "This is true. Tell me White Wolf, why do you come here?"

"The Pawnee are great warriors, but they are great hunters as well." Jehu stepped closer to the chief. "We have come to talk trade with the Great Chief, Straight Arrow."

"There is nothing more you want?"

"Only to trade for furs and to be the friend of Straight Arrow, and the Pawnee people," Jehu lied, his eyes moving slowly about the village.

Straight Arrow looked over at Pinto and walked slowly around the Appaloosa, admiring the animal's qualities. "He comes from our enemies, the Nez Perce people of the north."

"I wouldn't know. A friend gave him to me."

"Would this friend be a Crow with a scar across his forehead?" Straight Arrow looked into Jehu's face and smiled.

"You have seen this warrior?"

"I have seen him."

"Where?"

"He is our captive. He works for our women."

Jehu looked over at Pinto. "Got any ideas?"

"Little late now for ideas, I'm a thinking," Pinto whispered.

"Why is this warrior your captive?"

Straight Arrow looked over at Jehu. "You come to this place to trade you say, but for furs, or maybe Crow captive?"

Jehu knew he was caught in a lie. "I am here to trade for furs, but I will trade for your captives as well."

Straight Arrow spoke to a nearby warrior and turned back to Jehu. "Many Crow come to our village to steal horses. The warrior you call Running Dog, we captured when he tried to steal Pawnee woman and his horse fell under him."

"And the others?"

"They take horses and escape across river in the night."

A commotion started as Running Dog was dragged, fighting, and cussing, to the front of the chief's lodge. Seeing Jehu and Pinto standing among the gathered warriors, Running Dog straightened his shoulders and ceased to resist. Jehu could not believe his eyes. His friend, this once proud Crow warrior, was clad in the dress of a squaw and his long hair had been cut short. Pinto could hardly restrain himself from busting into a fit of laughter.

Jehu stepped toward his friend, only to be stopped by several Pawnee Warriors blocking his path. Straight Arrow raised his hand and the warriors retreated, lowering their weapons. Jehu approached Running

Dog and embraced him. No words were spoken until Straight Arrow sat down in front of his lodge near the council's fire.

"This Crow is your friend, the one you come to find," the chief smiled slightly. "You wonder how I know these things."

Jehu had to admit, it was a curiosity. As far as he knew, Straight Arrow had never seen him until the fight with Murdockkinn, and Running Dog was not even in that fight.

"Now, both of you are my captives."

"Is that why you let him live? You knew I would come here looking for him?" Jehu knew captive warriors were tortured to death quickly. It was too much trouble to guard them constantly, and most warriors made poor slaves.

"We knew someone would come. The warrior Murdockkinn told us long before he died about the great White Wolf, and his brother Running Dog of the Crows."

"I came here to trade with my brothers, the Pawnee." Jehu looked over at Straight Arrow. "What do you wish?"

"The Crow dogs ran off with many good buffalo runners when they raided our village."

"Those were Crow horses Murdockkinn and his raiders stole from our villages and the Paiute villages." Running Dog spit on the ground.

A warrior slammed his war axe into his back, knocking him painfully forward. Slowly, Running Dog straightened to his feet. Jehu walked over to his friend and looked at his back where a trickle of blood seeped through a hole the axe had made.

"If you speak again Crow, you will die," a subchief spoke up.

"Kill me Pawnee, but you have to keep me tied to do it." Running Dog spit again, this time at the warrior. "Free my hands and fight me like a warrior."

Jehu stepped between the advancing Pawnee and Running Dog. Looking over at Straight Arrow, he raised his hand. "If he dies, my Chief, you will never get your horses back, and you will lose good friends."

Again, Straight Arrow raised his hand. "How do you propose to get the horses back?"

"If you wish them back, I will stay here as your prisoner while the Crow goes after them."

"Lad, you can't be serious," Pinto spoke up. "There's no telling where them horses are by now, and your life will depend on Running Dog bringing them back."

"You don't trust him?"

"I trust Running Dog, but it may be impossible to find them horses."

Straight Arrow listened to the men talk. He wondered why a white man would trust an Indian with his life. Maybe this would be interesting to watch. "White Wolf, if he does not return in one moon with the horses, you die."

"I will wait here with my friend Straight Arrow, and his people."

"You saved my son, for that I gave you and your Crow friends their lives. Now, I owe you nothing." Straight Arrow looked over at Running Dog. "In this, I cannot help you, my friend. If he does not return, you will die a slow death."

"So be it," Jehu nodded. "The other white trapper will go back with the Crow to his own land."

"I will not," Pinto growled. "I'm staying here with you."

Straight Arrow nodded. "The Pawnee Killer is free to go."

"You know me?" Pinto couldn't believe his ears.

"We know you white man. Leave our lands and never return." The chief touched his knife. "Only because you are the friend of White Wolf do you yet live."

"Small world ain't it, laddie."

Jehu shook his head. "Hard to believe Straight Arrow knew all about us."

"I reckon Murdockkinn was a busy person," Pinto laughed lightly. "I'm surprised the old boy is letting us go so easily."

"Reckon he wants them horses back real bad."

"I reckon; you just never know what goes through an Injun's mind."

Jehu was surprised, Pinto and Running Dog were given their horses and an escort out of Pawnee hunting grounds. The Appaloosa was turned loose in the village to graze with the rest of the herd, and his weapons were not taken. He was allowed the freedom of the village, to roam at will. Bright Eyes, the son of Straight Arrow, followed Jehu everywhere throughout the village, fascinated by the tall white man that had spared his life.

Jehu and Pinto were lucky, Straight Arrow and the Pawnee wanted the horses back or none of them would have left the village alive. Jehu could not believe their good fortunes. He knew the chief put much stock in his youngest son, but to spare the life of an enemy like Pinto was hard to believe.

Two weeks passed and there was no sign of the horses or Running Dog. Time was running out. Jehu kept track of the passing days. Soon, he would have to attempt to escape if Running Dog did not return. He had faith in his friend, but as Pinto pointed out, what if the horses could not be found.

"You have still a few sleeps left for the Crow to return." Straight Arrow looked across the village as they ate. "Do you still have faith in the one called Running Dog?"

Jehu nodded. "He will come, with the horses or without."

"Without them, both of you will be dead men." Straight Arrow looked around his village. "But, I do not think your friend the Crow will return."

"He will come."

"Perhaps, I hope so. This will be a good thing." Straight Arrow nodded. "I have grown fond of you like a son. My son, Bright Eyes thinks of you as a brother. I too hope your friend returns."

Jehu bit into his meat and stared into the fire. Straight Arrow was a great chief and a good man, but if Running Dog failed to return, the chief would be powerless to help him. His word had been given, but the Pawnee people would demand his death for the raid on their village and the loss of so many valuable horses. Jehu knew the Pawnee had no animosity toward him. He was still unsure why the Pawnee allowed Running Dog to live after he was captured, but as Pinto said, you never know what goes through the head of an Indian.

Bright Eyes stood silently as the two older men talked. As things became silent, he stepped forward. "We are in need of fresh meat for the fires. We could go hunting for the deer that live along the river."

"If it is allowed, I will go with Bright Eyes." Jehu looked over at the chief.

"Teach my young son how to shoot the white man's rifle. Soon, he will be a man." Straight Arrow looked hard into the eyes of Jehu. "We have need of such knowledge."

Jehu nodded and gathered his rifle and shot pouch as Bright Eyes waited eagerly outside the lodge. Two Pawnee warriors followed them to the edge of the village, then turned back toward the lodges.

"I don't think they trust me to come back." Jehu looked back at the warriors.

Bright Eyes smiled. "They want you dead because of Murdockkinn being killed."

"You didn't like the Delaware?"

"No, him cause my father much trouble, raid other people, cause tribes to hate Pawnee."

"Tell me brother, why didn't the people kill the Pawnee Killer?" Jehu looked over at Bright Eyes. "He has killed many of your people."

"My father and the people know it was Murdockkinn and the renegade Pawnee warriors who many years ago killed your friend's people, and wounded him in the back."

"But it was a Cheyenne arrowhead that Pinto said was taken from his back." Jehu was curious.

"This thing happened many years ago. Murdockkinn had many renegade warriors with him from other tribes." Bright Eyes shrugged. "Maybe a Cheyenne warrior rode with him back then."

Jehu knew that could be the answer. Perhaps Straight Arrow and the Pawnee were trying to play fair, something Pinto would never believe. "You say Murdockkinn killed my friend's people?"

"Him come here with scalps of woman and bragging about killing three young ones. Maybe they are babies of your friend."

Pinto had only spoken of the arrow in his back and his hatred for the Pawnee. Lowrie told Jehu about the death of Pinto's woman. Never had Pinto mentioned the killing of his wife. Jehu knew it was like Pinto to hold something like that inside him. Jehu knew the children were not Pinto's as the two boys wait, even now, in Red Hawk's Village.

A small buck stood twitching his tail, his eyes darting everywhere, and his nose testing the air. Jehu and Bright Eyes knelt in concealment alongside a small stream a few miles downstream from the village. The buck was still out of range for the youngster's bow and any attempt at stalking closer, across the open ground, was bound to cause the deer to sense them and dash away.

For Jehu, it would be an easy shot with the Hawken. Instead, he placed the rifle slowly into the boy's surprised hands. Earlier in the day, he went through the rudiments of cocking and aiming the heavy weapon. Bright Eyes slowly balanced the Hawken over a limb of a maple tree and aimed. Twice he took a deep breath as Jehu instructed him. He then rubbed his eyes and waited. The deer turned sideways, giving the lad a perfect shot. Jehu wanted to take the rifle, from the excitement of the hunt. He watched the brown finger tighten slowly, as the explosion of the rifle broke the stillness of the surrounding woods.

Jehu looked through the smoke to where the small buck lay; twitching in his last throws of death. Patting Bright Eyes on the back, he showed him how to reload the still smoking weapon.

"We will eat tonight, my young friend." Jehu smiled as he looked at the face of the bewildered boy who was still looking at the weapon in awe.

"This weapon of the white man is much more powerful than the bow of the Pawnee." Bright Eyes stared at the rifle. "To be strong, the Pawnee need many such as these."

Jehu looked over at Bright Eyes as he walked toward the deer. He knew the young lad, with one shot, immediately understood the power of the white man's rifle. He was aware; someday the foresight of this warrior would enable Bright Eyes to become a great chief as his father before him.

"Rifles, my young friend, are very expensive." Jehu smiled as they dressed the deer.

Bright Eyes held out the heart to Jehu. "For the White Wolf of the Crow, and the friend of Bright Eyes, and a great warrior."

Taking the still warm heart, Jehu held it up to the sky as he had seen warriors do and bit into the bloody meat. "Thank you."

"It is no matter what the rifles cost. If the Pawnee are to survive, we must have them." Bright Eyes looked over at Jehu. "Will my friend help me get rifles for my people?"

Jehu knew the Crow had a few old muskets and the Assiniboine people of the north had been given rifles by the British of Canada. Soon all the tribes would be trading for the white man's weapon. He could see no reason not to help the Pawnee get rifles, but first he would talk with Pinto.

"We will see," Jehu nodded. "But like I said, they are very expensive."

Another larger deer was brought down with the rifle and Bright Eyes was overjoyed by the power the weapon had given him. Never had he felt such power. He looked at the weapon in his hands and then across the flats at the dead deer. Quickly dressing the deer, Jehu shouldered the heavier one and started toward the far off village. Bright Eyes carried the smaller deer and the rifle. Admiring the Hawken, he raised the gun and smiled at Jehu. "I must have a weapon like this."

"When Running Dog returns, I will see about getting you one."

The youngster stopped and placed his burden on the ground. "I will tell you something White Wolf my friend, before we go further."

"What?"

"My father, Straight Arrow says for you to leave this place and not return to the village with me." The boy nodded. "He says Murdockkinn followers want you dead. They are not to be trusted."

"And if Running Dog returns?"

"They will still try to kill you." Bright Eyes shrugged. "They will not go against Straight Arrow's word, but they will wait and kill you when you leave the village."

"They tried that once before." Jehu shifted the deer over his shoulder. "And what would my friend Bright Eyes have me do?"

"I am young, my voice has no consequence," Bright Eyes shrugged. "You have given your word to stay until your friend returns. To run away would be the act of a coward."

Again, Jehu looked at the youngster who had such a grasp of leadership, way beyond his young years. "Come, we must take this meat to your mother for supper."

Bright Eyes smiled; hefting the deer over his shoulder, he followed Jehu toward the village.

Pinto, Running Dog, Owl Man, and Tall Grass sat their horses beside the Republican. Twenty-two horses stood bunched up, ready to ford the river. Their horses were tired from traveling. The time given for them to return to the Pawnee Village ran short. They had been pushed hard. Running Dog was again dressed in the warrior attire of the Crow. Only his short hair reminded him of his capture by the Pawnee.

"I will take the horses into the village myself." Running Dog looked across at Pinto. "Wait here and cover our retreat if it is needed."

"We will ride with you." Tall Grass kneed his pony forward.

Running Dog held up his hand and shook his head. "No my friends, wait here. My foolishness got my friend White Wolf in danger. I must ride in alone for his safety."

"It is White Wolf's fault. If he did not show weakness for the Sioux and Pawnee children, we would not be here now," Owl Man spoke up.

Pinto looked over at the warrior. "You mean, because he didn't kill that Sioux boy or the Pawnee boys?"

"Yes, they are the enemies of the Crow," Running Dog nodded. "Our friend, the White Wolf is a great warrior, but he still thinks like a white man."

"It's all in the past now," Pinto nodded. "Running Dog is right. If we all go, they may kill Jehu before they see we are friendly."

Straight Arrow looked surprised as Bright Eyes and Jehu returned to the village carrying the deer. Hanging the two bucks on a rack for skinning, Jehu watched as Bright Eyes rushed to his father's side. The youngster pointed several times at the rifle Jehu held, then pointed his hands as if he was sighting the weapon.

"My son is very excited. He says the rifle is much better than the bow for hunting," Straight Arrow smiled. "I thank you for teaching him of the weapon."

"For one so young, he has much foresight." Jehu looked to where the boy was talking excitedly to some other boys. "One day he will be the Great Chief of the Pawnee."

"He says the Pawnee should trade for these weapons." The chief eyed the Hawken. "He says nothing must happen to his friend White Wolf."

"Running Dog will come."

"He has only two sleeps left to bring horses to this place."

"He will come."

Running Dog crossed the Republican alone early in the morning, driving the small herd of horses before him. The horses were trail worn and tired from the several days journey back to the village. Traveling at a slow trot, they followed the lead horse straight into the Pawnee Village.

Jehu came to his feet as he heard the alarm sent out by the squaws cooking over early morning fires. Bright Eyes yelled and waved his arms happily, running to where Jehu and Straight Arrow stood waiting for the Crow.

Running Dog rode his gelding proudly through the village, his head held high, his shoulders square and straight, and his eyes looking only forward. Jehu noticed the change in his friend. He had aged, matured, and no longer did he have the wildness of youth. The short internment of being a captive and going through the embarrassing ordeal had done what battle and fighting had failed to do, it made him older. The bravado was no longer evident in his features. It was true, he was still proud and arrogant, but Jehu believed the warrior had been taught humility as well.

Reining his horse in and letting the younger Pawnee boys take over the loose horses, Running Dog looked down at Jehu. "I was worried my friend, that I would not return in time."

Jehu reached up, shook the Crow's hand, and laughed. "I was not worried. You had two more days.

"The others wait for us at the river." Running Dog slid from his horse.

"The Pawnee Killer did not think it wise to come to the village."

Straight Arrow looked at the Crow warrior. "Sit with me and eat. Then we will smoke the pipe of peace between us."

"As a captive or as a Crow Warrior?" Running Dog asked calmly.

"As a highly respected enemy."

Running Dog followed Jehu and Straight Arrow toward the morning cook fire. Elders of the village studied Running Dog, as they had never seen him before.

Bright Eyes walked in front of Running Dog and looked up at the warrior. "He knew you would come back with the horses."

"That is why we are friends, young one." Running Dog placed his hand on the boy's shoulder. "We trust each other, and that Bright Eyes, is why we are strong."

"You have changed, my friend." Jehu sat with Running Dog, watching the Pawnee women preparing meat over the cook fires.

Running Dog nodded slowly. "The Pawnee women taught me, I am not as important as I once thought I was."

"You no longer like the women?"

"I didn't say that White Wolf. I said I found out I wasn't as invincible as I once thought I was in my youth."

Jehu nodded slowly, looking at Running Dog's shorn hair. "My mother used to tell me of a man in the bible. They cut his hair and it changed his attitude."

"Why did they cut his hair off?"

"They were scared of this man. He was very strong, a great warrior."

"He had many enemies?"

"Many."

"What tribe was this man from?"

Jehu looked deeply into the fire. "I'm sorry my friend, but I have forgotten some of the story."

"Did he die?"

"Yes, only after he defeated all of his enemies." Jehu looked at his friend.

"Did he kill many?"

"In the book, it says this man killed thousands with just the rib bone of a buffalo." Jehu changed the words slightly, making it easier for Running Dog to understand.

"That many?"

Jehu nodded. "The book does not lie."

Running Dog nodded. "This is the way I will die someday."

"Your hair will grow back, and like the man in the Bible, you will be even stronger."

"Do you remember this warrior's name?"

"I believe it was Samson. He lived a long time ago."

"Is this a true story, or do you tell me this to cheer me up my friend?"

Jehu smiled. "My mother told me the story. She was a religious person."

"What is this religious?"

"It means a person believes in their medicine."

Running Dog smiled like his old self. Jehu could see his friend come back to life. "The mother of the White Wolf would not lie."

Jehu agreed. "No, she wouldn't."

The drums were beating a steady rhythm throughout the night as Jehu and Running Dog sat with the elders of the tribe and talked. Jehu noticed Bright Eyes kept touching his father on the shoulder.

Looking over at Jehu, he grew solemn. "My son wishes for me to speak with you about the rifles."

Running Dog looked sharply over at Jehu.

"What does my young friend wish to know?" Jehu asked.

"My son wishes to trade for the white man's rifle."

"These rifles are very expensive, my Chief."

"We have horses, furs," Straight Arrow looked again at Jehu. "Tell me, what you want."

Running Dog leaned over and whispered. "Whoever owns these weapons is strong, stronger than their neighbors."

"The Crow already have rifles," Straight Arrow added.

Jehu shook his head. "I must talk with the Pawnee Killer before I will know if I can get the rifles you wish to trade for."

"The white trapper is at the river you call the Republican." Straight Arrow smiled.

Running Dog jumped as if he had been shot. "How did the Pawnee know Pinto waits at the crossing?"

"To answer your question my friend, my scouts watched as you crossed the river with our horses." Straight Arrow smiled crookedly. "This time we were not caught off guard. We have been following the progress of the horses since they entered our country."

"You sly old wolf," the Crow whispered to himself.

"I must ride to the river and speak with the Pawnee Killer before I can give you an answer on the rifles."

Straight Arrow nodded. "The horses have been returned. You have kept your word. Now, you and the Crow are free to go."

Jehu looked across to where Bright Eyes stood beside his father. "You will have a rifle, my young friend, this I promise."

Pinto yelled a greeting and ran out to meet Jehu and Running Dog as they splashed across the Republican. Smiling up at the young trapper, he walked beside their horses as they rode toward their small camp. Tall Grass and Owl Man rose from where they had concealed themselves until the new arrivals were identified.

Pinto picked up the battered coffee can used to boil coffee and poured Jehu a hot cup, then settled down on the soft sand beside the fire. Tall Grass, Running Dog, and Owl Man drifted toward the crossing and disappeared into the tall weeds lining the river. Jehu trusted Straight Arrow, but some of the followers of the dead Murdockkinn were not to be trusted. Sipping on the scalding coffee, he looked quietly at his old friend. The trapper, known to the Indian tribes as Pawnee Killer, never seemed to age or change in any way. Occasionally, he would trade his worn hunting shirt for a new one, but other than that, Jehu could tell no difference in the trapper that had brought him west. Even the deep lines in the weathered face, seem the same. The wide set eyes and the friendly smile were all exactly as he remembered.

"Straight Arrow kept his word and released you and Running Dog."

"Did you have any doubts?"

"I did; figured the old heathen would go back on his word."

"Well, he kept it," Jehu raised the cup, "but I have a slight problem."

"Problem?" Pinto looked up from the fire. "What problem?"

"Straight Arrow has asked to trade for rifles." Jehu watched his friend's face, knowing how Pinto felt about the Pawnee. "I told him I had to speak with you first."

Pinto looked down along the river where the Crow Warriors waited and watched. "Did Running Dog hear him ask?"

"He did."

"What was his reaction?"

"He said nothing, but I don't think he was very happy with the idea."

"I should think not, laddie." Pinto retrieved the pipe from his pocket. "The Pawnee and Crow were natural enemies. If the Pawnee get their hands on rifles, they would be very dangerous foes to contend with."

"He said nothing, for or against the idea." Jehu shrugged.

Pinto looked toward the river. "He wouldn't, you are his friend. He respects your judgment."

"Maybe I don't deserve his respect."

"You do, you saved his bacon back in that village. No other man, red or white, would have ridden into that village for a friend." Pinto set a burning twig to his old pipe. "Maybe I should give the Pawnee a few rifles to kinda make up for the wrongs I've done them."

Jehu smiled. "You have done them no wrong, my friend. The young one, Bright Eyes said it was Murdockkinn and his renegade Pawnee warriors that killed your family and put the arrow in your back."

"But it was a Cheyenne arrowhead. I saw it with my own eyes."

"Bright Eyes said it probably was stolen in a raid, or maybe a renegade Cheyenne warrior rode with Murdockkinn against your family."

Pinto looked over at Jehu, and nodded. "No matter, it was a long time ago. The Pawnee let you and Running Dog go. It is finished."

"And the rifles?"

Pinto whistled a shrill call that sounded up and down the river. The three Crow warriors trotted easily toward the camp. "They are your friends, ask them."

Tall Grass had not been idle as they sat along the riverbank. A large catch of fish hung from a stringer he carried. Jehu waited as the warriors cleaned, gutted, and hung the fish across the fire to cook.

Finally, seeing he had their undivided attention, Jehu looked over at Pinto and nodded. "My friends, I need your counsel."

Running Dog looked across the fire. "About the rifles?"

"Have you told the others?"

"No, it is a thing that should be discussed by all."

Looking over at Tall Grass and Owl Man, Jehu dropped his eyes into his empty coffee cup and stared at the grounds. "My friends, the Pawnee want to trade for the rifles of the whites. I have told Chief Straight Arrow, that we would speak in council and give him our answer."

"The Pawnee are our enemies," Tall Grass spoke up. "They would use the weapons against the Crow."

"Straight Arrow spared the life of Running Dog and myself. I believe him to be a good man. If he gave his word not to attack the Crow, he would keep it."

"He would keep it, but what of the next chief to follow him?" Owl

Man shifted his feet nervously. "What of the ones that followed Murdockkinn?"

Jehu looked at Pinto for help. "White Wolf only means to let the Pawnee of Straight Arrow's village have a few rifles."

Tall Grass waved his hands. "A few kill the same as many."

"You are my friends. I will honor your wishes, but I say this; I have promised the young one, Bright Eyes a rifle and I will give him one, but only one, if my friends say no."

Pinto looked over at Running Dog. "You have said nothing."

The warrior nodded his head, but did not raise his eyes, only continued to look into the small fire. "It does not matter. Soon, some white trader from the north or from the big river will bring guns into this country."

"My ears do not believe my brother's words." Owl Man hit the side of his head. "You wish the Pawnee dogs to have rifles?"

Running Dog looked over at his friend and nodded. "If we make a truce with Straight Arrow, there might be peace between our people."

"Has the great Running Dog become a woman, afraid of the Pawnee?"

The black eyes spit fire as Running Dog glared across the fire. "Does my friend think this?"

Owl Man averted his eyes. "No, we are as brothers; I say no more."

"We will have the Sioux and Cheyenne to fight with, and they are worthy enemies," Tall Grass spoke up.

"Seems to me, that's plenty," Pinto agreed.

"We will vote, my friends," Jehu pulled his skinning knife, "and whichever way it turns out, it is finished. Nothing more will be said."

All heads nodded, agreeing, as each man pulled his own long knife.

Running Dog looked across the river toward the west. "Should we vote or let our chiefs decide such an important thing as the rifles?"

"We vote," Owl Man looked at Jehu.

"A knife standing up means no guns. A knife lying down means yes." Jehu lays his sharp, bone-handled knife flat on the ground. "Everyone must agree or no guns will be traded."

Pinto was next; his knife lay next to Jehu's knife. Running Dog and Owl Man drop their knives to the ground flat. Each man waited expectantly. Only Tall Grass still held his knife.

The warrior studied the faces of his friends, slowly turning the knife he held. "The Pawnee are women; maybe if they have guns, they will become greater enemies and give the Crow more glory." Tall Grass smiled and laid the knife flat.

Pinto stood to his feet and walked over to the saddles and packs. Pulling a rifle from the bundled tarps, he handed it to Jehu. "For the boy, the one you promised a rifle."

Jehu took the extended weapon and nodded his thanks. "A forty-five caliber Hawken, thank you Pinto, thank you."

"That rifle cost me twenty prime pelts. They'll come out of your traps, come fall," Pinto laughed.

"Done." Jehu examined the weapon. "It is a dandy."

"How are you planning on him getting the gun?" Pinto sat down.

"Simple, I'll take it to him." Jehu poured himself another cup of coffee. "I do believe the fish are ready."

Daylight hardly broke over the village as Jehu rode alone into the midst of the Pawnee. Straight Arrow sat before his lodge with the elders of the tribe as the squaws prepared the morning food.

"It is good to see the White Wolf of the Crow people." Straight Arrow motioned at the steaming bowls of meat. "Eat with us, my son."

"Thank you, my friend." Jehu dismounted. "I have come to see your son Bright Eyes and to talk with you and the elders."

"Eat first, then we will talk."

Jehu looked around the peaceful village as he swallowed the steaming bowl of meat and wild berries. It reminded him of the Flathead Village of Alamette. He missed her and his new son. Soon he would be with them once more. He wondered, were the Pawnee and the Crow so different that they couldn't be friends?"

Bright Eyes came trotting toward the lodge and took a seat beside Jehu. "You have come back to the Pawnee people."

"Yes, it is good to be back here and see you."

Straight Arrow set his empty bowl beside him and looked over at Jehu. "You have spoken with the Pawnee Killer about the rifles?"

"Yes, my Chief, we have spoken."

"What is your decision?"

"If we are to trade guns for your furs and horses, I would ask one thing of Straight Arrow." Jehu walked over to the Appaloosa and pulled a soft deerskin scabbard from the saddle. "This is the rifle I have promised Bright Eyes."

"What do you ask, White Wolf?"

Jehu removed the beautiful weapon and ran his hands over the smooth stock of the Hawken. "I will have your word the rifles I trade you will not be used in warfare against the Crow People."

The mumbling elders could be heard as they listened to Jehu's words. "We have always fought the Crow."

"And we always will," another spoke up, leaping to his feet.

"Then I cannot trade with the Pawnee people of Straight Arrow." Jehu handed the rifle, along with shot and powder to Bright Eyes.

Straight Arrow nodded his head and smiled. "My son thanks you."

Jehu smiled as the boy admired his new rifle. "It is a good rifle, the best the whites make. It has only the small scratch on the stock which is hard to see."

"Thank you, my brother," Bright Eyes smiled. "I will ride with you to the river."

Reaching out, Jehu shook hands with Straight Arrow and mounted the Appaloosa. Looking over at the frowning, grim faced elders, he shook his head. "Is peace such a hard thing for two peoples to negotiate?"

Straight Arrow nodded grimly. "The Crow have been our enemies even before my father was Chief of the Pawnee. Our elders or young men will never settle for peace between us."

"And the rifles?"

"The white traders from the north will give the Pawnee the rifles we need." Straight Arrow stepped back. "Go White Wolf; we have known each other's heart. You are the brother to the Crow. We can no longer be friends."

"This saddens me, my Chief."

"As it does me, now go and do not return," Straight Arrow smiled. "Bright Eyes will show you safely to the river."

Several times, on their short ride to the Republican, Jehu showed Bright Eyes the proper use and care of the Hawken Rifle. The Pawnee boy was quick witted. He mastered the rifle easily. Jehu smiled; the lad reminded him of himself many years ago.

Shaking hands with the young Pawnee, Jehu kicked the Appaloosa into the cold water of the Republican. "Maybe we will meet again Bright Eyes."

"When I am Chief of the Pawnee, the White Wolf of the Crow will be welcome in the Pawnee Village once again."

Jehu pulled the gelding to a stop in the belly-deep water. "Tell me, why would your father not trade for the rifles?"

"The elders of the tribe are old, too old, but they still are the elders of our people and their words must be listened to," Bright Eyes shrugged. "My father is chief, but only as long as he listens to the people."

"No matter that the rifles would make your people stronger?"

"It is the way of our people," again the boy shrugged, "perhaps when I am Chief of the Pawnee."

Chapter 18

Cloud's Trading Post came into view as Jehu and Pinto rode along the banks of the Big Muddy. Running Dog, Tall Grass, and Owl Man turned off north, toward the land of the Crow people, eager to return to their home. Again, the two white trappers were in the vast lands along the great Missouri. Jehu smiled as he looked across at his friend. It seemed they were in the same place only a few days back, instead of almost three years.

"We have only a short time to meet Lowrie on the Yellowstone." Pinto sat his horse quietly as he looked out across the great river.

"I know." Jehu looked behind him at Alamette and his young son hanging from a cradleboard on his mother's saddle. His heart swelled as he looked at the beautiful woman, then down at the bundle at her knee. Never had he known such happiness as he had on their ride from the Flathead Village to Clouds.

"Will you be going with us this year?" Pinto asked.

Jehu nodded. "I have signed the paper. I will keep my word to trap with him this season."

"And the next?"

"I have saved money. Maybe I will buy myself a farm."

"Would you be happy farming?" Pinto took a deep breath of the sweet woods and the clean air that blew across the river, and he knew the freedom that made a man love the mountains.

"I don't know Pinto," Jehu shrugged. "My father was a farmer; he liked it."

"Well, we'll see next season, won't we, laddie?"

Jehu looked toward the stockade that surrounded Clouds. "I guess we will."

"Lad," Pinto followed Jehu's gaze, "Cloud ain't real happy with you right now. He put a lot of stock in the black, Benje."

"Then he should have kept him on a leash."

Pinto looked at the man he had known as a youngster and that lad no longer existed. The young man he picked up, what seemed like so many years ago had matured, turning into a man, a strong mountain man of the Rocky Mountains. Pinto doubted any two men he knew could outfight the tall Jehu. Never would he have thought the young lad would turn into the respected trapper and hunter that sat beside him. He had watched many a time as strong, brave men walked softly around Jehu. Pinto's chest swelled; he was proud, proud of his prodigy.

"While I ride into the post, perhaps you and the lady should wait here for me to return."

"Cloud already knows I am here," Jehu shrugged. "I will ride in with you."

Pinto looked sharply along the banks of the river. "Have you seen something I missed?"

Jehu nodded. "Two of his blacks have been watching us for the last couple miles."

"I must be getting old. I sure missed them."

"They're gone now."

"I reckon they've gone back to tell Cloud that we're here." Pinto blew out a breath of air. "We need traps, supplies, and a few fixings before we head west. We might as well ride in."

Pinto had been right; the blacks had already announced their presence to Cloud, who met them on the porch of the trading post. The cold, black eyes of the trader looked coldly at Jehu, as they reined up in front of his post.

Pinto smiled widely as he looked down from his horse. "Ah, Charlie, me lad, we've come a long way to trade with ye."

"Did your young friend here tell you he killed Benje the last time he came through?" The words were filled with hatred.

"I have heard, but let's let bygones be bygones." Pinto watched the small man closely, knowing the violence that lay within the man. "We need supplies, and you need the plews that we will bring here in the fall."

Cloud looked at the bulging shirt of Jehu. Muscles rippled every time his arms moved. Creole blood in Cloud made him hot-tempered and very dangerous, but he was not stupid enough to let his anger get him killed. He had seen the power in Jehu when he killed Benje with his bare hands, something he did not think any lone man was capable of doing.

Cloud wanted Jehu dead, but he knew if he was lucky enough to kill the young friend of Pinto, he would have to kill the older trapper too. He was a businessman, and killing the trappers would cost him the furs they would bring in the spring and probably the furs from other trappers that were their friends. Pinto was well known and well thought of, and Jehu had become something of a legend among the trappers and the wild tribes.

"So be it; the supplies are yours," Cloud gritted his teeth. He could always settle with Jehu later. "Take what you need. I'll look for you in the spring with your pelts."

"I'll pay cash for the supplies." Jehu swung down from his horse. "The pelts will be yours in the spring, providing the price is right."

The summer was long gone. Jehu and Pinto stopped briefly on their return trip to the Flathead Village then rode on, toward the Musselshell. Jehu wanted to ride to Martin Carter's farm to check on Chauncy, but there was no time to waste if he was to meet Lowrie. The ride was going to be long and hard. Jehu tried to convince Alamette to wait for him in her village, but she refused. She was adamant; never would they be separated again.

Jehu had led the small group on to the Crow Village in search of Running Dog and Tall Grass. They would need the warriors for hunting and scouting when they reached the valleys where Lowrie planned to hunt this season.

The village was alive with excitement as they rode slowly past the colorful tepees looking for the lodge of the Crow Chief, Red Hawk. The chief would know where to find his nephew, Running Dog. Jehu only hoped the two warriors were in the village and not out on a horse raid somewhere. The women looked up at Alamette, then tried to touch the baby who stared out at them from the cradleboard.

There was no time to lose, Lowrie would be waiting on the banks of the Musselshell this year and the snows were coming soon. The cold would affect the fur bearing animals making their pelts thick and rich, ready for the traps of the Brigade. The trappers were ready to start laying their trap lines. They were in a hurry to start trapping and harvesting the furs that would make them money and provide the supplies needed to return each year to a life they loved.

Red Hawk stood before his lodge with his arms folded. He was waiting for the whites; he already knew were coming through his village. It had been several months since he had seen his friend the Pawnee Killer. Running Dog told of the fight with Murdockkinn, of his capture, and how the White Wolf had ridden alone into the Pawnee Village to barter his release. The praises of the young white trapper had been sung around the campfires of the Crow for several days after the stories were told.

One their way home, even with the loss of the horses, Tall Grass and Running Dog had managed to steal more horses. Tall Grass was able to produce the horses he needed for the bride price to her father. Never had Running Dog or Owl Man seen their friend so happy. Running Dog even joked that maybe, one day, he would have to try marriage.

Pinto dismounted and greeted the Crow Chief, then waited as protocol required before he could talk. Red Hawk motioned for Jehu and Alamette to dismount then ordered women to bring them food. Taking the baby from his cradle, Alamette handed him to Jehu, who set the baby in his lap.

"It is a boy?" Red Hawk questioned and smiled at the baby.

Pinto slapped his leg, he was as proud as Jehu. "Ain't he something, Red Hawk?"

The chief nodded. "Running Dog will be jealous. Now he can't say he's the prettiest warrior in the Crow Nation."

Everyone enjoyed a good laugh as Pinto looked about the village. "We have come to get Running Dog and Tall Grass for the winter hunt."

"Running Dog is not here. He and Owl Man went to the west on a hunt for the shaggies."

"And Tall Grass is he here?"

Red Hawk shrugged his shoulders. "He is here, but he will not go with you."

Pinto frowned deeply. "Why not?"

"He is now married. He will not leave her," Red Hawk laughed. "Tall Grass is now an owned man. He is in love."

Jehu was curious. "What's he mean, owned?"

"Don't quite know for sure, but maybe he means Tall Grass ain't his own boss anymore."

"You mean, his new squaw kinda tells him what to do, and when to do it."

"Something like that I reckon."

"I don't believe it, no sir." Jehu thrust his jaw out. "Tall Grass is a great warrior."

"Was a great warrior," Red Hawk shook his head sadly.

Jehu was not about to believe his friend was being told what to do by a woman. Leaving Alamette and the baby in Red Hawk's care, he walked in the direction the chief pointed. With Running Dog and Owl Man gone from the village, they needed Tall Grass more than ever. Lowrie was counting on them for scouting and hunting for the Brigade while they trapped.

Jehu recognized a small claybank gelding staked beside a well-kept lodge, the same horse Tall Grass captured in the battle with Murdock-kinn's warriors. Tall Grass sat wrapped in a blanket outside the lodge, his back to the approaching white man, completely unaware of Jehu's approach. Stepping in front of the warrior, Jehu looked down at his friend.

Leaping to his feet, Tall Grass grabbed the tall trapper in a bear hug. "White Wolf, it is you, my friend."

"Yes, it is me," Jehu smiled.

"It is good to see you. Is the Pawnee Killer with you?"

"Yes, and my woman and baby." Jehu led Tall Grass away from the lodge and probing ears. "We have come for you, Running Dog, and Owl Man."

"You wish me to go to the mountains to trap the flat tail ones?" Tall Grass looked back, toward his lodge.

"The White Chief Lowrie needs scouts and hunters." Jehu pulled the warriors attention back to him. "He will pay you well."

"I am married now, my friend."

"So, bring your woman with you. Lowrie will pay her to cook."

"I don't think so."

Jehu studied the face before him. "Red Hawk says Running Dog and Owl Man are away hunting the shaggy ones."

"They have been gone many days. Maybe they are on their way back."

"Why didn't you go?"

"I told you before, I am married."

"We need hunters; we need you Tall Grass."

Again, the warrior looked at his lodge. "No, I must stay here."

"Don't you eat anymore my friend?"

"I eat."

Exasperated at the warrior's answers, Jehu turned to leave. "We must leave in the morning to rendezvous at the great river with Lowrie. We have little time. If you are going, be ready with the new sun."

A tall, big-boned young squaw, stood outside the lodge where the claybank stood tied. Jehu figured this had to be Tall Grass' new bride. She was a beautiful young woman, but the look of pure meanness coming from her eyes made Jehu understand why the warrior was tied to his lodge. Jehu shook his head, as he wasn't even married to the woman and she scared him. A bloody skinning knife dripped blood from where she had been skinning a deer, and the look coming from her eyes said she wouldn't mind using it on him.

"Did you find Tall Grass?" Pinto questioned Jehu. "Is he going?"

"I found him alright, and he ain't going."

Pinto rubbed his face slowly. "Why not? We need hunters. The men can't be out hunting for game and running their traps at the same time."

"Well, like Red Hawk said, Tall Grass is kinda tied to his lodge." Jehu walked on by Pinto. "The men will just have to eat beaver tail all winter is all I know."

Scratching his head, the old trapper watched Jehu retreat as he disappeared behind a lodge. "Beaver tail; I sure ain't telling them that." He spoke under his breath, rubbing his chin.

Early the next morning, Pinto took the lead with two heavily loaded mules tied to his saddle horn. Alamette and the baby followed him and Jehu brought up the rear with another mule loaded down with traps and trade goods for the winter. Pinto was still swearing under his breath, trying to figure out what he was fixing to tell Lowrie. No other Crow warriors could be coaxed into going with them. There was no way they were gonna be cramped up with forty or fifty white trappers all winter. The trappers had a bad reputation among the tribes of entertaining themselves throughout the winter by aggravating and playing jokes on the younger men. None of the young Crow thought getting their hair shaved off or waking up smeared in bear grease was worth the money or trade goods they would earn. Before leaving the village, Pinto left word with Red Hawk to hurry Running Dog and Owl Man after them, when they returned.

"What are you grumbling about, Pinto?" Jehu could barely hear the words coming from the trapper.

"I said, ain't nary one of these long-haired heathens you can trust to keep their word, no sir."

"I don't remember any words being given."

"Well, it was the same as giving their word."

"And what was that." Jehu shook his head and grinned.

Pinto turned in his saddle and looked back. "They didn't say they weren't going this year, and to me, that's the same as saying they were going."

"Uh huh."

The morning was too beautiful to argue, and Jehu was not about to let Pinto sully it for him. Early fall was in the air with the fragrance of the falling, yellow leaves, filling the air with their fresh smell. Meadowlarks and doves flew up in front of them as squirrels barked from the high limbs. A huge grey wolf darted across the open ground far down the narrow path, seemingly unafraid of the horsemen coming down the trail. Jehu was enjoying himself. The slow plodding of the Appaloosa, his family and best friend with him, he had never known such peace.

Only the thought of Chauncy and wondering if she was alright, darkened the day slightly. He wanted to ride by the farm before going with Pinto, but there was no time. Knowing Lowrie, he was probably at the rendezvous waiting, pacing, and cussing with every step he took. Next spring, after trading with Cloud, he would ride east with Alamette to check on his sister.

Pinto pulled in his gelding and grinned widely. Before him, sitting across the narrow trail, was none other than Tall Grass. Behind him, astride a small war pony that she made look even smaller was his new wife, Sun Flower. From where he sat, Jehu could tell she wasn't the happiest Crow Woman around, but at least they had a hunter for the coming trapping season.

Pinto looked curiously at Jehu as he rode up beside him. "Reckon what changed his mind, or hers?" He could see the wicked gleam in Pinto's eyes.

"Wouldn't know, you know women better than I do. You got any idea?" Jehu looked across at Tall Grass. Jehu was suspicious, as he had already seen the tender way Sun Flower dismounted from her horse and the submissive way she acted toward Tall Grass. "Alright Pinto Stade, what did you do?"

"Nothing, I'm telling you," Pinto kicked his horse. "Let's head out."

"Nope, I ain't moving until you tell me how or maybe I should say what you done to get him to come along."

Turning his horse slowly, Pinto grinned smugly. "I just told him how my old pappy used to get his way with my mam."

"And?"

"That part, laddie me boy, you don't need to know." Pinto looked over at the sweet-faced Alamette. "With her, you'll never need to know."

Jehu shook his head in wonder as he looked up at Alamette. He had his suspicions, but said nothing. Tall Grass seemed happy, and Sun Flower had lost the hardness in her face, so whatever it was, apparently it worked.

A hard two weeks later, they looked across the Musselshell and waved at the gathered trappers. The bandy-legged Lowrie stood in front of the men pacing back and forth. Kicking their horses into the cold, rushing water, they followed Pinto across the river and waded ashore to the yelling and cheering of the Yellowstone Brigade.

"Where you boys been?" Lowrie looked at the two women waiting close to the river. "We've been waiting fer ye."

"It's a long trail way out here, old friend," Pinto dismounted and shook hands with his friend, "or have you forgotten?"

Shaking hands with Jehu, he nodded at Tall Grass and the women. "Who does she belong to? I know Alamette, and where is Running Dog?"

"Slow down, old hoss, can't say for sure."

"About the woman or Running Dog?"

Pinto motioned Tall Grass and the women closer to the trappers. "This is Sun Flower, the woman of Tall Grass."

"And Running Dog?"

"He'll be along in a few days," Pinto lied as Jehu shook his head.

"Well, he'll have to track us, cause we're pulling out come sunup." Lowrie turned and walked away.

True to his word, Lowrie had the Brigade headed due north, further into the Rocky Mountains than they had ever trapped before. The trails were sometimes pure rock and other times pure dirt, but they were always straight up. Tall Grass led the brigade steadily north, then finally turned northwest. Sun Flower rode behind Alamette helping her with the baby and the packhorse.

"I ain't liking this none, laddie."

"What's wrong?" Jehu looked out across the seemingly endless high peaks and mountain ranges. He knew he had never been this far to the northwest.

"If'n I ain't missing my guess, we're heading right into Blackfoot Hunting Grounds."

"You sure?"

Pinto nodded. "Me and Sublette were gonna trap these valleys one winter."

"Just the two of you; what happened?"

"When those Blackfoot got through with us, we were buck naked, hip deep in snow, and two hundred miles to the nearest white man."

"Well, we got a whole Brigade backing us this time, and Lowrie guaranteed us the best catch of our lives."

Pinto laughed. "You remember them words when you hear the

Blackfoot war cries and their arrows start flying by your ears."

"There are beaver up here, ain't there?" Jehu looked at his friend.

"Yes, lad; they're as thick as fleas on a hound's back."

Running Dog and Owl Man had followed the trail laid by the Brigade easily through the mountain passes and back down into the watery valleys. Small lakes, numbering in the hundreds, lay among the tall pines and other trees. Beaver signs, downed trees, dams, and beaver dens abounded everywhere. Owl Man dropped to the trail and picked up fresh horse droppings.

"They are near; maybe we catch up tonight."

Running Dog nodded, eager to catch up to the Brigade. The hoof prints and signs of numerous ponies showed Lowrie and his men were being followed. He knew slipping around the warriors ahead, and reaching the Brigade without being spotted was gonna be difficult.

Tall Grass looked out over the huge valley and inhaled the cold mountain air. Small clouds drifted lazily over his head, seemingly close enough for him to reach up and touch them. Suddenly, the claybank raised his head and nickered lightly. Tall Grass knew the sound could not be heard far, but he jerked the gelding's rein hard to quiet him. Hair stood up on his neck as somewhere close, another horse nickered back. Slipping quietly to the ground, he led the horse through the deep cedars and spruce trees, trying to lose himself in the deep timber.

The yell of discovery sounded as Tall Grass swung on the claybank's back and turned him toward the Brigade, pushing him into a hard run. Half-naked warriors seemed to materialize from every direction with their fierce war cries and screams breaking the quiet of the mountains. Whipping his horse hard with his bow, Tall Grass broke from the timber and raced across the deep valley, plunging ahead across water and deep ditches. The warriors, closing in behind him, were yelling in delight, as they knew they had their foe caught. Tall Grass urged the claybank faster, leaning to the side of his horse; he can feel the arrows, as they zipped past.

Tall Grass screamed his own yell of defiance as the race neared the end of the valley. Ahead was a small pass that led into another valley where he had left the Brigade setting up camp earlier in the day. Nearing the pass, Tall Grass pulled the claybank in hard as two warriors rode out, blocking the trail. Looking over his shoulder at the closing warriors, Tall Grass looked back at the pass in despair.

"If I were you Crow, I would leave this place quick."

"Running Dog, Owl Man," Tall Grass grinned in relief. Intent on escaping, he had not looked close enough to recognize the two warriors. Running Dog looked calmly at the oncoming warriors. "Why do you run, Tall Grass? Has marriage made you weak?"

"No, marriage has made me smarter." Tall Grass heeled the horse hard and rode through the pass with Running Dog and Owl Man pounding right on his heels.

A rifle sounded from behind them as they raced down the rocky passage, out onto another flat valley. Looking behind him, Running Dog noticed a lone warrior that had outrun his companions, leaving them far behind. Pulling his gelding to a sliding stop, Running Dog turned the gelding and charged straight at the oncoming warrior. Tall Grass and Owl Man shook their heads in disbelief as they pulled their horses around.

Running Dog notched an arrow, as the warrior bearing down on him was intent on reloading his rifle. Pulling the arrow back to a full draw, Running Dog released the string, sending the barbed shaft straight through the chest of the warrior. Sliding slowly from his horse, the warrior dropped to the ground, rolling across the grass. In a flying dismount, Running Dog scalped the warrior and retrieved the man's rifle, shot pouch, and skinning knife. At a run, he mounted the horse and kicked him hard to where the others waited, shaking their heads.

"You, my friend, are crazy." Tall Grass looked past Running Dog to where at least twenty enraged warriors were screaming their heads off in rage as they passed their fallen comrade.

Owl Man laughed and raised his arm at the warriors. "No, Tall Grass, our friend Running Dog is not crazy, he's insane."

"Maybe we should leave this place." Running Dog laughed again as the warriors raced to within a hundred yards of them. "I think these Blackfoot warriors wish to kill us."

Jehu heard the screaming war cries and looked across the valley to where three riders were being chased by several. One rider slowed his horse, taunting the followers by turning backward on his horse and waving his arms at them. Jehu grinned; only one warrior, he knew, could ride like that or would dare to ride like that at a dead run with so many chasing him.

Lowrie paced back and forth furiously as the three warriors rode laughing into the Brigade's Camp. The old darkened pipe blew a steady stream of smoke into the pure valley air as the trapper ranted and cussed. Several Blackfoot warriors rode in circles, taunting and daring the Crows to come back out and fight them.

"Well, the fat's in the fire now boys. They know we're here," Lowrie swore.

Tall Grass looked down at the man and shook his head. "Them follow you many miles. They knew you here before they start to chase us."

The Blackfoot sat their horses quietly out on the valley floor, watching the men beside the small fires talking among themselves. None made a move to come in closer. They just sat there, staring.

"What are they up to, Pinto?"

Pinto stepped further out onto the valley floor. "I figure they're counting our men, figuring out our strength."

"Then what?" The pipe belched smoke as the bright red face of Lowrie fumed.

"This is their prime hunting grounds. I figure they'll be back with more help to run us off."

"Or kill us," Jehu added.

Lowrie looked over to where Running Dog was still waving furiously at the Blackfoot. "Can you talk with them?"

The warrior reined his horse around at the words and looked down at Lowrie. "Them plenty mad at Crow right now, no talk."

"Go try; we can't trap beaver and fight with the Blackfoot all winter."

Jehu noticed the Hawken tucked under Running Dog's knee and the bloody scalp that dangled from the barrel. "Don't send him, Taff. It's too late for talking."

"Why is that? We can at least give it a try."

Jehu nodded over at Running Dog and motioned toward the scalp. "You see what he's got hanging from that rifle?"

"Yeah, I see alright." Lowrie looked again at the Blackfoot. "Great, that's just great."

"This one had to kill Blackfoot warrior. He try to shoot me with this white man rifle."

Jehu stiffened and walked to where Running Dog was brandishing the Hawken, showing it to the trappers. Taking the rifle, he ran his hands over the smooth stock, feeling the small scar that lay in the stock. Jehu shook his head. It couldn't be the same gun he had given Bright Eyes. It was two, maybe three hundred miles or better across the mountains to the Pawnee lands, but the scar was the same. Surely, no two rifles could have the same scar.

Pinto stepped closer and looked at the rifle. "What is it, lad?"

"It's the same Hawken, we gave to the Pawnee boy, Bright Eyes." Jehu passed the weapon to Pinto. "See for yourself."

"Are you sure?" Pinto examined the weapon himself. "These Hawkens all look the same."

"The scar; look at it Pinto, there can't be two like that in these mountains."

"I remember now. It's hard to believe, but it is truly the same rifle."

"I take from Blackfoot who try shoot this one." Running Dog held the rifle up as Pinto passed it back to him.

Jehu looked out to where the Blackfoot were still gathered, chanting their war cries and brandishing their bows. "You boys get mounted. If we can't talk with them, we'll scare the daylights from them, and send them on their way."

"Wait Jehu, if we kill any more of them Blackfoot, we're liable to be fighting them all winter." Lowrie held up his hand.

Mounting the Appaloosa, Jehu looked down at the Brigade leader. "A Blackfoot has already been killed, Taff. Now, I'm aiming to show them boys out there, we're not to be fooled with."

Lowrie looked across the valley at the mounted Blackfoot. "What are you planning to do?"

"I'm fixing to give those Blackfoot a lesson about us that they can take back to their villages."

"Are you sure, Jehu?"

Jehu nodded. "My word has been given to trap for you this season. I'm under your command. If you say no, then no it will be."

Lowrie studied the yelling Blackfoot, then looked around at his gathered trappers and back at Jehu. "You're the Indian fighter Jehu Wolf. On this, I trust your judgment."

"Running Dog, Tall Grass, Owl Man, let's ride out and talk with our friends." Jehu checked the priming of his rifle.

Running Dog grinned and bounded onto the back of his nearby gelding. Raising the rifle over his head, he yelled the war cry of the Crow.

"You ain't leaving me behind." Pinto mounted his horse.

"Nor me, Jehu Wolf." Ben Scott rode forward.

Jehu held up his hand as all the trappers started mounting their horses. "The rest of you wait here."

"But, they've got you outnumbered." Lowrie looked at the Blackfoot. "There are at least twenty of them red devils out there, against your six."

Jehu looked over at the set faces of the Crow and his face grew hard. "Outnumbered are we, Taff? I believe it's the Blackfoot who are outnumbered."

Lowrie grinned. "You may be right."

Jehu looked at the rifle Running Dog held, remembering the young son of Straight Arrow. Kicking the Appaloosa forward, he started across the valley toward the waiting warriors.

Suddenly, a running horse appeared off to the side, a black and white paint running full out, his mane and tail flowing in the wind, his rider sitting straight and proud on his back.

Jehu reined in and watched curiously, as the newcomer pulled up in front of his men and spoke for a time with them. The warrior pointed toward the six riders and motioned with his hand. A single rider came forward, stopping midway between the two forces. Jehu pointed at Tall Grass and motioned him forward. The two warriors met half way. Jehu couldn't hear what was said, their words were not audible. Tall Grass rode back to the waiting men and stopped his horse beside Jehu.

"The one who just rode here is a War Chief of the Blackfoot People. He wishes to know what we do here."

"Did you tell him?"

"I told him." Tall Grass looked over his shoulder at the waiting warrior. "Him say we leave this place now, or die."

"Uh Huh," Jehu smiled. "Go back and tell him we're gonna trap here this winter; we ain't leaving."

Nodding, Tall Grass loped his gelding back to where the warrior waited. Angry words erupted and Jehu heard a hard running horse ride up behind him. Looking back, he grinned as Sun Flower, the squaw of Tall Grass, reined her horse in behind the others. A war axe and skinning knife were held in her hands. The woman was an imposing figure, tall and big boned, but it was her facial expression, the blazing hard eyes that took one's breath. Jehu had been wrong. Here was a woman a man would be proud to have at his side.

Tall Grass turned his back on the Blackfoot and rode slowly back to where Jehu and the others waited. Seeing Sun Flower with the others, he smiled and nodded to her.

"His name is Chief High Road. He challenges our chief to fight." Tall Grass looked into Jehu's eyes. "He says if you win, you can stay."

"And if I die?"

"He wants the word of the White Wolf that the white trappers will leave the Blackfoot land."

"He knows me?" Jehu was surprised.

Tall Grass looked down at the valley grass, not wanting to meet Jehu's hard eyes. "He carried two more Pawnee scalps in his horse's mane."

"Bright Eyes and his friends." Jehu remembered the young boys.

"High Road says Pawnee tell him of you before he died." Tall Grass shook his head sadly. "He says Pawnee tell him White Wolf will kill High Road."

Jehu stepped from the Appaloosa and pitched Pinto his rifle. Pulling his leather hunting shirt off, he remounted the gelding and rode toward the waiting Blackfoot without speaking.

High Road looked at the pale skin of the white and grinned.

The two magnificent horses sped towards each other, their riders brandishing the heavy war axes over their heads. Both white and red watched as their leaders charged together, one to protect his hunting grounds and people, the other to avenge the death of a friend. Pure hatred poured from Jehu's eyes as he neared the Blackfoot Chief. High Road only had a minute to see the look in the white man's eyes, but it gave him a cold shiver. Never had he seen such hate as this one possessed.

Jehu took no chances as he had with the Sioux warrior. Reining the powerful Appaloosa straight into the oncoming Paint at the last moment, Jehu tensed ready for the collision. Men and horses went down in a pile, both riders tried to clear the jumble of kicking hooves and heavy bodies.

The Appaloosa rolled to his feet, trotting away from the downed Blackfoot horse. Jehu walked shakily toward the warrior's horse and the rider that lay pinned under him. Jehu raised the war axe and stared into the dark eyes of High Road who tried unsuccessfully to pull his leg free. The Paint lay still, his neck broke from the fall. Jehu swiped the white mane, cutting loose the dried scalps of the Pawnee. Looking into the eyes of the War Chief of the Blackfoot, Jehu turned and gathered the reins of the Appaloosa. Several Blackfoot Warriors raced to their leader's side and pulled him out from under the dead horse's body as Jehu rode off. Holding out his arms, High Road stopped his warriors from chasing after the tall white known as White Wolf.

Pinto waited for Jehu to put his hunting shirt on. "Why didn't you kill him?"

"He carried the scalps of the Pawnee, but he didn't kill Bright Eyes, another did." Jehu looked across at the Blackfoot. "Maybe by letting him live, we can trap these mountains in peace."

"I wouldn't count on it, lad."

Smoke curled from the rock and mud chimney of the small farmhouse as Jehu, Alamette, and the six-year-old Jeb Wolf sat their horses beyond the field staring at the farm. Jehu looked at Alamette and the small figure of his daughter hanging from her cradleboard and smiled.

Grey hair showed along the visible scar on his cheek and in the long hair of the man. The face was still young, but weather aged from the hard life, and the harsh winters of the mountains.

Jehu watched as a young boy carrying a rifle and a Bluetick hound walked slowly toward them along the edge of the cornfield. The face seemed familiar; Jehu nodded knowingly as it was him, years ago. The youngster was darker complected, but in other ways, his build and his walk, the boy reminded Jehu of himself as a young lad. The youngster stopped in surprise as he became aware of the tall man sitting before him on the Appaloosa. Glancing over at the Indian woman and children, he turned his eyes back toward Jehu.

"You're my Uncle Jehu, ain't you mister?" The boy overcame his shock at seeing them. "You're him; my ma told me of you."

Jehu nodded slowly. "How's your ma, lad?"

"She's fine." The boy looked over at the farmhouse where a woman shielded her eyes from the morning sun and stared across the field at them. "She wants to see you."

"What's your name, boy?"

"Ma named me after you, Jehu Wolf Carter." The boy looked up at Jehu. "If'n you're my uncle."

Jehu nodded. "Is she happy?"

"She is 'cepting, she worries about you."

"Tell her I'm fine." Jehu turned the Appaloosa around and stared back at the farmhouse where the woman started across the yard toward them.

"She wants to see you, Uncle," the boy repeated.

Jehu pulled on the reins slightly. Riding close to the packhorse, he pulled the Hawken rifle with the scar from a scabbard and handed it to the lad. Kicking the horse, he rode away from the farm, and headed to the west.

The youngster ran his hands over the smooth stock and smiled. "Thank you, Uncle."

"It belonged to a young man your age; good-bye Jehu Wolf Carter." Jehu called over his shoulder. "Take good care of it lad."

"Ma still wants to see you."

Jehu looked once more at the figure of Chauncy standing at the edge of the field, and then nodded at the boy. Harsh feelings would always exist between him and Martin Carter. He knew it would be best for him to ride on. Kicking the Appaloosa, he started back to the west.

"Where do we ride, husband?" Alamette looked at his strong wide back.

"We'll ride to our valley until fall."

"Do we trap with Lowrie again this season?"

Jehu raised his arm and pointed toward the tall mountains, far away. "When the time comes, we will rendezvous with Pinto and his sons, and Running Dog will meet us northwest along the Yellowstone. The time of the hunter and trapper is almost finished."

"But, we just left Pinto on his new farm near his friend Sutton," Alamette said. "Running Dog now has a new wife. Will they come?"

Jehu smiled sadly and kicked the Appaloosa into a trot. "The time of the beaver trapping is almost finished, but we'll meet them for one more season. They'll be waiting for us, the mountains are in their blood, and they're calling to our friends."

The End